Stag Rider

Tim Bennett

Acknowledgements
Sarah Quigley – Editor
Cover Design – Tim Barber
Interior Design – Polgarus Studios

To the unseen, for believing in me.

The Magician

Merlin stood at the empty round table, his eyes glazed over, staring down at the ghostly-still forest. The giant slice of ancient oak was the only souvenir he had granted himself from the golden days, but there was no longer anyone to sit around it. He walked its circumference, running his fingers over the bark and the worn sections of smooth wood marking the place settings. The wood was still in perfect condition thanks to the safe haven Merlin provided it with, away from Earth's elements. Each rippling growth-ring was clearly defined and imbued with the energy of the thousands of conversations about quests for the Grail, and otherworldly magic and prayer that had flowed across the table when they were all together.

Merlin's dream of a humanity united in the preservation of his dearest love, Mother Earth, lay in tatters. His lunar life suited him, far away from the toxic atmosphere and butchering of his beasts. He had grown accustomed to the solitude of his celestial observatory – perhaps too much so – but even with such distance he was still comforted by the ebb and flow of the seasons as they changed the glens' canvases; frosting peaks white and quiet for winter, before the warmth woke hibernating wildlife into the glory of the Scottish wilderness. Merlin was all too familiar with the cycles of life and death; they had shaped his reclusiveness in so many ways. Restlessness stirred inside him. His domed amethyst ring swirled with cosmic energy as he remembered how the table had served them well back then. He longed for adventure, but had vowed never again to interfere in man's affairs, at least not directly. He was tired of feeling Mother's pain as she withered from the strain of supporting humans racing toward destruction and he could no longer deny the slow onset of depression caused by detachment from the land he loved so dearly. A surge of anger rose up from somewhere inside him, and there were oh such dark places there.

'Old friend!' he shouted. 'Arthur, where are you?' His deep bellow was lost in the cold lifeless miles of space. He closed his eyes to remember the musty scent of leaves, bark and earth. He turned his face upward, searching for the first drops of a storm's rain. 'All is never lost. Now then, where are you, Aaron?' he said, stretching and cracking his fingers with a mischievous smile as he turned his mind's eye to the only contact he allowed himself with the land and its people.

Aaron was a man like any other, in as much as he had his fair share of flaws and insecurities, but he had something different, too. Something Merlin thought was dead in men and which Aaron hadn't shown until now — faith in the unseen. He'd watched Aaron drink from the healing water of Lourdes, praying it would arrest the disease and insanity growing secretly within, and Merlin had learnt about the strange power of Led Zeppelin from Aaron. The volume of the poetic, bone-shaking *rock music destroyed speakers and damaged their eardrums: a small price to pay for the effect the sounds had on their souls. Merlin was fascinated by this young man and how they stood on such distant yet constant ground. He recognised Aaron's drug-infused madness, having spent years roaming the wilderness, surviving on grubs, berries, roots and acorns, lamenting the loss of his sons and their mother. Merlin chuckled as he remembered watching the carefree hippy tripping his own forest-nuts off on LSD, running naked and wild for days in the forests of Vermont, until lightning struck him down. He shook his head in disbelief as he watched Aaron walk towards the trees and stop to read the sign on the metal gate, remembering when the ancient Caledonian Forest had covered the very same land which had felt his own mad bare feet as he ran away from the world.*

'I wonder,' Merlin said, stroking his beard as a crow circled above Aaron. 'Let's see.'

The leaves drummed with the first pitter-patter of rain. Merlin pursed his lips and blew softly, calling the wind. He brought his hands to his lips to pray and slowly separated his palms, parting the clouds for the sun to merge with the raindrops and throw coloured prisms over the forest. The sights, sounds and smells intoxicated him. He started to move his right hand with the grace of an orchestra's conductor. His thumb and forefinger pinched an imaginary baton; he had never needed a wand to weave his magic. The combination of his hand's brisk movements and soothing strokes, synchronised with the sunlight, wind, and dancing leaves. Merlin's head rolled as the orchestra gathered momentum. 'Louder, faster!' he shouted.

The clouds blackened the canopy, eliminating the rainbow-fairies to make way for a more serious force of nature capable of great endings – or of forging new beginnings. Merlin thrashed his hands as the distant rumble hurled into the secrecy of the forest.

'Hell hath no fury like a sorcerer's thunder and lightning!' he cried, holding his hand high above his head before slamming it down with gritted teeth. The bolt hit the forest floor. A mushroom-cloud of leaves and earth shot into the sky, high above the trees. Merlin caught himself; he sniffed at the suggestion from his conscience that he had interfered. The opportunity was too good to miss. Aaron so intrigued him. A mischievous smile sprang across his face as he sensed Cernunnos' response deep in the Underworld. Was this the day he'd been hoping for?

'It's been a long time since I rock'n'rolled!' he shouted, thrashing his hands to the opening drum-beat of Led Zeppelin's anthem as the music danced with his soul, and Stag stirred deep within the fertile forest earth.

ONE

Logan Mackenzie, author of 'The Sacred Mystery of the Ardnamurchan Volcano', lived a reclusive life on the small beach of Singing Sands bay on the westerly tip of Scotland. His book was elusive, with my exhaustive searches of libraries and second-hand book shops proving fruitless. The collapsed remains of the volcano attracted frequent interest from geologists worldwide. Of the many online journals available, discussing various theories on its structure, I had found a solitary article which described 'disappointment at the sudden and unexplained withdrawal of Mackenzie's eagerly anticipated book'. Mackenzie was a highly respected anthropologist who specialised in the field of ancient tribes and their sacred methods of connecting with the land. I was hooked on finding this man. He was a piece of the giant jigsaw I'd just started to put together.

I looked at the sign on the gate which read 'Singing Sands. Danger. Unexploded Munitions. This area was formerly MOD property and items containing explosives occasionally may be found in the forest, dunes, or washed up on the beach'. The words made me clench my teeth. A burst of anxiety hit me, triggering my hand-tremors. I tried to hold my right hand flat in front of my eyes, but it shook uncontrollably. My dark side was roused by an opportunity to play Russian roulette for the first time in years. Not since I'd shot line after line of cocaine up my nostrils, hoping one of them would have enough ammunition to explode my heart, had I felt such twisted excitement. I watched clouds of my misty breath float into the cold February air and listened to the tapping of a distant woodpecker on the Sitka spruce trees beyond the gate. The ebbing tide slipped away from the mudflats of Kentra Bay, while the ensemble of nature sounds and my relatively new ability to revel in the present moment steadied my hand. A doctor had told me the tremors were a side-effect of active addiction and that they would lessen in time, but the pounding I'd given my nervous system meant it could take years for them to cease.

Years of drug-abuse and alcoholism had left their mark, but four months of rehab in Cape Town had put me in good stead for a promising recovery. While the inevitable divorce was still a recent memory and had left me shell-shocked, near the end my drug-ravaged heart was incapable of true love, so it let go of the married years with ease and the freedom of single life soon became exhilarating. I still, though, found it easy to question every decision I made about my future; especially the one I'd made to come to Scotland.

I had changed from a place so deep inside myself that everything I heard was clearer and the things I touched felt so new to me, but it was my vision that had gone through the biggest change. Life presented itself in high definition. The sun shone brighter and my relationship with nature deepened. I felt connected to it all, especially to my half-brother, Crow. He was always with me, waiting in the wings, watching over me.

I scanned the trees for his blackness, listening for his caw, hoping for guidance or one of his fleeting conversations after which he'd leave me with a riddle, or plant a seed of suggestion in my head. He loved goading me to take both a leap of faith and the next step forward on this new path. One thing I knew for sure about Crow was that he would never be gone for long. The cause of my bond with him remained a mixed-up collage of memories and flashbacks from an LSD trip in the ski hills of Vermont, and a magical afternoon in Newlands Forest on the lower reaches of Table Mountain. Part of me relished the adventure this new-found path was taking me on, and the other, dark part wondered if I was still insane and clutching at straws.

Only twenty-four hours earlier I'd stood at the edge of the gangway at Gatwick, stepped inside the aeroplane and stamped a seal of commitment to fly to Inverness and whatever lay beyond.

'Okay, I'm in,' I whispered to the unseen as I fastened my seatbelt. Quite what I was *in* for was a complete mystery. Before rehab, all that happened inside my head was the noise of cravings bouncing around my skull. My complete surrender to the rehab programme had rewarded me with a profound healing I was on the verge of calling miraculous. Nothing could satisfy my new desire to visit the place I'd seen in my mind's eye while I was five thousand miles away, alone, and happy with who I was with for the first time in years, on the highest point of Table Mountain: Maclear's Beacon.

Why did I have a vision of the remains of an extinct volcano on the far reaches of the west coast of Scotland? Why was I being haunted every night by a dream in which a hand clad in a steel armoured glove repeatedly tapped its fingers on a shield… waiting for something, or someone? I wanted to know. The quality of my sleep deteriorated as the power of the dreams increased, and the weirdest thing is, they were happening in real-time. The tapping grew louder and the dents the fingers made in the shield deepened with every dream, playing their performance to me at night, or an afternoon matinee during my precious siestas as I tried to catch up on sleep.

Now I stood at yet another threshold, a manmade one, wondering what the hell I was thinking, crossing into explosive territory with only two hours of daylight left to find a man who had no idea of my impending arrival. The self-sabotaging voices pecked inside my head, telling me to ignore all the signs and messages which had brought me to Scotland. The louder they got, the more I wondered what they were trying to hide from me.

I pushed on. There was no going back. The rusted clasp of the heavy iron gate clanged loudly as it closed behind me. The startled resident birdlife hadn't heard the brash sound for years and evacuated the area to find quieter perches. I moved towards the tall wall of swaying giant green beings waiting to see what my next move would be.

Nature's silence listened to my muddy footsteps. I knew this domain well, having spent many a solitary night in the woods near my parents' house, with fire, drum and weed. The essence of the plant eventually drove me insane, but it was also a key which opened me up to the unseen, harmonising me with nature in a way I was still coming to terms with. Stepping into nature now returned me to my roots – to grow.

The path followed the estuary frontage. It was littered with small boulders the size of my head and flanked by a rugged wall on my left where veins of rainwater found cracks in the rock, leaving the forest in search of a new life as the sea. On my right, the path slipped down to the now distant tide, letting velvety brown grass and light green moss take centre stage. No cars or air traffic tainted the beautiful silence. I was alone with the land again.

'Caw!' Crow came out of nowhere like a firework, bursting my balloon of tranquillity. I tripped over a boulder, breaking my fall with both hands and hitting a puddle. Subtlety wasn't Crow's style. He thrived on raging winds, tightly packed trees and pigeons to ambush. He weaved in and out of the trees cawing loudly, shooting vertically above the canopies before plummeting back into the dense forest. I couldn't help but smile. For all my love of the present moment's peace and solitude, I never grew tired of his company. He and I were growing closer by the day.

I stood with my arms by my side, palms open, facing the sky. I closed my eyes, listened to my breath and psychically connected with Crow. A freezing gust brushed my face, parching my lips like dry ice; then I saw the trees dart past in the corners of my eyes with flashes of black feather. I heard his breath and his heart race like a child's on its first ever fairground ride. My fingertips felt the slightest brush of bark as he clipped the trees and the smell of pine needles filled me up.

'Get a move on,' Crow said. I opened my eyes to see him perched on a boulder with a feather that didn't belong to him stuck to his beak with the previous owner's blood. 'You won't find his cabin in the darkness.'

'Where is it?' I yelled as he departed and his delighted 'caw' was swallowed by the forest. Quite how much he knew about where I was going and who I was meeting was a mystery, but his persistence to make sure I kept my side of a bargain with the spirit world was, as ever, unbreakable.

The path curved away from the water and led me into the forest, gradually narrowing to a metre wide with its terrain changing from old brown tarmac to sodden brown sand. The pines stood to attention, curious about my arrival. Carpets of bright green lichen spread from the path and into the dark wooded realm. Half an hour passed. I repeatedly checked the small blue dot on my mobile map-app to track my painfully slow progress. The two-hour walk described by the owner of the guest house was a gross understatement. The light faded fast and my steps quickened to quieten my head as it raced with thoughts of turning back to the guest house for a hot meal by an open fire. To turn back, however, would leave my cup empty, but I had no idea what was supposed to fill it. My leading foot froze as nature paused the music and I became her statue: waiting, wondering about 'The Path' I'd opted to walk on. Yes, it was best to stay on path, but sometimes The Path was boring and straight and predictable, like the one I saw ahead of me. My eyes twitched left and right, into the murky land beyond the first line of trees. If I was going to follow a path, I could find my own way, not the one marked with large four-by-four tyre tracks. If spirit was guiding me and insisting that I follow its way, it could stop me stepping on an unexploded bomb – couldn't it? I hopped across the small gully at the side of the path and darted into the woods. Every step was charged with bursts of adrenalin and then relief, as I realised my legs hadn't been blown off.

The forest thickened around me, interested in my sudden arrival. Tall thin pines became giant dense Christmas trees. I reached for my phone to check my location. A shudder rippled through my body. The last remaining birds singing the evening chorus cut their songs short. Raindrops the size of marbles pelted the autumn foliage and a wind whistled through the trees, parting the clouds just enough to allow multi-coloured rays of the setting sun through the canopy. Swirling blackened clouds rolled above me, blotting out the brief light show. I sprinted back to the car park, overdosing on adrenaline when all went as dark as night. A lightning bolt split the blackness and thunder descended on the forest, putting the fear of Thor into me. Sticks and leaves hit my face, and an explosion sent me flying into the branches where I lay like a broken present, my ears ringing the alarm to get the hell out of there. I frantically checked my legs to make sure they hadn't been blown off. I had new gratitude for every part of me which lived and breathed since my body had managed to recover from the abuses. The branches dropped me to the ground where I sighed with relief as I felt my toes wriggle and watched a cloud of forest debris float around the canopy from my soft mossy pillow.

'Crow! Was that you?' I yelled. His reputation for trickery preceded him. I couldn't rule out the possibility that he'd been playing with unexploded bombs. He didn't answer. I brushed myself off and walked into the woods to retrieve my scattered belongings. It felt good to be among the green beings. The air was heavy with the smell of earth and foliage which lured me further from the path. I saw some of my money lying on an ant-hill; a two-pound coin rested perfectly on the top of the cone-shaped mound. The path was fading from view and for the first time on the walk I felt out of my depth; then, ever so briefly, the earth below tremored, throwing me off balance again. My hand fell into the ant-hill. Ants sprinted over my flailing arms as I swatted them off. I scampered to a different hiding place, but didn't know what I was hiding from. I heard branches move and something that sounded like a very large dog shaking itself dry. Soil rained down on me. I lay down, commando-style but scared, and looked through the gap between the ground and the bottom branches. All I saw was freshly dug earth; then, the sound stopped. I squirmed uncomfortably with the unmistakable feeling that someone, or something, was watching me. Sound-waves of slow rhythmic breaths reached me every few seconds, like the sound of giant bellows breathing life into the embers of a coal furnace; bringing it back to life. Something as hard as stone scraped huge long strokes against the bark before it let out a deep guttural 'roar!' I leapt to my feet and ran for my life, sprinting for the path. Branches scratched my face as I found myself in the midst of my own wargame and careered out of control, tumbling on the unpredictable terrain. As soon as my boots hit the path I ran with military precision towards my unsuspecting host, gibbering the Serenity Prayer for protection and never looking back.

TWO

The tranquillity of the Singing Sands beach washed over me as soon as I left the forest. Whatever I was running from had decided not to follow me to the sea. I was met by hundred-metre-long waves rolling into the beach, arcing with their last gasps and then flopping onto the shoreline with the sound of a maestro jazz drummer caressing his cymbals. A moody, low-hanging, pale-grey sky gave a dome-like feel to the place. The atmosphere alone was worth the fear and run through the forest.

I scanned the area for Logan's home. Footprints in the fine yellow sand walked past me into the sea. I traced them back to their origin, but they disappeared at the entrance to the tidal pools in the small cove to my left where the land jutted into the ocean, blocking the view of where the coastline went from here. Huge dark boulders and outcrops of stone gave way to more pine trees, but in the space between the sea and the trees I saw a cabin made of dark wood blending with the rock it sat upon. A tightly-knitted lattice of stilts raised it above the outcrops. Smoke rose from a round metal chimney poking through a slatted roof, which had seen its fair share of repairs. A front porch stretched the width of the cabin, its crooked and warped shape blended artistically with its nautical habitat. I made my way across the rock-pools toward the steps, marked by two old kerosene mining lanterns burning bright in the dusk light. My nerves jangled as I prepared myself for – what? I had no idea. There was a small square table on the front porch with two chairs and two places set for dinner. I wanted to turn and run before I was seen. I cringed at the thought of disturbing Logan and his companion, but I had come too far to turn back. As I stood with one foot on the first step and my hand on the bannister, memories of rehab and the most traumatic yet transformative time of my life returned to me. I'd been given a second chance at life. Something had guided me to Cape Town, and to this very moment in time. My head questioned every decision, but my heart knew that the Celtic land I stood upon was exactly where I should be.

'It's best to stay on path, Aaron. They will nudge gently in the beginning.' Crow's words pecked away inside my noisy head.

'I hope you're not a vegetarian!' shouted a Scottish voice. I looked back at the beach where a tall burly man wearing waders was hauling a small white boat onto the beach to meet the footprints. He stashed the oars and made his way through the rock-pools holding a brace of fish high in one hand and speargun in the other. His smile should've put me at ease, but I was unnerved by his over-familiar reaction to finding me on his doorstep. My head chattered with paranoid thoughts of how many gullible victims he'd done away with. I tried to see if the speargun was loaded, or whether his finger was on the trigger, and entertained the idea of sprinting for the forest again before he got within shooting distance. For a few seconds I felt hopelessly trapped by beasts: one behind me and another heading my way. Logan loosened the wader-straps on his shoulders and slapped the fish down on the stairs next to me. 'Not often I get this lucky with mackerel. I presume you're staying now you've come this far and seeing as I've set you a place at the table – Aaron, is it not?'

'Yes. H-how did you know my name?' I stuttered.

'*He* told me. Doesn't sound like you've met him yet, though,' Logan said, releasing his beard from an elastic band and unfurling the foot-long silver tail. He was as broad as you'd expect someone who wrestled bears to be, and a few inches taller than my six feet; nothing like the bespectacled, tweed-wearing bookworm I'd pictured him to be. What skin was left exposed by his beard and wavy fringe was brown and weathered. He looked at me with eyes that sparkled with all the sunlight they'd caught from the fishing trip, and held out his hand, smiling and nodding for me to accept. I sealed my fate with a firm handshake. I squeezed hard, determined not to be intimidated.

'Yes, I'm Aaron. Good to meet you, Logan. Who is "*he*"?' I asked, releasing his hand.

'Come inside for a brew. We'll get to that,' he said, patting me on the shoulder as we walked inside.

My eyes took time to adjust to the dimly-lit open-plan interior which was furnished in perfect symmetry and smelt of coffee – good coffee. Single beds were pushed against the left and right walls. A central living area with a three-seater sofa and a low oak table with live bark edges faced a large black wood-burner which threw its dancing orange glow over the dark creosoted walls. A small kitchenette was tucked into the far left corner and in the right corner was a door which I hoped led to the bathroom.

'Make yourself at home, Aaron, get yourself warm.' Logan nodded towards the sofa and lifted a kettle from the top of the wood-burner. He flipped the lid open with his thumb and inhaled the contents with a long slow sniff, closing his eyes and breathing in the steam which clearly transported him to the coffee plantations. 'Damn, that's good, eighty percent Arabica from Rwanda and twenty Nicaraguan Robusta. How do you take it?'

'I'll pass, thanks. Too late for me. I won't get a wink of sleep.' My relationship with stimulants was not a healthy one. Coffee was something I allowed myself only when there was a long drive ahead as it agitated my drug-frazzled nervous system when I had nothing to occupy myself with.

'Ha! That's the whole idea, laddie, there's a lot to be getting on with. We both know you're not here to sight-see. You came here to learn, did you not?' Logan poured coffee into two large metal camping mugs and placed them on the table. My brain was still trying to decipher what he'd said in his strong Scottish accent. He sat opposite me on the sofa, momentarily losing himself in the flames as the orange glow consumed his complexion. 'It's good to have your company, Aaron. You're most welcome… cheers!' He offered me my coffee and held his mug up to mine.

'Cheers, Logan, thanks for being so hospitable. I had no idea what kind of welcome I'd get coming unannounced.'

'Ha!' he laughed, dribbling coffee down his chin. 'You *were* announced, Aaron. Look up there, look laddie, look all around you.'

He pointed to the walls, which were covered from floor to ceiling with animal parts, instruments and objects I'd never seen before. A line of small turtle shells arched over the wood-burner, split in the middle by a giant tortoise shell. There were several brushes made with black hair and bone handles, one of which looked very similar to a human femur; there were parts of elaborate fur costumes and porcupine needle necklaces and skulls of small mammals surrounded by flutes, feathered fans, hand drums, rattles and dried plants, but it was a large painting framed with driftwood under the turtle shells which caught my eye. Praying hands wearing an amethyst ring emerged from a green mist. It had a heavenly feel. The skin seemed to change texture in the firelight. One minute the fingers looked as though they belonged to an old man, the next, like the branches of a tree. The hands oozed wisdom and power. A shiver ran through me as I imagined the glare of their owner from behind the green mist.

'Does it creep you out?' Logan said.

'A bit. Whose hands are they?'

Logan stood up and walked to the painting. He stroked his beard and ran his index finger over the outline of the hands, then placed his palm over the amethyst ring and whispered something.

'Merlin's… they're Merlin's hands,' he said.

'The wizard?' I asked.

'Ha! He wouldn't like it if you called him that. He's so much more than a wizard, Aaron, he's a master of magical arts, of beasts, and the forest.'

'Why are you talking about him in the present tense?'

Logan turned and faced me, holding his hands behind his back to find the heat from the fire. He paused and stared, as though he were hearing voices. 'I'll teach you what I can in one month. Tell me at the end of that time if you still need an answer to that question. Whether you stay for longer is up to you. Oh, and I don't charge a nightly rate. Just put a donation in the tin on the shelf in the kitchen. Whatever you feel is right is alright, laddie.'

'What are we going to learn? I've just come to ask you about the Ardnamurchan volcano. It's the only reason I'm here. I found a record of the book you were going to publish. I want to know…' My words fell away like the onset of premature dementia and I suddenly felt so lost. Surrounded by garish objects, listening to a man who thought Merlin was not only real, but still alive. 'To know… I don't know. I don't know what I'm doing here. Shit!' I smacked my head with the palm of my hand, trying to rattle the answers out of my brain. Nothing came. I felt sick. Had I made a monumental mistake?

'Shamanism, Aaron. It's the answer to all your questions. It will answer them all and bring you more, like why didn't I finish the bloody book? Shamanism has all the answers, as long as you ask the right questions.'

'What's shamanism?' I said, hoping it was one of the right questions.

Logan returned to the sofa and sipped the rest of his coffee. He lost himself again in the fire for a moment. 'See those flames, laddie? They're alive. Hear those waves?' He cocked his head to the side and froze, wide-eyed. 'They're alive too! Spirit lives in 'em. Those rocks the incoming tide is crashing on – they're so alive they'll tell you stories if you listen carefully enough. Those trees you walked through and the clouds floating over your head, they've all got their own spirit! Their own souls. Spirit is in everything, even…' He paused and leaned forward to look me straight in the eyes. 'Even that beast you ran from, laddie… even the beast. Shamanism is the ancient spiritual practice which helps us communicate with those spirits and nature energies. We can ask them for answers and teachings about the path we're on, and healing – oh yes, lots of healing. Doesn't that interest you?'

'Yes.' The tremors returned to my hands. Logan had spooked me. It was difficult to be at ease in the company of someone who knew so much about me, and I, so little about him.

'A shaman enters a trance-like state, usually by drumming or listening to a rhythm which alters the frequency of their brainwaves. It's then that they can let go of their physical body, while still being aware of it, to embark on a soul-flight. The physical part of you, Aaron, is the smaller part. Your non-physical self, or soul, is always flying. I've been waiting for years for someone to finish what I started – years, I tell you. Cheers! Ha!' He held out his mug and smiled.

Hearing him call me by my name set me at ease. 'Cheers, Logan,' I said, clanking our mugs together.

He set about gutting several mackerel with the finesse of a master-chef.

'Finish what? And what about the beast?' I said.

'We'll get to *him* soon enough. He's not really a beast, though.' Logan stopped filleting and held up the knife, accentuating his point with the razor-sharp blade. 'More a lord. I know you've got more questions, hold on to them for now. I promise most'll be answered. Let's eat! You can't journey to the spirit world on an empty stomach.'

He disappeared onto the front porch with the fish, leaving me inside to stare at the macabre array of tribal objects surrounding me in the flickering firelight. The glare from a bird type mask painted with a white and red Haida design made me feel uneasy, but at the same time I was intrigued. I'd always had a fascination for Haida art. The bold clean lines of bright brush strokes looked futuristic, like a race who'd travelled back in time to settle on the North West Pacific Coast of Canada and North America. I walked over to inspect it further with my face inches from the long wooden beak extending two feet away from the wall. I touched the point of the beak with my fingertips and closed my eyes, expecting to feel a buzz of mystical energy.

'See you've met the Thunderbird then, nice, eh?' Logan appeared with a burning stick, startling me. I tripped backwards, my heels snagging on the edge of a black bearskin rug as I retreated quickly from the mask. 'Come outside and get some supper, the light's leaving for the night. It's a beautiful time of the evening; when magic can happen, especially when I'm cooking, ha!'

The smell of sizzling butter wafted from a cast-iron frying pan resting on a wire mesh over half an oil drum which had flames jumping from it. Logan threw a generous handful of fresh herbs into the pan and shook it back and forth, making the fish teeter on the lip before flipping it pancake style and seasoning the other side.

'What's a Thunderbird?' I asked.

Logan motioned for me to sit at the table. The sea turned twenty-four carat gold as the sun sank beyond the horizon.

'Call them storm-bringers if you like. They have a wrath you don't want to ever experience, but their rain is sacred and all-healing.' Logan paused and lost himself in the sky with the pan poised for the next flip. 'Belief in the Thunderbird is common among all natives of the Pacific North West.' He switched back on, flipping the fish. 'They know it as an enormous super-being. A half-human, half-eagle form living in the mountains. Thunder comes from its wings, and lightning from the forked tongue of a fish living in its wings. Celtic mythology talks of a similar supernatural being living in the Highlands. There's parts that are still truly wild, where no one's been for centuries. Here you go.' Logan slid a plate of fresh fish and herbs over to me, triggering salivation. 'Not so fast. We make an offering before we eat.'

He moved a small bowl into the centre of the table, placed a piece of his fish in it and raised it to his mouth to breathe on the food before passing it to me.

'Breathe on it, for the spirits. Our breath is our signature, so they know who it came from,' he said.

I placed some of my food in the bowl and breathed on it. Logan took it back and stood holding the bowl head-height. 'So here we are, here we are. Thank you to the ones swimming in the sea, I'm sorry I took you away from your home, but I thank you for feeding us, for this meal, and for the plants, the still ones, the herbs which make such a beautiful aroma and flavour. Thank you thank you thank you, to the soil and the rain and the sun which grew these beautiful vegetables and to you, Mother Earth, for holding them safe in the ground until they were ready for us. Thank you thank you.' Logan walked to a bolder on the beach and placed the bowl on it. 'Repetition is good by the way, for when you do the next blessing. Everything revolves around gratitude. Let's eat.'

A distant flash of lightning signalled the majestic elevation of a super-moon above the tree line. I felt a burst of gratitude for the situation I found myself in after running blindly through the forest not knowing what I was going to find. A deep rumble of thunder called out as the final waves of the day detonated on the beach. Logan stopped eating as he listened to it and looked at me. We exchanged smiles and finished our food in silence as nature's magical sound-and-light show played on.

A second cup of coffee washed down an exceptional plate of seafood and sharpened my mind. I felt ready for whatever Logan had in store.

'Lay yourself here, laddie. This is to cover your eyes when we start.' Logan handed me a piece of pristine velvet material long enough to tie around my head. He sat with his back to the wood-burner, his aura lit-up by the flame. 'Your first journey is always to the Underworld to find your first ally; your main power animal. Don't listen to the sound the stick makes as it hits the drum-skin, listen to what comes afterwards. Listen to the reverb.'

'What drum?'

'This one.' Logan stood up and pulled a round frame-drum from the wall next to the painting of Merlin's hand and gave it to me. It was made of a light wooden frame about five inches deep and nearly two feet in diameter with a pale skin stretched across it. On the back of the drum was a perfectly symmetrical criss-cross of threads of the same skin, branching from the main piece, all finding their own places in small holes expertly drilled into a fork-shaped branch. 'The frame is oak, the handle is ash and the skin, reindeer. The Danish make the best drums… in my opinion, that is.'

'What do you mean, the Underworld?' I said.

'The unseen world of spirit, as far as shamanic tradition goes, is divided into three worlds. The Underworld where the animal spirits reside is a place of primal power where our ancestors dwell. Then there's the Middleworld, this place right here where you're sitting – the land which we live and breathe on with just a veil separating us from the realm of spirit. There's no need to go up or down – spirit dwells alongside us all. Then there's the Upperworld, a place of great knowledge where our teachers reside. Your first journey is, in some ways, the most important, as your power animal will, if you continue to pay it attention and respect, become your life-long ally. But the spirit will choose you, not you him. Once you have found each other you never journey anywhere without your ally. He is there to help you and protect you. The Underworld is a place of wondrous landscapes and cosmic skies; it's where we replenish our energy and renew our connection to spirit if we feel the need. Before we start, though, you need to think of somewhere to start your journey from, somewhere you've actually visited. You start the journey from this same place regardless of where you are journeying to, be it the Upper, Middle or Underworld. It can be a tree, a cliff, a waterfall or a wishing-well. Just somewhere you know, a base you return to when the journey ends.'

I closed my eyes to find the shape of a tree I knew so well: the apple tree in my parents' garden where I'd spent five years of my childhood. I remembered the wild patch of grass which was never mowed by my dad. It circled around its base where I played with my toy soldiers. Dad told me it was always important to leave an area in every garden wild for the nature spirits to do their work. So I role-played battle scenes with my toys which defended the patch at all costs. I remembered the scratches and bruises on my arms and legs from the climbs and falls from the tree's branches, and the pyramids of fallen apples I made in the autumn. Most of all, though, I pictured the small hole in the middle of a knothole, just big enough for a sparrow to make its home and stay safe from the watchful eyes of the sparrow-hawk which patrolled the area. For me, the hole was a place of daydream and magic where my imagination ran wild, where dwarves and trolls did battle and where baby dragons slept by day and ventured out to feed on the apples at night.

'Caw!' Crow's feet scratched at the cabin roof.

'Friend of yours?' Logan asked. 'Not many crows I know fly at night.'

'He's not your average crow. It's a long story – one I don't know fully myself, yet.'

'I think you'll do quite well at this. Just relax, keep an empty cup, as it were, for something to arrive and, most importantly, don't second guess or question anything. You'll need to remind yourself of that a few times. It can take years to trust that what you're seeing, hearing or feeling is real. Where have you chosen?'

'It's an apple tree.'

'Nice, a magical tree. When you start journeying, describe it out loud, tell me what's happening. It helps your subconscious validate the information in the early journeys. Cover your eyes and say your question out loud, then think it again when the drumming starts. When the journey ends of its own accord, or if you want it to finish, say "I'm back in the room" and I'll signal the end with a different rhythm. Remember, the spirit has to choose *you*… ride the rhythm, laddie, ride the rhythm.'

I remembered the deep rhythmic hum which had lured me to Table Mountain from day one of my rehab programme. Where was *this* rhythm going to take me?

I returned myself to the garden of my childhood and focused on the small hole. 'I am journeying to the Underworld to meet my power animal,' I said.

Logan started drumming. I took a deep breath. My body

sagged into the sofa as I exhaled. I repeated the question and the rhythm carried me into dark space. Everything swirled, I hesitated to use my voice in case I broke my concentration. My head moved in circles. I tried to stop it moving, but it wanted to rotate, dipping more to the left like a magnet was pulling me with its force.

'I can see myself standing next to the tree.' The sound of the drum held me close to its rhythm. 'I'm being sucked into the tree, its dark, I'm spiralling, twisting through the soil. There are roots, earthworms and stones flying by. I can smell the earth. I think there was a leg of a rabbit scrambling. Vines are following me, no, chasing me, green vines, now they've gone. It's dark again. I've stopped moving.' Nothing happened for a time, I had no idea how long. I tuned into the drumming and whispered my request again. 'A parrot flew at me, a Blue Macaw. There's a frog on the ground. I can see my bare feet standing on the shore of a small shallow lake, the stars are so bright above me they're reflecting in the water. An owl! There's an owl looking at me.' I stared across the water into the blackness on the other side. Logan's drumming sounded louder. 'Please show me.' I waited, my head twirled round, and then I saw him. 'There's a stag, he's looking at me from the other side of the lake. He's walking towards me through the shallow water. He's standing in front of me now. He's huge! – are you my power animal? He's bowing his head, his big brown eye is level with me. Now he's kneeling on the ground next to me, rubbing his head against my chest. His antlers are growing like trees; foresting around me. There's velvet on them; they're pulsating… so alive! The velvet is disappearing, exposing hard bone. God they're magnificent! I'm reaching out to his coat, I can feel it bristle as I run my hand against the grain of his fur. He's grunting, happy. I feel like climbing onto his back, he's watching me. He nods his head towards his back, I'm climbing on. I reach for the nearest antler and hold it with one hand. Green vines, like ivy, are growing from his antlers around my wrists. Warm green pulsating vines, yes, they have a pulse, I can feel his heart beating through the vines. I'm placing my other hand on the other antler, vines are growing around it. He's standing up.'

Everything went black again, I lost all visuals; just the sound of Stag's breath fading in and out with Logan's drumming. 'I'm in blackness, I can feel the antlers against my skin. I'm twisting my hands, like I'm revving a motorbike's handlebar throttle. Stag's feet are scratching at the ground. I'm revving; he's scratching, I'm so tense. He bolts! Now we're running so fast, charging. I don't know if I can hold on. It's gone black again. I can still hear his breath and see flashes of his hooves spitting grass in their wake as we sprint at full speed. We're running up a steep hill, it's almost vertical now. There's an explosion, lava is flying out of the top of the hill. It's too much, I'm out of control. We're surfing the lava flows. The vines tighten and the pulse quickens with our acceleration, there's reassurance in the grip they have on me now. I can hear my heart beating in time with Stag's hooves as they hit the lava and we descend the steep banks of the volcano. We're back on solid ground, still running, only the sound of hoof on earth with his breathing and mine together – as one. He's slowing, drawing to a halt. The vines release me. I'm climbing down from his back. His antlers climb into the sky until the tips are out of sight. We return to the garden through the hole. "Thank you," I say to him, pressing my forehead into his head. The brownness from his eyes engulfs me… a small flurry of white feathers blows through the hole and rests on the wild grass at the base of the tree. I am back in the room.'

Logan's drumming sped up to a frantic level and then wound down to a crawling rhythm, stuttering to a final drum beat until we were in silence. I realised my head had stopped rotating, but a new charge of energy pressed between my eyes. My hands fizzed with supernatural electricity, so strong, I hadn't felt anything like it since my first fateful Reiki initiation ten years ago. I bathed in the cosmic aftermath of the experience, eventually removing the blindfold. I looked at Logan who was busy writing notes in a journal bound in thick burgundy leather. He repeatedly twisted and unfurled his beard around his index finger.

'Be with you in just a wee sec,' he said.

I looked at my buzzing hands and then around the room to get my bearings, having just travelled to and from another reality. My brain bulged with the enormity of what had just happened; my mind began to pick it all apart, analysing and rationalising it all.

'Okay, Aaron? Second guessing, eh? Remember, it can take years for even the most experienced people to trust what happens. They don't call it "another reality" for nothing. Stag is with you now. You never journey without him, okay!

The first and only rule – you never, ever, journey without him,' Logan said sternly, his eyes blazing at me. How could I forget such a warning?

#

The sound of the sea woke me from the deepest sleep I'd had in months, and my first night's respite from the dreams of the armoured glove since they'd started on the flight back from Cape Town. For a few seconds I had no idea where I was; I gripped the bed for reassurance. The smell of the freshly stoked wood-burner brought me back to the here-and-now, grounding me. Stag loomed large in my mind: his presence, his gaze, the faint echo of his breath and the resonance of the pulsating vines around my wrists. I was quite happy with the outcome of my first shamanic journey, but I knew how powerful my mind was; it had sent me spiralling into the world of a junkie where I'd courted the dark contents of my shadow-side. If it could do that, maybe it could link my fascination with an extinct volcano and throw me a classic Scottish animal in the process. Wherever my mind had gone, I wanted to go there again.

Logan's bed was empty. He'd left a note on the table which read 'Porridge on the stove and fresh brew in the pot, laddie!' I ventured outside to a glorious sunrise and crisp air which brought my breath to misty life. The tide was so far-out, I struggled to see the threshold of land and sea. The sun had free rein of the sky and transformed the cove into an oasis of light and life. Its rays danced on hundreds of rock-pools, and the birds skimmed low over the water in perfect lines. I sat on the steps and soaked up the scene as I ate my Scottish oats, before walking to the beach with my hands hugging the warm metal coffee cup.

'Caw!' Crow dive-bombed me, manifesting out of thin air, clipping my head with his wing and depositing a mussel shell in my cup with expert precision which would easily have earned him a place in the Black Arrows aerial display team, if it existed. 'Caw caw, two points!' He laughed, disappearing into the forest before I had a chance to apprehend him. I was grateful for the reminders he gave me that he was never more than a wing's length away, but I was beginning to miss our impromptu chats. I was out on a limb here. No mobile phone signal, three miles of exploding forest separating me from the nearest neighbour and some kind of animal patrolling the paths. I wasn't about to throw away the very intriguing, if a little unnerving, welcome Logan had given me. I turned three-sixty, scanning the front-line of the forest to my right and across the empty beach. I found him to my left on the last piece of coastline that jutted out into the ocean before disappearing to the next cove. He was sitting cross-legged, facing out to sea. While alcohol no longer graced my gullet, I still retained the alcoholic drinking technique; I downed the rest of my coffee and shook the cup. The mussel shell rattled from side to side getting Logan's attention. He moved to a kneeling position, kissed the rock and stood up, stretching his hands towards the sky before hopping down to zigzag his way back through the rock-pools.

'Trust you slept well?' he said.

'Like a baby. What were you doing out there, yoga?'

'Meditation, laddie, it helps to keep my demons at bay. We've all got our own demons, eh?' He smiled at me. I was struck by the brightness of his eyes and the glow of his complexion.

'What meditation?' I said, instantly engaged.

'Just simple stuff, focusing on the breath. If you're gonna stick around for a while you'll need to learn that too. You could be spending a lot of time out there.' Logan nodded towards the rock he was sitting on. He turned to face me, putting his hand on my shoulder. 'There's potential in you, laddie… real potential. I'd be more than happy to help you find it. You can ask all the questions you like, but you'll need to get out there on that rock every day and meditate to find the real answers.'

'What's so special about that rock?'

'The rock is something to be experienced, I can't describe it to you. All will become clear when the time is right. Do you meditate?'

'Yes, I practise Transcendental Meditation, so, what about the volcano? Why do you think it's called me up here?' I kicked a stone out of frustration at Logan's aloofness as we walked along the beach. More of it was embedded under the ground. My toes crunched into it.

Logan nodded his head and made an approving grunt. 'No time like the present. Take these, they'll keep you going.' He threw me a bag of mixed nuts. 'Time to introduce yourself to the rock, you're in luck with the sunshine and the neap Spring tide. It will be back in an hour, best make haste.

That sea's got a sharp nip to it, but it won't cover the rock for another couple of months. Who knows if you'll still be here then, ha! Lady Luck's smiling on you today, laddie!' He skipped away excitedly with a jump and a click of his heels like an oversized leprechaun dancing to fiddle music.

'What about the volcano, Logan!' I shouted, but it fell on his selectively deaf ears. I remained none the wiser, and in his hands. I was grateful for my own company again and relished the space to keep my meditation programme going. Transcendental Meditation was the jewel in the crown of my first year of recovery. I'd returned to England without my cravings for cocaine and alcohol, but with a savage chain-smoking addiction in its place. I was relieved when the counsellors told me not to attempt to give up everything in one go. Nicotine helped me deal with the bizarre feelings of alienation and isolation I'd experienced when I first returned to England. I'd been away for so long, the only relationships I had were with my family. Friends who still drank alcohol never understood my restlessness if I stayed too long in a bar drinking lime and soda. Sobriety and clean-living was both the biggest breath of fresh air and the most hectic rollercoaster ride imaginable. My demons hadn't disappeared at all, they were tagging along for the ride, waiting for me to stick around the unhealthy atmosphere of a nightclub or pub for a minute too long, or to take the wrong turn down the wine aisle of the supermarket. Glasses and bottles stared at me and began talking.

'I taste good. Drink me. Remember how good we were together,' they said.

My frazzled nervous system was a long way from being cleansed. While I appeared to be functioning, on the inside I battled feelings of not belonging to this life anymore… but then I found Transcendental Meditation.

A few months after leaving Cape Town I went to a free talk and heard a teacher discussing a simple effortless technique which could, if practised regularly, help me find peace from the self-ridicule, the sabotaging voices. But it turned out that peace of mind just skimmed the surface of the treasures waiting for me.

I wasted no time taking the weekend course to learn my mantra and put the same practice, patience and perseverance that kept me focused on recovery into my meditation. I became religiously devoted to it. Nothing and no one stopped me doing my twenty minutes, twice a day, to access the oneness of the unified field of consciousness underpinning the philosophies of the world's religions. In those moments of transcendence I began to realise – no, I remembered – that I had potential. Lots of it. Once I'd been overcome by a tidal wave of love on a train journey, causing me to face out of the window to hide the tears of happiness streaming down my face. Meditation was bringing me closer to my Goddess, to Mother Nature herself. I was well and truly hooked on something new which gave me a natural high more powerful than any chemical I'd ever taken – I had found my new addiction.

I covered the top of my eyes with my hand to shield them from the sun and locate the rock. There was no need, though. Crow was perched on it, occasionally diving onto one of the many seafood treats laid out before him. Crab legs appeared to be on the menu today. The funny thing was, he didn't need to eat anything. Nothing from the spirit world needed food to survive, but he was so enchanted by the flavours on the earthly menu. I let out a long exhalation of misty morning breath; remembering the times Crow had enjoyed inhaling my cigarette smoke. Meditation had brought that slow suicidal habit to an end. As my meditation progressed, a feeling of inevitability started to grow inside me. My body started to talk to my head in a weird kind of telepathy. 'Stop killing me!' I heard it say. After three days of trying to make it through just twenty-four hours without a cigarette, I broke the cycle, reclaimed control over my health and never looked back. I left my life as a night-owl behind me and embraced meditation at the dawn of each new day. They were such sacred times.

I gingerly made my way to the rock, resorting to a final scramble along the pathless coastline where the returning tide lapped over limpets clinging onto their jagged abodes. When I reached the end of the cove's left arm, I stopped, stunned, by the sudden smoothing of the plinth-like surface which had one small step. It was the perfect place for sitting cross-legged and drifting in and out of a mantra with the ebb and flow of the ocean. The tree closest to the rock had one unusual protruding branch, as though it were reaching hopelessly for a touch of the water. It was a strong straight branch with clean lines, perfect for pull-ups if I could jump to it. I had worked hard on my physique since rehab. Addiction had ravaged my body, stripping away forty kilos and leaving me close to major organ failure, but my new muscles and physical strength fortified my spirit, keeping the ghost of my gaunt junkie-reflection well and truly at bay. The tree held its hand out to me, and a chance to keep the muscle I'd built. I crouched low and leapt vertically with both arms high above me. My hands found the bark with ease and its texture made it easy to hold. I repeatedly pulled my chin above the branch until my arms burned. As I dropped to the ground I moved straight into the press-up position and kissed the stone with my chin until my chest and arms failed me. The setting invigorated me. No television monitors or whirring treadmills with people checking their mobile phones ambling along on them. I felt the pump in my muscles and I wanted more, leaping to the branch again, looking for the burn and the endorphin high.

When I was finally spent, I shovelled a generous helping of nuts into my mouth and sat down on the plinth. I waited for my heart-rate to return to normal and took a farewell glimpse of the ocean before diving into my own sea of consciousness. A sea otter poked his whiskered face out of the ocean in front of me and quickly disappeared, shocked that he hadn't seen Logan.

The ease of the present moment dawned on me as I sat surrounded by nature. I stared at the sea in wonderment, at the way it moved and the way the clouds' shadows scudded across its surface. Peace washed over me, and I realised I had just been granted the serenity I'd been praying for.

THREE

'The Upperworld is where you'll meet your spiritual teacher. You start from the same place in front of your tree with Stag, but this time you travel upwards. You've travelled down the roots of the Tree of Life, now it's time to climb its branches. This is cosmic exploration at its finest,' Logan said, stubbing out the embers of a giant cigar-shaped clump of sage which he'd smudged around the room. The Thunderbird mask stared at me through lingering clouds of a sweet heady aroma which had me reminiscing over the pungent smell of cannabis I'd been so used to. He reached for his drum. 'Don't be surprised if Stag keeps his distance a bit when you arrive. He'll still escort you there and back. No need for a running commentary this time, just focus on within.' Logan flung his beard over his shoulder and crouched down to the wood-burner with his arms spread out, embracing the flames, drum in one hand and beater in the other. He closed his eyes and whispered unintelligible prayers. 'Thank you, thank you, thank you,' he finished.

'When are you going to tell me about the volcano, Logan?

I've come all this way and you won't give me anything.'

Logan turned his head and half-looked over his shoulder at me with the air of a school teacher rebuffing a petulant pupil. I knew my timing wasn't perfect, but my curiosity grew constantly and I wanted to know what, if anything, was waiting for me in Ardnamurchan. I grabbed the front of my shaved head, trying to tug at a clump of the absent hair out of frustration.

Nonetheless, I was eager to journey again on the rhythm of the drum after the dawn's hectic meditation on the rock. Nature's tranquillity didn't always guarantee me a peaceful meditation; the stress-release triggered by meditation was unpredictable. Be it anger, resentment, fury, sadness or profound peace and love, rollercoaster rides of emotion were not unusual, but the calm after the ride was exquisite. My head quite rightly objected to being taken into its quiet realms where the sludge was waiting to be stirred from the nooks and crannies of my frazzled nervous system. This morning's meditation was constantly clouded by Stag's presence. I heard his feet scraping at the dirt and caught glimpses of his flared nostrils breathing orange sparks as his silhouette appeared on the brow of a hill, baying loudly at the moon and running full-pelt on rivers of lava. The sense that he was near distracted me from my mantra. I had turned repeatedly to check the line of trees behind me for movement and the onset of an explosive gallop.

I blindfolded my eyes, uncertain of what mood I'd find Stag in, and smiled, thinking how well the phrase 'power animal' suited him. I took myself to the apple tree where

Stag waited for me. He bent down, bringing his huge eyes level with mine. I felt a telepathic connection with him that wasn't there before. There was no need for me to speak, I knew he understood me, and I him. I heard his heart beating and felt his breath brush against the back of my hand. I placed one hand on his antler and as my fingers grasped it, the long grass surrounding the tree glowed bright. We'd been given the green light.

He stooped down to me; strands of ivy grew out of his antlers as I reached for them and wrapped them around my wrists before we sprang to the top of the apple tree. I swung rodeo-style onto his back just before his front legs hurled us into the sky. The rhythmic sound of his breath replaced the absent drum of his feet on the earth. Blue sky turned to black in the blink of an eye. An owl watched us fly by as we moved into the starlit skyscape: not a hint of vertigo, only exhilaration. The moon shone like an airport's runaway guiding us in for landing, Stag knew where he was going. The crater loomed in front of us. He flew faster with every stride. I waited for him to slow down so we could rest on the moon, but he had other plans and accelerated to ramming speed. His breaths turned to aggressive grunts as the crater's circumference surrounded us moments before we smashed into the moon's surface. I held on tight, white-knuckling Stag's antlers, hiding my face in the thick fur of his neck, bracing for impact, but a loud splash replaced the collision I thought was in store for us. Our pace slowed momentarily, all movement slurred. Panic set in as I realised we were underwater. I kept my lips tightly pursed together, praying we were about to surface for air. My cheeks ballooned and I waited for my lungs to start burning, but nothing changed. Surrender to suffocation never happened. I transitioned smoothly into my new amphibious body and phased my focus, like a volume control, in and out of Logan's drumming and the room my body sat in. The sound of the beater drumming an unfaltering metronomic rhythm reassured me. I had two hearts beating. One for my earthly body and one to power the spiritual engines propelling my etheric soul. I was very much alive and flying high. A silver slip-stream of bubbles escaped from Stag's mouth as we darted like a comet through the dark lunar sea. I focused on Logan's drumming to steady myself and with no end in sight I opened my mouth, gasping for whatever cosmic reality had in store for me. The relief was brief and sweet. I sucked in the watery air and relaxed my grip on Stag's antlers, giving him a kick of my heels to tell him I was fine and to speed on to our mystery destination. Stag's pistons kicked us to the surface where light shone, and someone waited for us to make our ascent: a tall bright white figure, his outline blurred by the surface of the water. Stag was spurred on by his presence. We swam faster and the figure started dancing, clapping its hands, hopping up and down in an excited jig. The sound of crashing cymbals filled my ears as we burst out of the water. The change in density hit me hard, making me lose grip of the antlers. I clung onto Stag's neck as he slowed his step onto a beach with fine white sand. The ivy released me. I fell to the ground and lay there, sprayed by a shower of crystal droplets as they exploded into the sunlit air from

Stag's coat as he shook his body like a dog fresh back from a trip to the doggy spa.

Logan's drumming was steady and unfaltering, anchoring my physical body while my soul flew to a reality I had easily become accustomed to. A dense bamboo forest lined the back of the beach; each stem was several inches thick and spaced with barely enough room to walk between them. I held a fistful of the fine egg-timer sand in front of my face and watched it slip through my fingers. A large hand appeared in front of my face with its outstretched palm offering to pull me to my feet. The body faded into a cloud of white light where the shadowy outline of a man's figure was barely visible. Long wide fingers, which had their own small set of biceps, gently curled and straightened, beckoning me. A ring adorned the middle finger, its purple light glowing like a cosmic traffic-light to give me the all-clear that it was safe to take the offer. Stag stepped back as I held the hand and it pulled me to my feet. I peered through the cloud to see who my ally was, but his shape retreated. He pointed to the bamboo forest, indicating I should follow him as he weaved between the stems toward a clearing where firelight flickered. I heard no words, was just conscious of thoughts and feeling flowing to me with strong intention.

'Who are you?' I said out loud.

'All in good time, young man, all in good time,' he said. We made our way through the bamboo to a clearing where firelight flickered. I glanced over my shoulder to the beach where Stag stood sentry.

The clearing was a perfect circle of bamboo stems. I walked inside it, towards a second inner circle of tree stumps surrounding the fire. Daylight turned to night, and the fire burned brighter. Flames licked the air above my head, releasing sparks into the sky where they joined a perpetual stream of shooting stars, all carrying my wish that this magical journey would never end. I went to sit on one of the stumps, expecting to start a conversation with my host, when his hand rested firmly on my shoulder and turned me to face him. His other hand appeared from the cloud with its fingers held straight and rigid in a karate-chop pose. I watched, paralysed, as his hand drifted slowly towards me with dagger-like certainty and pierced my chest. At first the blood dripped, blotting the white sand with small splats, but as his hand pushed in further, my ribs cracked like twigs and blood gushed out of my chest. I waited for the pain, but it never came. Instead, the pull of his eyes through the thinning cloud of light kept me in a trance-like calm, and the horror at bay. I stared down at the hole in my chest as his hand withdrew, holding my heart in its palm. I felt life-force flowing through me from his other hand as it strengthened its grip on my shoulder, keeping me alive while I watched my diseased aorta stutter to a standstill. There in front of me was the decay of alcoholism and drug addiction. I'd always wondered how deep beneath my skin the damage went and whether my liver escaping the tirade of abuse was just a façade. The heart murmurs and palpitations all made sense now. In my darkest addicted hours I had prayed endlessly for it all to end, hitting my heart with every drug I could find. I'd thumped my chest, cursing every beat in the hope that hell would open and swallow me whole.

He held my gasping heart into the fire where it crackled and spat while alchemy had its way. I watched in wonder, oblivious to the gaping hole in my chest. When his hand retreated from the flames a fading image of my heart remained, just a ghost of the organ, but something new began to take its place. Faceted outlines appeared first, shooting diagonally like lasers in perfect symmetry as the image of a diamond took shape. He cradled the finished product in his hand, briefly checking the blood-flow from my chest, and nodded his head in approval from within his misty aura. The diamond formed two pyramids mirroring each other with their vertical tips, pointing to Heaven and Earth. Its crystal-clear panes revolved in his hand, reflecting bamboo and comets as they trailed across the sky.

The drumming amplified as his hand guided the diamond into my chest. The alchemist's arms embraced me, bathing me in whiteness before vanishing in the blink of an eye. I found myself next to Stag on the beach and we flew with haste through the stars, back to the apple tree.

I placed my hand over my heart to feel its beat. Logan began the quickened call-back rhythm, increasing the beats per second to end my trance and bring me safely back to the cabin. I stroked Stag's neck in thanks. As we both looked at the tree, a long white feather floated down from the portal above the canopy and settled on the grass in front of me. I picked it up, twiddling the quill between my thumb and index finger, admiring its length and purity, like fresh snow on a stick. I couldn't think of any bird big enough to own a feather as long as my arm. The drumming slowed and stopped. I moved to uncover my eyes, but froze, distracted by the face of a horse staring at me in the darkness, so close! His breath pushed against my chest. Tears filled my eyes as I remembered where I'd seen him before. Pinocchio's solitary white horse from the Romanian orphanage appeared in the darkness.

'I am back in the room,' I said, delaying the removal of the blindfold to let my tears dry. I wasn't ready to cry in front of Logan. He moved his hand slowly up and down in front of my face to make me blink. My body fizzed with energy. If the cabin roof was suddenly removed, I would've launched myself into the sky.

'Okay, laddie?' Logan asked.

'I'm not sure.' My hand stayed glued over my heart. I blinked and looked up at the painting of Merlin's hand wearing the same ring I'd seen in the journey.

'Tell me about it.' Logan stroked his beard and smiled.

'I met someone who wore the same ring as that one up there.' I pointed to the painting of Merlin's hand. 'There was a beach and a fire burning in a circular clearing of a bamboo forest. He stuck his hand inside my chest and pulled out my heart, then he replaced it with a diamond or crystal of some kind. I feel weird.'

'You are weird, I mean, you should. You've been given an upgrade. That's the kind of thing *he* does when you first meet him. He doesn't do formalities. Why are you finding it so hard to say his name?' Logan said, crouching down next to me.

I opened my mouth and tried to speak; nothing came out.

'Merlin! Why don't you believe you met him?'

I looked away, embarrassed, but the painting pulled me in. 'Why would he be interested in me?' My old self-sabotaging demons tried to sap the excitement and steal my moment. My ego ballooned one minute with acknowledgement of my connection with Merlin, and shrank the next, as I dissed such a preposterous idea. How could I connect with such a power and legend? 'I couldn't see him properly anyway, just his hands and the faintest outline of his eyes,' I said.

'That's because you didn't believe... the more you believe, the more you see! Come on, we've got to go somewhere. That's if you're sticking around?'

'I'm not going anywhere; you haven't told me anything about the volcano. Why won't you give me something, just something about it? Why the hell am I here, Logan?' I struggled to keep up with his marching pace to the back of the beach and into the trees. 'Logan!' I shouted.

He stopped in his tracks and stood with his back to me. I watched his shoulders tighten and his right hand rise to twiddle his beard. Then he turned and pointed at me with a move that was John Travolta inspired.

'Shortbread laddie! I've been off it for months... can't resist the cravings any longer. Come on, the shop won't stay open all night.'

Logan walked into the woods, turning off the path to a huge bivouac. I helped him pull away the branches and then a tarpaulin to uncover a vintage army Land Rover with a Scottish flag on the bonnet and glass missing from the windscreen.

'Hello dear,' Logan said quietly, removing debris from

the empty shell of the wing-mirror with his hand. He patted the flag gently. 'Remember, laddie, everything is alive.' He smiled, hopped into the cold khaki seat and started the engine first time. It growled and rattled as we trundled toward civilisation. Logan was in no hurry. He savoured the fresh aroma of pine needles and sank further into his seat. His body wobbled in tune with the uneven surface of the single-track road as he teased the steering wheel left and right with two fingers. He pulled a pipe from his shirt pocket with the other hand and lit it. Smoke bellowed from his mouth and nose, trailing behind us like a steam-train as he sank into the worn seat and drifted off to la la land where the shortbread's sugary coating sparkled like diamonds; any chance of volcanic conversation was lost in the smoke. Doubt seeped into my head. I began to wonder whether he would ever give anything away about his book, or the piece of land I felt compelled to visit and learn about.

I sat, liberated by the lack of seatbelts, yet wary that we would soon pass the area of woods where the explosion had happened. Crow flanked us on the left, his blacker-than-black silhouette was clearly visible; even with the darkened forest behind him my shadow was never far away, bringing safety and calm as I sank further into the worn-out seat.

'I see you,' I whispered, casting my mind back to how he'd chaperoned me to Heathrow on the day I left for rehab. My mind and body had been shot to pieces, but Crow had showed me there was a way out as he had followed my dad's car, landing on top of the lamp-posts, turning them on with his magic touch.

I took deeper breaths and focused my eyes beyond him further into the forest as we passed the site of the explosion. A dark brown shape caught my eyes. At first, it faded in and out of view, but it became clearer the longer I peered into the Scottish jungle. The flick of a blurring heel, a spike of antler and a flash of slanting snout. It ran level with the Land Rover, straight as an arrow, never slowing to negotiate the trees. 'I see you too, Stag.'

After we had cleared the forest, I opened the gate for Logan to drive through and looked back one last time before closing it and returning to the Land Rover. I squinted to focus my eyes in the dying light, framing a small patch of forest with my hands. Something at the edge of the forest disturbed branches, preferring to keep within the boundary. I squinted as hard as I could and deciphered the image like a photographer looking at a negative. Crow's fiery eyes marked where he was perched on Stag's highest antler tine; his breath, hot from the run alongside us, sent up clouds with a strange purple glow to them and Logan started humming 'Oh Flower of Scotland' as he relit his pipe.

'Not far now, laddie,' he called from the Land Rover. I wondered if someone so Scottish could've travelled to all of the countries his regalia had come from, or were they all online purchases? Parasitical doubt seeped into my mind again.

'Please give me a sign.' I prayed, asking the Universe to show me something which would prove my flight to the moon was real. We waited at a junction for a lorry to pass before pulling out to follow it, slowly encroaching on the emblem which covered its large rectangular rear-door. The image I saw was forever etched on my mind. Painted on the lorry was a giant picture of the moon and a single crater with a bat flying past it and the words 'Fly by Night Couriers' written across the top of the lorry. I caught my breath, stunned.

Never one to settle for moderation; I wanted more. Something to seal my commitment to this as yet unknown quest. Logan turned away from the lorry at the next junction. The Ardnamurchan peninsula was a remote and quiet place. Out of season it was rare to come across more than a handful of vehicles during the two-hour round trip to the ferry stores and petrol station in Kilchoan. We had full rein of the road as it narrowed and widened from single-track to short stretches of two-way carriageway. I checked ahead before asking again. 'Please give me another sign that my journeys are real, just one more, please,' I prayed.

The blue light flashed in the rear-view mirror, like a distant firefly distracting Logan from his soft whistling through the tube of his empty pipe. He slowed the Land Rover and pulled into the next passing place to wait for the vehicle to pass. It gave a brief blast of its siren in thanks, and accelerated away. I leant forward to see the sign on the back doors of a van, mouth aghast, as a huge red heart shone in our headlights. I felt my own strong heartbeat and looked across at Logan who was grinning at me, as the blood donor van disappeared into the night and the synchronicities called me back to The Path.

FOUR

Time flew by after my first encounter with lorry-divining. I was no stranger to synchronicity and my belief in the hidden meaning of coincidences grew every day. After one month at Logan's I felt at home, which was strange considering the limited amount of socialising we did with each other. The couch was a cosy place to sleep and my organic diet of game, seafood and Scottish oats mixed with clean sea-salty air was a tonic for my recovery, like a further progression of the rehab treatment programme as I woke and counted my blessings which had seemed to grow daily since meeting Logan. No technology to distract me, no traffic noise drowning the beautiful soundscapes welcoming me into each day. Every morning I'd find my breakfast waiting for me on the table outside, along with a hot water bottle wrapped in a blanket if the weather was spitting wet or biting cold, or both. He'd return from checking his traps in the woods or from the sea in his small boat with the day's special in his hand, holding it aloft with pride, just as he had the first day he walked across the beach to meet me. I stopped asking him about the volcano, because it was clear he wasn't going to tell me anything until he was ready. He was looking after me, so I had no qualms about filling the kitchen tin with my divorce money. For the first few weeks I made a donation every weekend. The time soon blurred blissfully and I gave up remembering what day of the week it was as I succumbed to the magic Logan wove into Singing Sands bay.

My morning meditations started earlier with the approach of Spring. I couldn't wait to get onto the rock to witness the sky and wildlife waking for another pure day. The lack of access to televisions and telephones kept my mind unclogged and in tune with my surroundings. Logan postponed any more shamanic journeys and told me to put more time into my meditations. I didn't object. Getting lost in the quietest realms of my mind was actually helping me to find myself again.

'Caw! Open your eyes, Aaron,' Crow said, bursting out of the ether. He hopped across the rock in front of me as I meditated. 'It's time… you've got a visitor.' Maybe it was the way I released full ownership of my body during meditation which stopped Crow from startling me. Or perhaps it was the connection we had with each other. The burn scar on my back heated up: a mark of initiation by the elements when I was lost in an LSD fog of my own making, unable to find my way out of a New England forest for days. Back then, my drug use was experimental with new paraphernalia and techniques to try, and just one responsibility – to enjoy myself. I'd done well until that fateful 'trip'. Being struck by lightning had always been a bizarre fantasy of mine. I wanted to know what it was like, but I never expected it to actually happen. Thunderstorms stirred a side of me I didn't understand, half aroused and wanting to go to war; and half petrified by Thor's distant flashes and rumbles. I felt like the hunter and the hunted.

The scar burnt for the first time since rehab, when I had taken myself into Newlands Forest on a day-release and experienced the first visitation from the Native American. I opened my eyes with a downward gaze, peeking through the slits to ease myself back from the cosmic sea of consciousness to the one lapping on the rocks in front of me. The hazy morning sunshine was shielded by a close sea mist which left a short stretch of the sea visible before whiteness covered it. I looked behind me to find Logan's cabin, but the mist encircled me, making it dangerous to attempt the walk back to base along the uneven shoreline. The birds made their familiar exit, just as they had before the chief appeared through the South African forest. I sat and watched the mist thicken into a dense screen of fog, and waited for whatever was about to play out.

'Your buddy chose this place well, Aaron.' Crow spread his wings, catching a soft breeze which lifted him to eye level. The fog behind him swirled into a vortex. 'You've always wanted to know more about *us*; well, now you're ready. When you get back to the hut try asking Logan again what's so special about this rock.' Crow's voice had an excited edge. He tilted his wings and veered out of sight. I stared at the whirling vortex as it moved back and forth, hypnotising me. One minute it seemed close enough for me to touch it, and the next it retreated from my outstretched hand.

I heard the familiar sound of small bones jangling around his ankles and smelt the same pungent aroma of white sage which had lulled me a year ago in Cape Town. Birds squawked and screeched in the fogged forest as they crashed into the trees, unable to find their escape routes from the energy that pressed itself against me. His strides were rhythmic and definite this time, compared to the surprise and trepidation he'd previously approached with in Cape Town. There was a purpose and knowing behind the weight of his feet as they boomed and splashed across the ocean like a Native American Jesus, risen again to bring me his sermon from the spirit world.

My scar throbbed with heat, brought to life by the huge warrior I saw walking towards me. I instinctively checked the tremors in my hands to try and link his appearance to the irreversible damage caused by my junkie days, but I couldn't deny what was happening. I'd spent years denying my connection to the spirit world. All the drugs and alcohol in the world couldn't numb the psychic gifts I'd never had the courage to own until I embraced the darkest night of my soul, and most of the plant-based drugs had had the opposite effect, opening me up even more to the unseen.

I stood to greet him as he stepped smiling onto the rock and opened his arms to spread mottled brown feathers from his armpits down to his wrists. I stepped towards him, opening my arms to return the greeting as rivers of tears flowed from both our eyes.

'Son,' he whispered, closing his winged arms around me.

I waited for the darkness of the warm feathered cave to lift, but the darkness deepened. I spun out of control. My arms and legs flailed everywhere as the earth suddenly fell away. I closed my eyes and surrendered; I was good at that.

The sound and smell of a crackling fire brought me to my senses. I pushed my hands into the ground I sat cross-legged upon. The rock had gone. I kept my eyes closed and encouraged myself to open them as I clenched fists of desert sand and let it flow through my fingers. The last grains fell and I opened my eyes. The fire birthed yellow fireflies into a night sky gifted with a generous sprinkling of stars which arced over me as the world rotated slowly. A group of tepees stood to my left, and empty desert stretched far to my right. Giant rocks lay as stages for howling coyotes' haunting melodies.

I waited expectantly for someone or something to join me, but remained alone. The tepees didn't stir. The place was deserted. A shooting star fizzed across the sky and I wished with all my heart that everything happening was real.

'Please show me,' I said, closing my eyes as the supernatural fire burned louder. Remembering my journeys to Logan's drumming, I looked to the unseen for answers and when I opened my eyes, they came. The fire suddenly roared, towering above the tepees, spewing a cloud of sparks and smoke which engulfed me. I expected the same immunity to suffocation as I'd experienced underwater on the way to meet Merlin inside the moon, or wherever the crater took me, but instead my lungs burned, reminding me of over-eager blow-backs from joints of weed which took me to Stonedville. I ran away from the inferno, freaked by the reality of it all. The supernatural wasn't supposed to be so real – was it?

I tumbled onto the sand as the smoke lifted. Night had passed to day and the dry desert sand gave way to the clear running water of a stream where the body of a juvenile crow lay. Its wings twitched from the movement of the current. I reached forward to pick it up, but froze when I saw the colour of my hands had changed from white to brown and the soft tickle of black hair brushed across my shoulders. For someone with a shaved head it felt bizarre. I cradled the soggy black body in my hands and looked at my reflection in the shallow water where he lay. There, staring back at me, was the face of the Native American youth I'd once seen in my vision nearly twenty years earlier; all time had dissolved. My past life became present.

I smoothed the crow's feathers over its body and cupped my hands softly around it, blowing gently on its face; and as I tapped the tip of its beak with my finger its body trembled. I quickly moved it to the grass and picked a variety of herbs and grasses which covered all but its head, marvelling at the intentional way my hands selected the specific plants. I made a small circle of dry tinder grass around it and shuffled through the stones on the riverbank looking for two very specific types of rock before scampering back to the crow and striking them together repeatedly until my hands bled and the fire caught. I danced and hopped around the flames mumbling prayers for the bird, squeezing drops of blood from my hands onto its body as a gift to the healing spirits in return for their help.

Finally, when the fire had died and no more prayers escaped from my lips, I sat exhausted, waiting for my black phoenix to rise from the ashes. I heard a deep, distant rumble and looked for storm clouds in the distance before realising the sound was coming from underneath me. The ground tremored. I placed my hands either side of me to keep my balance as the action rocked the crow's body, sifting the herbs and ashes of the fire into the earth. I stared at the symbol nature had drawn: a black ash circle with a black bird, like a road sign that would be forever ingrained on my soul to signpost the way to my destiny.

As soon as the rumbling stopped, the crow hit me in the face with a barrage of flapping wings, claws and gnashing beak. I fell into the stream and lay on my back enjoying the cool flow of the water against my skin. I marvelled at how my senses translated everything I experienced while in such utter detachment from my present-day location in the Scottish Highlands, but this wasn't as strange as it had first seemed. I had always felt Native American spirit running through my soul and now, through the exploration of my more indigenous Celtic roots, I was learning more about where I'd really come from.

I smiled proudly and sloshed water into my mouth while I looked up at a bird who was never going to leave my side. Crow stared down at me, twitching sparks of light from his damp feathers as Mother Earth's magic worked its mojo on him.

'Caw!' he said.

'You're welcome, my friend.'

I closed my eyes and drifted with the soft sound and motion of the stream, watching years of our childhood friendship play out in my mind's eye. He was my night-time watchman for both animal and human threats to our safety. Having his unique bird's-eye view, Crow found the best places to stalk and set traps. We always shared the bounty. I threw pieces of meat to him. We watched the sun rise and set together; perched on the same rock. The silence between us was strong and full of energy at those times and fuelled by the same orange ball of fire which helped to bring him back to life. I cherished my beautiful black bird of *pray*.

'You are Lakota Sioux! We never give up, never lay down to die!' a man's voice said, making me spring to my feet where I found myself in the middle of a settlement as it burned around me. Blood-curdling screams echoed everywhere. My eyes turned red and a surge of anger brought me to my senses. I looked at the knife in my hand and then at Crow perched on the smoking skeleton of a tepee. We ran into the smoke, blinded by our frenzy and slashing at the flesh of our attackers. There was such freedom in the slaughter. The frenzied sounds of Crow cawing and my excited screams got louder as I tore into human flesh with my knife and hands, flailing in all directions like a whirling Dervish killing everything in its path and enjoying the main course of human scalp. Crow was always close for seconds, replicating the surgical skills he'd shown me during my darkest addicted hours when he extracted snails from their shells, but this time the human eye was what popped out of its skulled home. We were always first into the fight and the last to leave, addicted to death-fuelled adrenalin, but also to magic.

A crack of lightning peeled back the macabre scene of the battlefield to signal the start of drumming, and another vision. I danced with Crow in the middle of a circle I'd drawn in the sand with an arrow. He hopped across my shoulders as I whooped and hollered, revelling in the spectacle taking place around a huge fire. Two men danced around the flames on all fours. They danced and jerked in time with the quickening rhythm, feeding off the crowd's fervour. Occasionally they would stop still to stare at each other before pain seized them and sent them back into the possessed dance again. It seemed there was nowhere higher or faster for the voices and drums to go, but they always found the next level, pushing Crow and me out of our own comfort zones where his razor-sharp beak made glancing lacerations on my back and I retaliated theatrically with my prized arrow before: Boom! It stopped with one sudden drumbeat. I stood panting, with my hands on my knees and Crow peering over my shoulder at what was unfolding. I wiped a droplet of blood from my brow with my finger and passed it to Crow for tasting. The tribe were silent. The two men walked out of the circle of brown skin and feathers as it opened in a horseshoe to set the men free. A shaman covered in paint, fur and bones stood with a bow and arrow primed for firing high into the air. The two men stood behind a starting line, their heads hung low and their shoulders slumped, zombified.

'Caw!' Crow couldn't hold his excitement. His feet dug

into my shoulder as we waited, barely breathing, for the magic to start.

The shaman screamed at the sky as he fired the arrow and the two men suddenly dropped to their hands and knees. One instantly shapeshifted into a wolf, the other into a horse; the drumming and chanting started again and they were gone, racing for the arrow.

The vision changed from a scene of magic to one of tragic, with my adult body lying between a fire and a solitary tepee. Crow's lifeless adult body lay on my chest, his wings outstretched, embracing me with his head resting on my heart. The familiar rattle of small bones came from the tepee and then the flames started dancing to the snake-charming hums and chants of the Chief's voice inside. He burst through the flaps and danced low to the earth, singing to it as he approached our bodies, shaking a rattle in one hand and a bow in the other, the feathers of his full-length headdress rippling with every passion-filled stomp of his feet. He reached up to the sky and down to the ground, throwing pinches of tobacco from a small leather bag hung around his neck, tied tightly to keep its contents safe. He rocked from side to side, stamping and drumming with superhuman force. The ground quaked, throwing up the sand as he danced. With each movement of his body, he cried, softly at first, crouching down, asking Mother Earth to hear him. The small bones rattling around his ankles turned into owl feathers; his toes, to claws. The fire responded to him, fuelled by his anger, sorrow, and deep burning love. He wailed at the sky. It answered with a flurry of shooting stars which pulled furious clouds with their tails, closing the curtain on a beautiful starry night. The sky swirled with elemental forces. Sparks of light cut through the coalblack clouds as they hovered directly above our place in the vastness.

'I am Oka!' he shouted at the clouds, sending desert critters scurrying underground and silencing the coyotes' calls. The fire calmed and the clouds stilled, recognising his name. The faint sound of giant wings bellowed far away on the other side of the clouds where the stars and moon still shone. Overcome by something, Oka dropped his ceremonial instruments. He crouched again, kissing a handful of earth, crying, muttering prayers, throwing more tobacco in all directions. He hid his face in the flames as feathers covered his legs and arms. His body shuddered, ruffling his plumage into order. Picking up his bow he stood and shapeshifted into a giant muscular owl and hailed the storms in the sky with his wings.

In a flash of movement Oka picked up the bow and pulled a feather from his headdress, placing it into the taut string of the bow.

'Silver,' he whispered, kissing the string as he pulled it to his lips and aimed it skyward where the clouds breathed expectantly, bracing themselves for the union about to take place. The feather birthed a silver arrow which shot fast and high. Oka threw his wings out wide and retreated far from our bodies to where the darkness of the desert began. He crouched to the ground again, covering himself with his wings to form a perfect egg-shaped cocoon, camouflaged in the brown sand.

The fork of lightning descended, hitting Crow where he lay dead-centre on my chest. Thunder followed its strike like a mythical atom bomb. The rain cried down, drenching the fire. Oka opened his cocoon to inspect the magic's aftermath, his sodden feathers gave way to rain-dappled skin and he crouched low to where our bodies once lay, sniffing a handful of sand deeply as if it was the first summer rose he'd ever held.

'Go well my sons… go well,' he said.

#

The familiar smell of sage and burning wood woke me. I was cocooned in blankets on Logan's sofa and I struggled to focus on the hazy flames of the lanterns which lit the room, telling me time had moved from morning to night. Rain lashed at the windows and wind howled around the cabin looking for a way in. My head ached and my fingertips had softened and wrinkled from water saturation. I tried to sit up, but I had no strength to raise myself. I squinted repeatedly; every clench of my eyes made a flash of forked lightning dart behind my eyes, intensifying the pain in my head. My eyesight cleared to see an object swinging in front of me on the end of Logan's finger.

'What the hell happened? I said. Images of Oka, giant owls and shooting stars flashed into my head.

'Caw caw caw!' Crow called from the roof of the cabin.

Logan looked up at the ceiling, spinning the object around his index finger several times before catching it in the palm of his hand. 'Are you okay, laddie?' he said, folding his arms to keep the object hidden.

'I… I think so.'

'You know, my grandmother always used to tell me that if anything ever goes wrong in the world – get yourself to Ardnamurchan. So that's what I did, years ago. I'd had enough of everyone. Whenever I turn on the radio or the television I never hear anything positive, only crap about a new war, a crime or another mass shooting, some new financial crisis or a disaster killing thousands. Sometimes it's not even about an actual event, but an ominous message of impending doom. I can't say I blame Mother. We haven't done her any favours, have we?'

'Er… no. What happened to me?'

'I searched around the rock and in the forest for hours. I found you on the rock. The storm was in full force; any longer and a wave would've claimed you for King Neptune himself, ha! Your friend up there told me you'd appeared, I could hear him cawing, even above the thunder.'

'What is it about that rock, Logan?'

Logan stared at the painting of Merlin's hand. '*That* rock is more alive than any rock I've come across before. It has a ley line running through it, which is part of a grid of energy lines running all over Mother Earth. Much like our own acupuncture meridians. Some of them run through sacred sites like Stonehenge, Avebury and Iona, which isn't too far from here. West Cornwall alone has over four hundred sacred sites; some are linked by the lines to others in the Highlands. These lines beneath us were the communication networks of bygone eras. By tuning into the energy where it concentrates at a sacred power spot or stone circle, people communicated with each other miles apart. I asked you to meditate on the rock so you'd have time to soak in the Earth's energy: where you'd catch the sun's rays, feel the sea's spray and the rain, and where you'd feel the wind as it comes in from the Atlantic. Do you see, laddie? All the elements found you there while you lowered your metabolism and raised your vibration by meditation and transcended into the Unified Field you spoke to me about. Earth, fire, water and air – they opened the door for your senses to expand and cross over to the unseen. The others never got it, but I hoped you would. I felt something different about you the second I saw you standing on the beach.'

'Others? What others?'

'You don't think you're the only one curious enough to look for me and pick my brain about the book, do you? You're the seventh laddie, laddie, ha! Oh, well, one was a lassie actually.' Logan slapped his leg in amusement. 'That volcano's been reaching out to people for years, ever since I moved here. Mother keeps looking for the right person, maybe it's you. You're the only one who connected with the rock deep enough. Most got so impatient and frustrated with sitting on it all day, they just packed up and left; who knows how close they were to the miracle happening… seconds, maybe. Only you fully transcended to the spirit world. Recognise this, Aaron?' He hung a small leather bag on his finger, and it swung back and forth from the small drawstring which kept it scrunched closed. Hearing him say my name for the first time in a month pricked my ears up. 'Tick tock tick tock… time's up,' he said.

'What the…' I grimaced as my head swelled with pain. The revelation was too much. 'I was meditating on the rock… I saw a Native American… he came out of a sea mist, covered me with his wings and took me to a desert. He shapeshifted into some kind of owl being. His name is Oka, he called me his son. Crow was there… he wore that bag around his neck.'

'Fascinating, absolutely bloody marvellous! Here, drink some of this, it'll see you right.'

I cupped the warm metal cup in my hand and inhaled the reviving ginger-steam, sipping it to the back of my dry sore throat.

'Well, he gave this to you, it was hanging around your neck. It's a crane bag, shaman use it to keep their power pieces in. It's empty now, except for the smell of sacred tobacco. You'll have to fill it with your own power objects now. Things you find yourself, and those given to you by spirit. The crane bag holds things from both worlds.'

'I'm not a shaman. I wouldn't know where to begin with magic.'

'No, laddie, but magic has begun with you. It found you first!' Logan leaned in to me, cautiously looking left, right, then behind him for invisible eavesdroppers. 'So you want to know about the volcano, do you… about my book, eh?'

'Why didn't you publish it? Did you even finish the book?' I shied away from his intense glaring eyes.

'Och aye. The book was finished, it just doesn't exist anymore. I destroyed every last page of it. No one will ever read that book, but its story might still be told. That depends on you, though. You know, we only see four percent of matter. This world we live and breathe in; cars, furniture, nature, buildings, each other, it's just four percent. The other ninety-six percent is dark matter – the unknown and unseen. It's where this wee bag came from. We all yearn for home. I just haven't found mine yet. It's beyond the veil, somewhere in that ninety-six percent.' He reached behind him for his drum, holding it close to his ear, eyes closed, stroking the skin with the palm of his hand. 'There's been a lot of geologists from all over the world visiting Ardnamurchan with their fancy equipment, trying to find out how many magma chambers fed the volcano and such like. I could've told them that… there's only one!' Logan hit the drum with his hand. 'There's a reason my grandmother knew about the safety of this place. All drums provide protection, like your body's eardrum acts as a shock absorber, protecting the solid organs of the body. The volcano is an Earth drum. That huge magma chamber used to play Mother's sweetest rhythms; all volcanos did. You can still hear her voice in those areas if you listen well enough. Ardnamurchan, the world's most ancient Celtic drum, stopped playing one million years ago… it's your job to make it play again, laddie. There's a song of the Universe so deep and primal it can take years of meditation to hear it. Somehow you've got a head start.' Logan stood up, went to the door and pushed it open. 'It's the song of the birds singing.'

'Caw!' Crow responded on cue.

'Ha! Love that bird of yours, a one-off he is. It's the song of the sea crashing into land, and the soft hum of the wind moving the clouds into place; it's the sound of the sun rising and setting; of the grass growing, and all the world's water moving above and below the Earth. It's the primordial hum of the Universe present before God had even thought about making anything called creation. Within that song we all have our own under-songs, our own unique roots of connectivity – the ability that only we as individuals have.'

I froze, mid-sip, with the hot ginger's steam wafting over my face. I'd been searching for confirmation ever since the booming bass drumming filled my head on the first day of rehab, luring me to the forest on Table Mountain's foothills. I'd craved some sense of direction ever since the volcano's image flashed into my head as I sat next to Maclear's Beacon on the tabletop.

'How do I make it play again?'

'You'll have to find that out yourself. Where's the fun in knowing all the answers? You can't understand everything, you're not supposed to. Appreciate the uncertainty of mystery. Keep an empty glass so something can enter your life, like that volcano out there; something's waiting for you just like it's waiting for me.' Logan drifted off into one of his vacant senior moments. 'Time to rest. You'll need all your strength to keep up with that stag out there.'

I closed my eyes, too exhausted to react to his teasing and ask another question. Logan was a mystery in his own right. I rested my head on the sofa's thick fur lining and placed my hand over the rhythm of my new crystal heartbeat and wondered about Merlin. My eyes lost focus in the wood-burner's yellow flames while my mind drifted lucidly, half dreaming, half journeying to vast landscapes which offered a mere taste of the sacred geography of the other worlds. Deep down I knew Logan was right. He'd helped to ground me in the basics of soul flight and introduced me to nature's fluid matrix of time and space. I dreamt that I stood stranded in the desert surrounded by a thousand animals with Merlin peering down on me from the moon as my heartbeat boomed like a cannon. Then I heard the sound I hadn't heard for weeks.

'Tap tap tap, tap tap tap BANG!' The armoured fingers drilled their imprints into the shield, followed by a thump of the pummelling fist.

I woke with a start; throwing cold ginger tea into my face. The morning sun streamed through the windows, highlighting shafts of smoke and dust. The wood-burner's flames had died long ago. I looked around the room for the source of the smoke, but found no signs of fire.

'Logan!' No response.

There was an eerie emptiness to the cabin, as if it hadn't been lived in for years, and gaps on the walls where some of his artefacts were missing. The giant tortoise shell sat upside-down on the table beside me, surrounded by a scattering of tobacco. The Thunderbird mask sat next to the shell with an envelope perched on its bottom jaw. In between the shell and the mask was a bowl of water with half a lemon floating in it. I stretched my jaw and touched my cheeks to feel a tight crust over my face. I picked up the envelope which read 'Laddie, before you do anything else, go look in the mirror and wash yourself. Don't freak out!'

I freaked out. Wincing and shivering as my body adjusted to being upright, I felt disorientated, like I was coming to after a blackout from a drug binge. The feeling of dread was just as crippling this time. I shuffled my way to the small mirror in the bathroom. My jaw dropped as I saw my face greened-out; even my eyelids were painted with a dark green mud-mask, caking my complexion. Dazed and confused, I wiped my face with the corner of the blanket Logan had wrapped me in. The back of my hands and feet had small stars painted on them with the same substance. I walked back into the lounge with my skin sore from the scouring and stopped to take in the scene.

Four grey boulders the size of footballs stood on metre-high wooden pedestals in the middle of the walls. Each was a different shape, with north, south, east and west painted on them. A fifth boulder lay on the floor in the middle of the room with 'Mother' written on it and a sixth, clear quartz-crystal sphere hung from the light-fitting in a fishing net. My fingertips tingled. I stood under it and held my arms above my head, palms facing upwards, offering myself as an empty cup for energy to fill me up, but Logan's letter dragged me back to the present. What had he done here? Where was he? The questions piled up. The envelope was sealed by a small wax circle with the letter 'L' on it.

'Dear laddie, I didn't say goodbye, because it isn't. You are sitting in the centre of a vortex I have only made once before: for myself when I arrived in Ardnamurchan to ask for permission and blessings from the spirits of Singing

Sands to live here. I fell in love with this land, but it will never be my home. I belong elsewhere. This portal is closed now; there are others I'm sure you'll find if you choose to continue with your quest. Which I hope you will. You have a natural connection to the spirit world I have not seen before; dare I say, you may belong there more than here. I am so glad you decided to find me. I took the liberty of asking my guides to help with your expansion and quest across the veil, but remember… it isn't all about visiting the spirit world, we also need to invite them to this reality. We need their help now more than ever, or our sacred land will turn to dust. Forgive my lack of conversation. I never had all the answers. I was only here to offer you shelter and a place for nature and spirit to initiate you. If the tincture I put in your ginger tea worked, you have been asleep for two days, during which time the spirits will have done their work and you may now see and hear the Universe in all its glorious spectrums of light and sound, but remember, this may not always be a smooth boat ride. Keep your allies close to you and more than anything, I hope you find peace, clarity and inspiration out there and that I have not done you a disservice. I only ask one thing from you: that in helping you to find your destiny, you do not deprive me of mine. When we meet again – you must kill me. More than you can know at this time depends on it, so don't stray. All will become clear. Remember, laddie, it is best to stay on path. Wild blessings, Logan. P.S. There is some spirit cake for you in the kitchen to keep you going on your quest.'

I dropped the letter, disoriented, angry, scared. What had

Logan done to me? How could he disappear leaving such a confusing letter? What about the volcano… why was I here? The questions lined up again. I felt like killing him right then and watched for the door to open so I could fly at him with one of the tomahawks he'd left on the wall. My gaze remained on the door. I placed my hand on my heart, breathing in through the palm and out of the back of my hand; the rage subsided. Scratching came from the other side of the door, and the handle wobbled up and down. I looked at the tomahawk again as the door slowly opened with Crow balancing on the handle.

'Is there anything you can't do?' I asked.

'Not much,' Crow said. 'Welcome back. I was wondering if you'd ever wake up, you took a battering in that storm.' He flew to the Thunderbird mask, landing on its beak. 'Interesting mask,' he said, pecking one of the eyes. 'Some Native Americans say the storm the Thunderbird brings will help to save mankind, can't say I'm surprised, birds have a knack of saving you lot. Just like my cousin, the raven, who stole the moon, stars and sunlight from the old chief to give back to humanity.'

'I thought that was just a myth,' I said.

'Sure, a myth just like you and me. Try telling *that* story to someone else and see if they believe it. Why do you think Oka fired the sacred arrow into the clouds? You heard the wings flapping, right?'

'Yes, I heard them.'

Crow hopped onto the back of the sofa to be at eye level with me, something he always did when he had something important to say and which always unnerved me as he was pecking distance from my face, but it gave me another chance to see the flames burning in his black eyes.

'You missed a bit of the green stuff under your nose, makes you look like that German. Not a good look. What you saw then was the last time the Thunderbird was summoned in that lifetime. Each tribe can only summon it once, for the good of the whole tribe. Oka was banished after the ceremony you saw. He stole the headdress which holds the magic arrows and took our bodies to the desert to summon the Thunderbird for us – not the whole tribe. Oka will never know true rest now. That was his sacrifice for us. To forever roam between the veils. We're in this deep now, Aaron, so deep.'

'In what so deep?'

'The quest! Aaron. We're on a quest!'

'Seriously? Me, on a quest?'

'We've been on one ever since that lightning bolt hit our bodies. Just like your buddy counsellor, Troy, told you in Cape Town, remember? Our souls are intertwined forever, expanding into greater awareness with each lifetime, but this could be the last lifetime. The world's going crazy, Aaron. There's only so much Mother Earth can take. She is humanity's placenta! Why so few people understand that, I will never know. Look at it out there.' Crow pointed his beak to the sea as it rolled back and forth under dawn's rising sun. 'The greens, blues, yellows… it's so beautiful, but the fish are full of mercury; skies cry acid rain and the soil is contaminated. Think how that feels on Mother's skin and when it sinks down to her core. Long ago, this planet's poisonous atmosphere was uninhabitable, but she used these trees to take all the toxins deep into her core to make it safe for human beings to start living here. What did you do? You cut down the trees as fast as they grow and scavenged Mother for her minerals while filling the air with the very same poisons which she tries to protect us from. All those mineral deposits are parts of her sacred heart, Aaron, and her heart also keeps the nature spirits here, working alongside us. We live in unity, even if some of you can't see or speak to us; we are here for all of you. We love this place too, but if people don't start waking up to smell the roses, there won't be any left. No roses and no magic.'

Crow's words saddened me. Like Logan, I'd chosen the solitary track to find inner strength rather than join the outward struggles others participated in, but now I was being drawn into these struggles by this huge force propelling me forward into the unknown. Out of the gloom Crow had spoken about, pieces of the jigsaw began fitting together. I saw how Mother's deep rhythmic hum resounded from the depths of Table Mountain, calling me to the spiritual antennae on her highest point where I received my first destination – Ardnamurchan. Logan had gone, but I wasn't alone. I had my allies Crow and Stag. I'd chosen not to revisit the lunar landscape where Merlin waited for me near the bamboo forest. When I tuned into him I felt his power, his gaze. Stag remained in the shadows of the forest. I felt him there, pacing back and forth, alert, growing restless.

It was the first time I'd been outside the cabin since disappearing from the rock. The daylight blinded me like a vampire trapped in the first rays of the rising sun. I trod gingerly with bare feet around the rock pools to follow Crow onto the pristine sand where he teased the lapping waves. I'd grown accustomed to walking in bare feet, preferring to be earthed and feel the different textures of Mother's skin which grounded me: something I needed as my mind frequently escaped to star-worlds of eternally burning fires. The sand hadn't sung since I arrived. I had twisted my feet into the beach every time I began my walk to the rock, trying to hear the sound which gave Singing Sands its name, but it wouldn't sing. Today was different, though. Everything looked as though it had been polished. The clouds glowed pearl-white and the sky was a darker shade of blue than I'd ever seen before, like outer space had moved closer. I looked at the bone-dry golden sand. I stood with my legs apart, squirming and sliding my feet into the softness – and a squeak came from beneath my feet. I lunged and slid again, making a longer sound of some strange sand-bird, screeching in delight as I played with it. I spun and dived full frontal onto the beach, before returning to my improvised tap-dance version of Gene Kelly's 'Singing in the Sands', making the sand sing with every movement until finally I collapsed on my back, panting, staring at the sky, resting on the notes of nature's song and… 'tap tap tap!' ringing in my ears. The volcano could wait no longer.

The Saint

'Tap, tap… tap!' The armoured fingers ground to a halt; resting on the shield for the first time in centuries. Hundreds of years spent waiting in pain, nearly at an end. George let out a sigh of relief as he watched Aaron start the quest he'd been praying for ever since he killed her. He wasn't the only one depending on a recovering drug-addict to make it to rehab. He would have scratched his head in bemusement at the Universe's choice, if he could have reached it through the metal helmet. Why pick someone so fallible, once so consumed by consumption… someone who walked between worlds so naturally, but who was still so full of doubts and questions? But then he realised he was just the same; they were perfectly matched.

George forced open his rusty visor; the grating sound of the hinges always made him wince. He wiped away the perpetual tears which had streamed down his face from the moment he plunged his sword into her throat while consumed by greed and lust for glory. The dragon's death was so slow and oh so painful as he butchered her. Saints weren't born to cause such torture to the beings Mother depended on and loved so deeply. She was the only gatekeeper left protecting the volcanic drums. All Earth dragons were born from her volcanic wombs, but fear always got the better of her other family: humanity. Earth's last race of super natural animals – wiped out before any chance of living in harmony with each other could be achieved. And how tragic that England's patron saint should take the life of Mother Earth's last lava-blooded daughter, triggering the worst episode of female mass murder in the history of mankind.

George screamed out in disgust for the paradox he was trapped in. His visor grated as the weathered metal resisted his effort, keeping his face imprisoned. Spirits weren't vulnerable to the elements and Mother wanted him to feel it all with a life sentence of immortality. His penance was always going to be different, though. And oh so punishing. He had been laid bare to the Scottish weather to feel the bite of every summer midge, gale and freezing winter. Beheading was too quick for a man who had killed such an important dragon. He would've been glad to lose his head, to stop the incessant noise of their tortured screams. Mother Earth cared deeply for humanity, but her compassion could never forgive such a personal crime. She had run out of patience, seeing all her daughters meet their end at the hands of those which her ravaged land sustained. So there George would sit: in the barren remains of an extinct volcano, waiting, with the storm-winds whistling through the hinges of his armour – a fallen saviour longing for his saviour. The screams of her slow torturous death sent ripples through the Earth's energy field, causing chaos and imbalance. George had spent many a night watching her fly along the same piece of land, waiting for his opportunity to end her. Little did he know, though, of the purpose of her flight path: to keep Mother's divine energy lines vibrant and full of flux. How he regretted his actions now. Half a million women, the witches, Mother's gift to man of herself manifested in human form, now howling in terror as they burned for their crimes against no one. George could never have known how deep the damage would go: the wars he'd caused, men fighting men for no just reason, demeaning and raping the feminine, their masculine energy running rabid for power. He was desperate to make amends, to right the wrongs he'd committed against the Earth, and restore the land to its former glory.

FIVE

I peered through the curtains at a grey and brooding sky on the morning of my visit to the volcano. The guest house was a familiar base, but it didn't feel as homely after two months at Logan's home. The warmer May nights and lighter mornings lifted my spirits, but I was back with my own company again, and I missed his. Being on my own was a double-edged sword. I loved the solitude because it was easier to connect with nature, but I could only take so much of my own company before I felt in danger of falling into a cavern of loneliness with the beat of a heart which yearned for someone to share the wilderness with.

I was still groggy after a night disturbed by drunk, singing Germans in the lounge below my room. It made me grateful to be sober, and the realisation of the journey I was about to make set off fireworks of adrenaline inside me. I fumbled with my small backpack, checking its contents an unnecessary number of times as my nerves jangled like I was about to go on a first date. I was almost too nervous to eat, but forced some cooked breakfast down and left the dining room before the Germans woke.

I climbed into the quiet insulation of the truck where I heard my heart pound and my rapid breathing misted the windscreen. I white-knuckled the steering wheel as it dipped and dived around the single-track road like a rollercoaster ride, without the loops; my stomach somersaulted instead. The intensity of the moment held me rigid. It was almost too much to bear. I imagined nature giving me a spectacular fanfare when I arrived: some huge magical moment cheering me on with a spectacular display of gratitude, celebrating my trust in making the journey to the Scottish wilderness, miles from any significant civilisation. Houses making up small hamlets dotted the coastline, the sturdy walls made to withstand the wind's battering as it charged in from the sea. I passed a sign for Ardnamurchan's lighthouse, perched on the most westerly tip of the mainland where the Atlantic crashed into its precipice. I remembered Logan's grandmother's words about safety. Nothing could break Ardnamurchan. I relaxed my grip on the wheel and eased my foot from the accelerator. There was no hurry, but there was still fear of failure. What if there was nothing here but a barren wasteland where the few people of Acharacle lived their lives crofting in peace, huddling together through the harsh winters?

Crow swooped in front of the truck, dropping a shell onto the windscreen to remind me of my totem's presence. The truck's tyres rattled across a cattle grid, knocking the small bottle of Lourdes holy water I'd brought with me onto the floor. I retrieved it and idled in first gear while I sipped some of the old healing water and imagined holy light spreading throughout my body. I tucked it into the sun-visor where I kept three of Crow's feathers and drew a Reiki symbol of protection and power over it with my hand. I'd learnt a lot in rehab. The quiet moments I'd spent at the bottom of the garden every morning before the programme began had taught me the power of ritual, ceremonial times, when I reconnected with my own life force – and now I found myself drawn towards nature's heart, beating as if from a drum. I wanted to mark this time with an act, some kind of offering, magic or no magic, I had gratitude I needed to express. I remembered Crow standing on the door of Lourdes' room of miracle healings in the holy domain, near Bernadette's sacred Catholic shrine, where he'd first spoken to me. Heavy with denial and clutching divorce papers, I had rebuffed his notion that I could be my own miracle, being unwilling to admit that I was already swamped in the darkness of drug addiction. Yet here I was, living a childhood dream, driving a four-by-four into the spring sunshine as it shone its tractor-beam on me through a gap in the clouds, steering me towards my vision.

The remains of the magma chamber walls surrounded me in all directions as the road snaked through the eerie damp dark brown terrain. I pulled into an old quarry car park marked on the map as the best starting point to find the centre of the volcano. My heart raced as I fumbled with the zip on my coat. I hadn't seen Crow since I turned off the coastal road to head inland. I turned three-sixty, but he had gone for now. His absence heightened my anxiety, as I'd learnt he only left me when something big that didn't involve him was about to happen. I walked the track from the car park towards the brow of a small hill. I felt like a soldier about to confront an unknown army. Were they friend or foe? Were they there at all? My footsteps crunched loudly on the gravel path in the still air as a huge section of the broken volcanic walls loomed into view and blew me away.

'Wow!' I whispered, stopping in my tracks before a metal gate which opened without my touch, leading me into the crumbled remains of a vast natural amphitheatre. Deep bass notes filled my head as if the church organ player had collapsed on the keyboard. I didn't know what to do, or where to go. I suddenly felt like a child taking his first swim, out of his depth and pining for his mother, or Crow.

I felt the land looking at me, watching for my next move. I turned full-circle to look at the undulating walls of the three-mile wide crater, formed when the magma chamber had collapsed during the volcano's massive eruptions. The sea was visible through one small section where the walls dipped low, briefly showing me an oasis in the distance before the lava terrain climbed high, hemming me in. The beauty of the circle of concentric rings I'd seen on Google Earth was nowhere to be seen at ground level. There was a foreboding air about the place. I took one more crunching step and as I did so the wind barged into my back, then pressed into my chest and stopped me in my tracks before roaring into my ears. Normal wind didn't change direction so suddenly. This one had an angry guardian-like presence.

I thought about returning to my truck to wait it out, but the new me was someone who didn't turn back: not after turning my life around, not after coming all this way. What was I expecting? A choir of angels bathed in bright orange lava playing their golden harps and singing songs of joy at my arrival? That would've been nice, but the Scottish wilderness had its own way of welcoming, or testing me. I pushed into the wind as it squeezed water from my eyes. I looked for refuge and saw a doe with her faun climb onto the crest of a small rounded hillock twenty feet from the path. I took the detour, making high long strides, stumbling over the tussocks and sinking knee-high into camouflaged pockets of bog. The deer spotted me and sprinted away, oblivious to the wind they'd known since each had taken its first wild breath. I clambered towards the hillock, determined to take the shortest route to find shelter. I pulled my legs out of a patch of bog as it made one last attempt to suck me in. The wind kept pushing and pulling me like a ball of wool at the mercy of a cat's playful but deadly paws, and I fell unceremoniously face down. Thick husks of grass gouged at my eyes. There was no sound, no hint of its invisible abuse. Just the sound of my breathing.

'I bet that feels nice,' a man said in a muffled, shaky voice as though he were close to having a nervous breakdown. 'What does she smell like? Mother Earth, what does Mother smell like? Tell me, dammit!' he snapped.

I froze, covering my head with my hands to push my face further into the land, praying my head was playing tricks on me.

'God grant me the serenity to accept...' I skipped the beginning of the Serenity Prayer and went straight for the courage, lifting my head to look at the figure wearing a suit of armour sitting above me on the crest of the hillock. His armour was tainted by patches of rust and dried blood which allowed him to blend into the landscape. The visor was open enough to leave a slit for his bloodshot, teary eyes to see me. His elbows rested on a shield which had small dents in it.

'Tap tap tap.' He drummed his fingertips on the metal where some of the holes were. 'Recognise this tune?' he said in a broken monotone. 'Re... cog... nise this tune!' he shouted, smashing his fist into his helmet with each syllable. I mentally located my truck keys in the inside pocket of my jacket and mapped out the route to the car park, wondering if I could escape. I wanted to run. I looked for other members of the medieval re-enactment group he looked like he belonged to, but we were alone. The figure bottom-shuffled down the slope toward me with the grace of a broken dustbin, clanging and gibbering to himself as he moved. I heard snippets of what he was saying: 'Don't go. Please don't go.'

I scrambled backwards as the man approached, now sobbing, pausing to bang his helmet with his shield, which prompted more muffled madness from inside the helmet. 'Shut up, Mother!' he screamed, head-banging and yelping, like a dog being beaten with a stick. He seemed to receive some form of respite from whatever torture was going on in there and continued his advance towards me. Eventually he sat with his head between his knees, motionless. I stood up as stealthily as possible and looked at the obstacle course of grass-clumps and bogs between me and the gravel path. Volcano or no volcano, I had escaped years of my own type of insanity and I wasn't going to get murdered by some weirdo in the middle of nowhere.

'Don't you recognise me, Aaron?' he whispered as soon as I made my first step. The arrival of calm in his voice stopped me.

'Tap tap tap… tap tap tap… tap tap tap.' He banged on his shield again and the world slowed to help me hear it properly. 'Do you know how hard it is to get inside someone else's dreams?'

I froze. Curiosity kept me rooted to the spot as the mad blood and mud-covered knight, or whatever he was, trundled towards me with his hand held out to greet me. He cleared his throat and tried to stand up straight, but dents in his armour kept him crooked.

'George. So pleased to meet you… after hundreds of years of waiting,' he said.

I weighed up the situation and decided against upsetting him. As I took hold of his hand, images of a spear piercing reptilian skin shot into my head. I saw it twisting and gouging into flesh, blood gushing, and a writhing mass of panic and death hit me – followed by the sounds of a man shouting and the terrifying, blood-curdling screams of an animal that filled me with a sadness so terrible, for a split-second I wanted life to end. I was overcome with grief and let go, slumping on the ground, cursing Logan. What had his concoction done to me? A macabre fascination for the terror I'd felt made me check again.

Clang… clang! I knocked on George's helmet. Each strike of his armour filled my head with more flashes of the horror film. The dread lingered like a hangover.

'What is that?!' I said.

He knocked twice on my shoulder and then grabbed it for support as his body slumped. No deathly horror filled my head. Forcing a smile, he squeezed tears from his sore eyes as he stared at the dark stones of the deserted village of Glendrian peppering the land a mile away.

'I never knew if all of Mother's curse was real. I only heard their screaming, but now I know I am never to receive another's touch. Not in greeting; especially not in love. Who would want to touch this foulness?' he said, and began to cry.

George was distracted and lost in his sadness, offering me a chance to run away, but I pitied him. I couldn't leave the weirdo alone to starve in the middle of nowhere and my mind was unravelling things in the background.

'At least their screaming's stopped,' he sobbed.

'What screaming?'

'The witches… hundreds of thousands of persecuted women; screaming, ever since I killed the dragon.'

'Don't tell me you think you're Saint George. Look, I can get you to a hospital if you'll come with me, but you'll have to sit in the back of the truck.'

George laughed from inside his dark hole, sniffing repeatedly to clear his nose from the sobbing and failing badly at wiping his nose through the small gap in his visor.

'Oh, that's kind of you, Aaron, but we are now joined at the hip. What do you think you saw being murdered in those visions? Who do you think this belongs to? Watch this.' He scraped some of the dried blood from the armour on his leg with a finger and flicked it away. I watched the snail-trail disappear as the blood grew back. 'It will never wash off. I am never to forget the pain I caused. I am cursed with immortality; never to receive the loving touch of another living thing without causing them pain from memories of my murderous act. I was banished to be the guardian of this empty place when I pierced her throat with my lance. She died so long and slow a death. As did all the women when they were burnt, drowned or tortured in the witch hunts which followed the dragon's last breath. You see…' George moved closer to me, placing his hand on my shoulder and looking left and right. He smelt like a slaughter house might. 'She was Mother Earth's last daughter. I could only see glory and a sainthood in front of me, for saving my people from a monster, not what she really was.' He let go of my shoulder and looked at the sky. 'I wish I could see her fly again. She was spectacular in flight, you know, full of wind and fire!'

I decided to test how deeply the weirdo believed he was Saint George by embracing his fantasy. 'You didn't just kill her, did you? I've just seen what you did to her. You butchered her. You didn't stop slicing her flesh when she was dead.'

George flinched at my gall. His mask hid his distaste for my unforgiving words. 'No, I did not, but it was only afterwards that I learnt the dragons were the force of light and life that hold and define the world we live within. They were divine feminine energies which flowed through everything Mother created, the mountains, rivers, trees, animals, plants and eventually humans, but we are more complicated, more unreliable and doubting than the innocent consciousness of nature. It took us time to believe in magic. Your technology still distracts most from its presence. In my time, this energy flowed strongest through the women of our land. There were never so many with psychic abilities, but my crime caused havoc: an imbalance of the divine feminine and masculine. Her death sent a surge of magic through the women with her last dragon breath. It is their screams I heard for hundreds of years, until your arrival gave me respite from their pain. How long this peace lasts is now your decision. We are one and the same, Aaron. We have both known the darkness and we both seek the light. Do you see?'

'You really believe this, don't you?'

'Caw!' *Ting!* Crow arrived unceremoniously, landing on George's helmet.

'If your bird shits on my head – I will end him.'

Crow flew away, shitting on the ground dangerously close to George's leg. He landed on the ground facing us where he pulled a long worm from the ground and sucked it in, spaghetti-style.

'Psst! Get lost!' I hissed. Crow spread his wings and sailed out of sight.

'You have quite the menagerie with you, don't you?' George pointed at the deserted buildings where a set of huge antlers bobbed up and down above the jagged outline of the ruins. Stag appeared in the gap between two walls and stood, watching, waiting.

'Amazing! All I need now is for Merlin to show up.'

George lowered his hand and jerked his head sideways, making a painful grating sound of metal on metal as his weathered shell resisted all movement. 'So you've met him too?'

'I think so, in another world, beyond the moo....' I stopped mid-sentence, stunned.

'You know Mother Earth has bound us together, you and I,' George said, poking a thick piece of grass inside his helmet to relieve an itch. 'You heard me through her. She has brought you here – for what? I don't know, but I know you've heard the same pain as me, at the edge, where hell waited for you, but you changed, didn't you? And now you want to give something back.'

'Okay, you're freaking me out. Where are the other guys in your re-enactment group? They shouldn't have left you alone like this. Did you get a bash on the head in one of the battles?'

George picked up the shield and moved his other hand over the dented surface where the faint markings of a red cross remained. Sparks flew from the palm of his hand onto the steel, magically drawing a detailed outline of the British Isles. The map glowed and flickered softly as though the sea were lapping gently at its shores. The dents made by George's fingers on the underside were fittingly placed to pinpoint the mountains of Scotland, Wales and the Lake

District. Small volcanos came to life all over Scotland, their peaks gently glowing red and orange with silver letters inscribed by an invisible pen spelling out… 'Glen Coe… Edinburgh, these are your first destinations, Aaron.'

'Why do I have to go to Edinburgh? Who the hell are you?' I slapped him on his breastplate, knocking him flat as a dragon's face screamed inside my head.

'I was placed here, Aaron!' he yelled. 'I killed the dragon in the south and Mother took me to the north, far away from her daughter's grave. I don't know how I got here, but my purpose was ingrained on me. To make sure this piece of earth remains untouched by everyone, even crofters.' He pointed at the ruins of Glendrian. 'See, no one must be allowed to blemish the energy of this place. You heard her, didn't you?' he said, straining as he propped himself up again.

I'd wondered what had caused them to leave homes they'd spent years building. 'Yes, I heard her, all the way from Cape Town, five thousand miles away, clear as a bell. Why am I here? Why are you here?'

'Too many questions will blind you. Just trust. Go to Edinburgh, ask for help at the right time and it will be there.'

'I'm not going anywhere until you tell me what the hell is going on!' I dropped to my knees, mortified that my adventure was coming to a ridiculous end at the hands of a madman dressed in armour. It was difficult, though, to ignore the magic I'd seen with my own eyes rather than in a shamanic journey.

'You won't believe me, you just need to go to Edinburgh.'

'Try me. If you really hijacked my dreams and dragged me all the way to this godforsaken place… try me!' I felt an uncomfortable surge of anger rise in me.

'You're here – no, actually, we're here – to bring back King Arthur. Mother wants him back. She says he is the one king who cared about the land and its people.'

'Okay, nice knowing you, George, or whoever you are. I'm not listening to this anymore.' I began a hasty retreat back to my truck, close to tears.

'Tap tap tap… tap tap tap.' George's fingers stopped me in my tracks. 'We all have a purpose, Aaron. What have you got to lose?'

I hadn't visited Edinburgh for years. Not since a shopping trip with my ex-wife to buy some shoes for our ill-fated wedding. I drifted back to the pub crawl we'd had and remembered the strange magical mood of a city which kept both white and black magic alive.

'Yaaaaaawww!' Stag bellowed from the top of the hillock. It was only twice the height of my truck, but it was steep and high enough to give him centre stage of the volcanic cauldron. I didn't see him leave Glendrian, but the track of splayed grass and chunks of mud left in his wake showed how fast he had run. His breath moved the air around me, wafting wisps of sage smoke up my nostrils.

Stag startled George who clattered over and impaled his head in a bog. 'Not again,' George said, his voice muffled from inside the wet bucket he had on his head.

I watched the arrival of the huge beast with his nostrils gasping and his heart drumming through his skin. Stag's white-tipped candelabra of antlers stood magnificently on his head. Light streamed from the highest points, reaching for the sky. A thick silver-sheened beard covered his throat, giving him the air of royalty. He stamped one foot hard into the sodden ground, splashing water into my face, before sprinting away to an oval of flattened land the size of a tennis court, encircled by waist-high grass so green and pristine it looked like a team of gnomes had been designated the sacred oval's gardeners.

'He wants you to follow him. Go! Meet him!' George shouted, struggling to turn himself over and get onto all fours.

I side-stepped to the foot of the mound, clutching my empty crane bag, half-hoping Oka would appear to take me back to the desert. I didn't know how this was going to play out. Stag seemed agitated and restless. I started to sweat as I walked toward him. He lunged forward and ploughed his antlers into the grass, flinging lumps of turf so high into the air that they rained down on me like meteors, thudding into the ground around me. Then he did it again and again. He was digging! As I drew closer I heard him grunting as he frantically propelled his head into the earth by leaping into the air. His antlers creaked under the pressure, nearly separating from his skull from the impact as he ploughed into the soil.

'Hey!' I shouted. He stopped and looked at me. Clumps of turf dangled from his antlers. I got ready to run in the other direction. His size and speed scared the shit out of me, but then I remembered – he was my ally!

He was here because I was. Stag had chosen me. He grunted and shook his head to clear the debris. A chunk of turf pelted George in the side of the head, knocking him over again. He lay still, resigned to another battering as part of his eternal penance.

I edged closer, holding my hands open, as if something so huge and supernatural would feel threatened by little old me. Stag looked down at the turned earth; stamping and dragging his front foot with a grunt, longing for something… or someone. It wasn't until I reached the outer circumference of the oval that I realised he was crying. I stepped across the long grass threshold of the oval and looked up at his face, holding out the palm of my hand to catch one of his tears as it seeped from his eye and trickled down the sodden tracks in his fur. His hot breath bellowed out of his flared nostrils and clouded over me.

'It's okay,' I said, holding the tear and placing it over my heart. I didn't know what else to say or do, but I wanted to show him I now knew my own heart and that it knew him. I stood still, silent, as he walked around me like a sergeant major inspecting a soldier at roll call, but instead of scrutiny, there was an air of interest and fascination about him. We had only met in the other world, the one I'd visited with my eyes closed and with drumming filling my ears, taking my soul to new supernatural landscapes. I had never been so close to any deer, let alone an alpha male, and yet he was clearly not a normal stag, breathing sage smoke and running with the thundering speed of a cannonball. I watched his antlers appear next to me as his snout brushed my back, just as the white horse had on my last day at the Romanian orphanage. Stag came full circle; faced me again and stood as still as a statue.

'He's wondering what you're waiting for. Don't you realise you're telepathic, Aaron!' George shouted from the top of the mound. 'Remember, it's better to stay on path… my saviour! Ha ha ha.' Laughing, he rolled down the back of the hill, rattling like a battered biscuit tin.

I looked at Stag, closed my eyes and took a deep breath. He was gone when I opened them. I walked back to the path, my trusty path, and stayed on it.

SIX

I pulled the Nissan into the empty car park at Glen Coe's visitor centre for a pit-stop, having left before sunrise with a flask of Logan's finest coffee and his spirit cake for sustenance. The cake was no morsel, though, no, it was the size of a small brick packed with dense sponge and currants and sultanas and walnuts and glazed in honey. It had been a quiet night-time drive, with only an occasional trundling lorry and the random light tap of Crow's beak on the roof of the cab for company. I was in paradise – alone with the land. Crow wasn't going to distract me from processing the surreal meeting with St George – or should I say, George – or the stupendous revelation that I was, in some way, to be his saviour. I'd been waiting for something like this all my life and the realisation that I was to be implemental in bringing about the return of King Arthur was both fantastical and at the same time, totally believable to the ever-present daydreamer in me. George was right, yes! To make a difference! I realised why I'd never felt as if I fitted in anywhere without drugs or alcohol inside. Perhaps I was destined for other worlds, and they for me.

I walked to a small bench in front of the visitor centre which took in the view of where the Glen Coe massacre had taken place. I looked for the moon above the dull rims of the Glen where giants lay tucked up in bed as they waited for the sun to rise. Merlin's celestial observatory was hidden. The moon would never be the same again to me, with its largest crater a portal into a bamboo beach paradise where the eternal fire burned. I sipped coffee and smiled at the synchronicity of how the tale of Merlin's madness in the forest helped him see nature spirits, blended with mine. His insanity opened him up to see the world as it really is – multidimensional. The physical world was only the tip of the iceberg; my own drug-induced madness had done the same. I was seeing everything – the whole iceberg, with a little help from Logan.

There was an eerie atmosphere to the Glen in the half-light. I felt as if I were sitting in an empty football stadium, frequently looking over my shoulder for Crow, or a car to arrive in the car park to keep me company. The energy made me uncomfortable, but there was no turning back. This was a hiker's playground, yet the worst type of murder 'under trust' laced its soil where thirty-eight men, women and children had been slaughtered and countless others had died of exposure as they fled their homes. I flinched as I heard the echo of distant screams and was filled with a feeling of dread which made me feel sick.

The history was the only connection I had with being here. I retraced my exchange with George and remembered the unpleasant flavour of the conversation being one of slaughter, torture and heinous crimes against the divine feminine and the sacredness of this earth. Now he had sent me to a place resonating with the same darkness. The seed of the quest had sprouted with a bright shining light. I foolishly held the ideal of twinkling magical lanterns signposting the way, showing me how to negotiate my way down the Yellow Brick Road where rainbows shed their light on every jolly step I took to meet the wizard.

Instead, I had left Ardnamurchan with the shocking news that I was going to have to kill someone I had become very fond of, even if he had coshed me with sacred herbs and indigenous tribal rituals. The twinkling knight in shining armour manifested as a destitute, cursed and banished for his crimes against nature. The Path followed extinct volcanoes and ancient landscapes. I relished the exposure to the elements, but there was no guarantee of solitude or escape from city life. Edinburgh held memories tainted by alcohol and nearly-forgotten love, but within its borders lay two extinct volcanoes, at Arthur's Seat and Edinburgh Castle. There would be no escaping tourists, traffic and memories.

The sun peeked its nose above the hilltops as birdsong ruffled the blanket of sombreness I'd covered myself with. I shook my shoulders and decided to test my new connection with the spirit world. If I was on such an important quest, surely the cavalry would be there for me when I needed them. I grasped my crane bag and closed my eyes.

'Stag, be with me,' I whispered.

I heard the drumming of his feet from far down the Glen

before I could see him. Then a cloud of dust, spitting grass and soil appeared. He slowed his pace and stood ten feet from me like a supernatural Road Runner. No sense of exertion in sight as the slip stream of debris peppered my face.

'You know, he could've just appeared in front of you, but he loves the charge!' Crow said, parachuting onto the tine of Stag's highest antler. Stag remained still, unaffected by his new companion. Crow flew away, but I wasn't ready for him to depart without conversation. Instinctively, I stretched up my arms and pretended to pull a rope towards me in a heave-ho motion.

'Cawww!' Crow yelped as, to my astonishment, he began flying backwards as I kept pulling my pretend rope until he was flapping and flustering above Stag's head again. 'New trick?' he said, finally resting on the antler as I dropped my hands. The flames in his eyes flared with annoyance.

'I didn't know I could do that, it wasn't supposed to work,' I said.

'We are of the same soul, Aaron. This is your domain, so you can play kite if you wish, but you may find shit, on fire, hits your head if you try it again. You may invite spirits to meet with you and you can take it one step further by using embodiment to blend with their energy. You are learning and changing fast and you are capable of more than you realise. Think of a bottle of water: add a few drops of oil and you have a mix of self and spirit ally, which is good for speaking to people with more wisdom than you alone can give them. Mix until you have half-and-half, well, then you have a mixture to work deeply with people in need of healing. Shake the bottle! And hey presto! The spirit ally is in the room, but this is for ritual use only. You may find that embodying Stag happens more naturally at first, when you have crossed the veil into the other world.'

'How do I do this embodiment?' I asked.

'First, you need to ask how to stop it.' Crow hopped onto a lower antler to be at eye level with me, something he always did when making a serious point. 'Never start an embodiment until you know how to stop it. Once you know how to end it, then you ask how to start it.'

I looked at Stag, waiting for some kind of telepathy to hit me, presuming that if I could hear Crow in my head I should be able to hear Stag, but there was silence. He brushed his nose against the thick heath grass and puffed out a small cloud of sage. It lulled me, bringing Oka to mind. I lay back on the bench and zipped my coat up to my chin. My hands prickled with energy. I scanned the skyline and saw Oka's face drawn in the pure white canvas of a cloud. Small gaps formed his eyes and mouth while grey tints accentuated his cheekbones as the rising orange, pink and red sunbeams projected a headdress of flickering feathers of light around his face. All I had to do was think of them, my allies, my guardians, and they appeared. I was without human company but felt so loved. I closed my eyes and surrendered to sleep, with spirit, as the light of a new day dawned on me.

SEVEN

I walked the half-mile from Edinburgh train station to my hotel, missing the isolation of the Nissan's cabin. The sudden onslaught of city noise shocked me. I felt like an alien, longing for the sight of mountains and hills or to feel buffeting wind and cleansing rain on my skin. People walked by me, expressionless, powered by headphones and the background noise of diesel engines and obsessions with their mobile phones as they tapped on their screens and bumped into each other, like some bizarre game of human pinball. I walked past a shop selling televisions and looked at the news scrolling across the bottom of the screen which read 'Breaking news – Eight thousand dead in Nepal earthquake… Passenger plane accidentally shot down over Russia… Financial crisis…' I wondered if Mother was still angry at the death of her dragon daughter and if the only time world peace had existed was before George's crime. But we were doing a pretty good job of self-destruction ourselves. A whisky shop was next door, with different height caskets and uniquely shaped hand-blown bottles with various shades of amber nestled into their own hay-lined display cases which were left tantalisingly open. Gravity seemed to let go of me as my eyes fixated on the window. Memories of whisky-tasting with my ex-wife during my last visit to the city flooded back, followed by flashes of the final days of my drinking as I threw half-pints of the stuff into my mouth and fell onto the nearest piece of furniture as alcohol burnt my throat and shot up my spine, numbing the distaste I had for myself and life. Saved by the next entrance to my hotel, I tripped up the final step into the lobby and composed myself.

'Your room's all ready for you, Mr Blake,' said the Spanish receptionist as she handed me the key-card. Her black hair was tied in a long pony-tail which draped over one shoulder, contrasting with her bright red lipstick and dazzling green eyes. Her creaseless white blouse was unbuttoned just enough to expose the first curves of her breast. She was a welcome, sobering sight.

The Waterloo was a four-star hotel in the centre of the city, a short walk from the Royal Mile. It was a large modern establishment with a swish cocktail bar just off the lobby, but more importantly, it had a gym, somewhere to sample the exercise-endorphins I'd developed a craving for.

I ordered a burger from room service and sat on my hotel bed, staring out of the window at a brick wall peppered with bedroom windows separated by an industrial-looking air-conditioning tube which climbed the height of the hotel. Any hope of a view of the old Edinburgh architecture, dashed by imprisonment. Cocooned in cement; denying the yearning coming from my heart to have someone to talk to and hold close. My mind flitted between analysing the steep, intense learning curve I was on, and the growing need for physical intimacy with a woman. I was so close to completing the year-long sabbatical from intimate relationships since finishing rehab. The advice to remain celibate and focused on building a relationship with myself had come from every counsellor I'd met in treatment, where Cassie had so nearly tempted me to fall at the first hurdle, and oh how I had felt like falling for her.

I retraced my steps to Maclear's Beacon at the end of rehab where I'd first seen the volcanic rings of Ardnamurchan, instantly seeing how far I'd come and the faith it had taken to follow the vision to its source. I was not a pawn in the middle of a huge game of chess, ready to be taken at the first blundering move. Nor was I a novice in the arts of magic or metaphysical occurrences. I'd always felt I had a healing touch. Was my purpose to heal, to bring light, the very same golden light which had returned to me as I loosened the chains of addiction from around my neck and the junkie's claws from the skin on my back? There was method in my madness: a light which shone brighter when the darkness came. There was never any more fear of the shadows. Here I was, exploring landscapes which once glowed lava-red with Mother Earth's blood; where death and hideousness tainted the light. Was I ready to heal the gaping holes in the hearts of the babies, children, husbands, brothers and sisters of the thousands of murdered witches? The very thought that my quest was to heal such ancestral trauma and herald the return of the greatest warrior ever to have lived overloaded my brain. Who the hell did I think I was?

Weary from the weight of expectation and the magnitude of the situation; I turned my attention to women of the present day, feeling the need for some Scotch beef and to explore the town. I needed a break from The Path.

'Room service,' a male voice said, knocking at the door of my comfortable cell with one hand while holding my meal in the other.

'Thank you for your life,' I whispered to the blackened burger before coating it in ketchup and clamping my teeth as far around it as possible. The concierge looked over his shoulder with an expression mixed with confusion and fear as he quickly closed the door and scampered away. I had never set out to become a shaman, but my encounters with Stag and Crow had taught me that, beyond all doubt, spirit was a force as tangible as any element and it lived in everything. The cow on my plate was no exception. Somewhere the spirit of that cow was resting or waiting for rest. My offer of gratitude to a beast which had no say in its slaughter felt the most natural thing for me to do.

I stepped outside the hotel and stared at the gothic Scott Monument, which looked like a rocket ship waiting to take me to see Merlin in the waning moon. I crossed the road to avoid the whisky shop window where the bottles were waiting to talk to me, instinctively holding out my hand to take a leaflet from a guy in a hoodie which read 'Speed Dating tonight at La Tasca. The perfect way to meet up to fifteen dates in one night. Come with a smile and an open mind'.

'Hello,' I said to the flyer, raising my eyebrows.

The pub scene was no longer an option to meet people. The energy was heavy and foreboding in bars. The noise of people jabbering away, surrounded by poison, sounded like insanity. I had tried it a few times, but seeing the madness of people calmly sipping alcohol and walking away from half-full glasses and bottles on tables was disorienting. The Four Horsemen looked on from every darkened corner of these dens of iniquity, waiting for me to slip up and revert to my old ways. Perhaps a tapas restaurant would be different. It was buzzing with chatter and the percussion of clinking glasses and cutlery on plates when I walked in. Fishing nets dangled from a low terracotta ceiling, strewn with red plastic lobsters and paella pans. I registered my arrival with the same guy who had given me the flier.

'First time speed dating?' he said in a camp Spanish accent, enabling me to tick him off my list as potential competition. My mind flitted through the other times I had reluctantly dragged myself to speed dating events in London to prevent myself from committing the cardinal recovery sin of isolating, secretly hoarding hope that I might find my true soulmate.

'No, but first time here,' I said, looking over his shoulder to catch a glimpse of who was waiting in the function room behind the red velvet curtain.

He pointed me to the bar for a complimentary drink where I perched on a stool and watched San Miguels crowned with lime slices being lined up on the bar.

'Last call for the daters!' called the camp master of

ceremonies from behind the red velvet curtain. I was disconcerted by the lack of toing and froing I'd seen between the function room and the main bar. I'd learnt not to get my hopes up too high as there'd been nights when I was obviously setting the bar too high for myself, but maybe tonight was going to be different. After all, I was on a spiritual quest, dammit! I made my entrance through the curtain and looked for an empty chair, of which there were far too many.

I watched the compere check his watch and look at the main door for late arrivals. The event was a dud. I turned around and speed-walked out of there.

The coolness of the night air distracted me from the confusion I felt, bringing a brief sense of relief and escape. I checked behind me for any sign of the Spanish compere, but it couldn't lift my low mood. The sense of anti-climax left a bitter taste and my self-esteem had been so easily shaken.

After two hours of flicking through the free-view channels I had succeeded in well and truly depressing myself with brief snippets of news warning of elevated terror alerts in several countries and how the number of missing in the earthquake was growing by the hundred. I threw the remote at the television and buried my head in the pillows until sleep found me.

#

I woke to the sound of intermittent knocks on neighbouring doors by room service and rolled over to stare at the ceiling, picturing the map George had shown me. I'd allowed myself two more days to explore the city and find the first pieces of the code needed to bring Arthur back. I planned to visit the castle first and make the walk to Arthur's Seat on my last day, but I had no idea where I'd be going afterwards. I just presumed George would show up somewhere to tell me where next. After all, he was my navigator and this quest was all about trust so I placed it all in him, and The Path, but George was nowhere to be seen.

Logan had equipped me with one of the best divining tools. Drumming was an innate sound to me, as if my mother's heartbeat had followed me from the womb. I could feel history oozing out of every brick in Edinburgh, but the subject was never one that stopped me daydreaming at school. The only thing from history lessons which stuck in my mind was the film of Nostradamus we were shown one rainy afternoon: fitting weather for a story about humanity's doomsday. The old man looked like he knew what he was talking about, or was it just that the media was constantly feeding us the negatives, instilling fear, creating dependence on manmade systems, blinkering us from the true wonders of nature and the human spirit?

I sat up on the bed, darkened the room, and put on my headphones, switching to a drumming track I'd found on the internet. I closed my eyes and said, 'Please give me a teaching about why I am here in Edinburgh'. I pressed play and took myself to the apple tree in the garden, inviting Stag to stand next to me. I repeated my request silently in my mind as I walked through the tree, crossing into the Middleworld, where Edinburgh waited. The black came quickly, enveloping us. I could still hear Stag's feet on the soft earth, brushing through grass, but there was no sight of anything: no sky above, no earth below foot and no fresh air. My shoulder brushed against a wall. Stag slowed and dropped back, leaving me to find my way. His feet started tapping on hard paved ground. The further I walked the blacker it became. I began to feel threatened and anxious. The light of a candle appeared in front of me. The tall flame stood still, petrified, shedding light on charred bricks which arced high above me.

'I am back in the room,' I said, as my anxiety suddenly peaked. I quickly retraced my steps back to the apple tree with Stag in tow. I opened my eyes, stared at the room's curtains to bring myself back to the present and sat pondering the journey's destination. The image of the candle lingered in my head and the unmistakeable sense that I had been underground, beneath the City of Edinburgh, remained with me. It didn't take long for Google to tell me about the night tours to the Underground City of the Dead where a whole population had once lived under the city in a series of over a hundred interconnected vaults. That's where my journey had taken me.

Desperate for fresh air and keen to introduce myself to Edinburgh's castle, I walked through the busy streets, flowing through the throngs of people as curiosity took my thoughts deep below the cobbled streets to the charred chambers. The one o'clock gun fired, startling me back to the present as I arrived at the castle's esplanade and watched the tourists snap away with their cameras at the views from an elevation granted by the three-hundred-million-year-old volcano. I had no interest in the landscape surrounding the castle; I couldn't avert my gaze from the esplanade. Everything moved in slow motion. My feet lolloped along as if I were a deep-sea diver with metal boots trawling the bottom of the ocean. I could hardly move; every step was exhausting. I sensed Stag near me, but I wanted to make his presence more tangible as it had been when we were in Ardnamurchan. If he appeared there, on volcanic ground, maybe he would appear here with me. I walked to a tomb at the side of the esplanade with an eagle engraved on it and closed my eyes, drawing perturbed looks from passers-by who thought I was a street entertainer without his statue outfit. I whispered the magic words. 'Stag, be with me.'

'Aaahhh!' I screamed in agony as Stag landed on my foot. I hopped and banged on the tomb before impaling my head onto an antler. Stag stared at me, blowing a cloud of calming sage. A group of Chinese tourists walked over to the tomb and stared at me as the sage loosened my body and removed the negative energy weighing me down. I looked at Stag, and he at me, then we both looked back at the Chinese who just raised their cameras, pointed them at the tomb and walked away. Unbelievers.

I opened my hand and pressed the centre of my palm onto one of Stag's whitened antler tines. The point pushed into the small patches of scar tissue where I'd burnt my hands with cigarettes in an attempt to feel something during the numbness of drug addiction. I lost myself in the moment, pushing harder, remembering, even revelling slightly in the pain. Stag remained statue-still, letting me revisit my past, reminding me how far I had come. Suddenly the dread hit me, but not from that time. My body had been freed, but my emotions were disturbed, fuelled by an unknown fear.

'Be with me, Stag.' I clenched his fur as panic set in. Nausea rose from my stomach, bringing me to my knees behind the tomb where I prepared to vomit. Then the screams came, quietly at first, like the faint whistle of a steam train bolting through a tunnel. I lunged for the side fence and threw my breakfast over the edge, sweating and retching as the screams pelted into my head and the panic heightened.

'Caw! Caw!' Crow called from the top of the tomb. His gravel claxon stopped the screams, but tinnitus remained as if my head had been slammed with cymbals. 'Wow! You can hear them, can't you?' Crow said. He flew off, perching himself on the trough of a small rectangular fountain flowing from the wall next to one of the gate posts. I followed him, reassured by the 'clipety-clop' of Stag's feet behind me. Tourists filed in and out of the castle gates, oblivious to the talking Crow and the giant Stag. I felt as if I had more in common with my otherworldly companions than the rest of the human race. I looked at the plaque on the wall above the trough, dribbling as my mouth hung open aghast and quivering like a dog recovering from an epileptic fit. The inscription on the plaque said the castle esplanade was where the Scottish witches had been burned during the most prolific hunts in Europe, but something about the word 'witches' didn't look right to me; its spelling seemed wrong, even though it was right. As my head cleared and my panic subsided, I ran my fingers along the cold metal of the memorial and held my hands under the slow flowing water as it trickled into the trough.

'Please show me,' I said, listening to my heartbeat and resting my palm on Stag's chest as our hearts synchronised. All sounds were muffled as the volume of our hearts' movement increased. Then the visions came – not witches brewing cauldrons with frog-legs jumping out in all directions, but women. I saw women holding their babies, nursing them and playing near water and in fields. There were sisters talking to each other, holding hands and singing. I saw wives holding their husbands close, deep in love, and children clamouring for their affection. I heard their soft voices, like angels wooing. The women moved toward me in droves, their auras glowing with rainbows, exuding nothing but goodness for their kin. My eyes welled up, and then the flames came, threading through lumps of wood, catching wisps of dresses and consuming them. I gasped as the panic and screaming returned, and opened my eyes with a jolt which pushed me backwards.

'Steady there, Aaron,' a voice said, as two hands broke my fall and stood me up again. Blood-curdling dragon squeals filled my head. 'To think, these poor souls were burned on top of a volcano, where Mother would feel their pain so clearly.'

I turned to see George peering through his half-opened visor. 'They're still here, aren't they?' I said, trying to push his visor further open. I was surprised at the audacity of my action, but I was glad to see him and there was a growing sense of camaraderie between all of us – the recovering drug addict, the fallen saint, silent Stag, and Crow. The rough rusted edge of the visor cut into my palm. It wouldn't give. I watched blood run down my wrist.

'Pass it to me,' Crow said, jumping onto my shoulder to sip the blood from my hand. I watched in amazement as the inch-long cut vanished. 'You're my blood, remember?' he said.

'Nice try, much appreciated, but Mother will not give me an inch until we have made way for Arthur's return. Yes, the women are still here,' George said. 'The land has kept them somewhere. Had they been burnt anywhere other than volcanic land their souls would have scattered, lost for eternity, but Mother has other intentions for them. Their persecutors had no knowledge of the magic of these molten lands. You have done well, Aaron.'

Crow settled on my shoulder, and for the first time I felt the unity between all of us as we moved forward on the quest. Heading to the underground vaults that evening was the right thing to do. My hands fell to my sides and Stag and George faded from view.

'The Path is not all made of roses, Aaron. This city has a murky past, but even I cannot see what lies below these streets. The blackness is too thick, it is darker than anything you met before rehab in the psychotic episodes of your tainted mind,' Crow said, perching on my shoulder and peering into my ear.

'If I have overcome my own demons, surely it puts me in good stead for whatever lies ahead?'

'Yes, Aaron, it surely does,' Crow said, unconvincingly.

EIGHT

The tour guide waited beneath St Gile's Cathedral clock tower at the top of the Royal Mile. I looked at her and felt underwhelmed, regretting enrolling on a night where it seemed the entertainment was going to be nothing more than an amateur dramatic performance by a woman who looked like Herman Munster's grandma. We were a mixed group of sightseers including European students, young-and-in-love couples, four chattering Japanese tourists and a single man on a spiritual quest to bring back the greatest warrior-legend of all time, or not, as the case may've been.

'BANG! Good evening, ladies and gentlemen.' The tour guide back-kicked the black advertising board behind her to grab our attention. The shock put my nerves on edge; I was unnerved at how easily I was unsettled. Something didn't feel right. 'Welcome to the Underground City of the Dead Tour. This is not going to be your usual history and ghost tour. You get to go to a place which is dark, dingy, nasty, smelly, horrible and drippy. The underground city does have an entity which will willingly interact and abuse you slightly.

You may get tickled, scratched, bitten, punched, slapped… or knocked-out.' She smiled, and we all smiled back, enjoying the theatrics, although my smile was more of a grimace. 'To give you a brief background on the history of the vaults we are about to go down to, years ago, when the English were invading the world, Edinburgh was a walled city. The wall was built to keep the English invaders out, but once it encircled the city, land disappeared quickly, so they built upwards, fourteen floors high. The first rickety wooden skyscrapers staggered high above the wall. As the population increased, so did its waste. The streets were covered in sewage and rubbish, the squalor created a class system with the rich living near the top of the high-rise buildings, far away from the festering smell and disease. They threw their sewage onto the streets, forcing the poor and underprivileged underground. But where to? We will be visiting the South Bridge vaults which were made from the nineteen arches of the bridge in the eighteen hundreds. The arches had floors and walls added to them, making about one-hundred-and-twenty different dark, airless chambers.' She quietened her voice, stepping into the semi-circle we'd formed around her with a torch shining up from under her chin. 'The vaults were home to some of the most depraved members of society and the class hierarchy continued underground. The lower you were under the bridge, the lower in the class system you were. The vaults were a breeding ground for serial killers, especially the body snatchers Hare and Burke who preyed on people for most of the fifty years the vaults were inhabited. Illness and satanic magic roamed its darkest corners. We are about to visit some of the worst memories of Scotland, where a malevolent presence still lurks called the South Bridge entity – so don't get left behind!'

I was grateful for the end of her speech. My eyes wandered high over the cathedral's architecture, then down onto the two young, white-blonde Scandinavian tourists huddled tightly together, stirring long-lost fantasies in my mind. The guide's description of the vaults made me question whether I was heading in the right direction, but Logan's voice echoed reassuringly in my ears. 'Never second guess anything, laddie, follow your first hunch.' At that moment, I missed the old bugger. I felt the first surges of adrenaline as we moved away from the meeting point. Theatrical tales of people being accosted on the tours weren't completely disregarded by yours truly. I'd had enough of my own experiences in addiction to know that there are energies eager to complicate things for the living.

My plan was to find an appropriate point in the tour to lag behind and ask spirit for a teaching about why I was in Edinburgh, and if there was anything I could do to help the women killed at Edinburgh Castle. We walked, single file, down zigzagging stairways, through narrow alleyways and a black iron gate underneath a pub into the first vault. The street light was sucked out of the room that was lit only by several large candles illuminating every single charcoal-black brick. I had learnt to welcome the darkness as it provided the perfect canvas for the golden Reiki energy, re-ignited inside and all around me since my ascent from rock-bottom.

'The darker the night – the brighter the light,' I

whispered, to reassure myself.

One of the students hopped onto a wide ledge at the back of the vault, nonchalantly leaning back on his elbow to listen to the guide tell us about the way overcrowded families lived down here. I did a double-take back at him as the faint image of an arm moving inside the bricks hooked him around his neck and tried to take him into the masonry.

'If anyone sees, hears or feels anything, please let me know,' said the guide. She looked around the group, pausing at me. She was well versed in spotting people's reactions to the paranormal. I kept my cards close to my chest and listened to the room, while the arm took another swipe at the student, then, clenching its fist in frustration, attempted to pile-drive it through the young man's face.

I explored how Logan had heightened my psychometric senses, trying to read what had happened here long ago. Suddenly the scent of ale wafted up my nose, eliminating the smell of damp bricks. I heard shouting, felt boisterousness, sensed people falling over. I felt anger come over me. I started to get restless as she talked more about how the vaults had become dens of iniquity, far beyond the reach of the law, governed by malevolence and flooded with chaos. 'This vault was used as a tavern, governed by a strong landlady who was known to have killed the men who crossed her,' she said.

I lagged behind the group as we moved through two more vaults, hearing more stories of how people on the tours *may* have heard or felt something in the darkness around them. There was no denying the ghastly atmosphere of the vaults, but her repeated attempts to scare us with hypothetical happenings soon wore thin.

'So, here we are in the final vault of our tour,' she said. I hadn't expected the tour to end so soon. She had dragged out the time with her stories, showing us a mere glimpse of the one-hundred-and-twenty vaults. I was flustered, given no choice but to remain behind or go through the whole tour again. 'We are standing in the most haunted of the South Bridge vaults where an evil entity known as Mr Boots has been seen. There is also, some say, the spirit of a small boy who people have seen running around from vault to vault.' I tuned out of her speech and into the atmosphere which felt no different to the other vaults, but her story of Mr Boots made me regret not leaving the group in one of the earlier vaults. '... and that is the end of the tour. If something follows you home tonight and things start tugging at your bed sheets, don't be alarmed, they usually return to the vaults after a few days. Follow me to the streets!'

I stood my ground until the last chattering Japanese tourist disappeared, tempted to throw in the towel and run like hell after the Scandinavians to break my year-long vow with some blonde rough-and-tumble, but my confidence was short-lived; the black dampness held me still. Goosebumps climbed up my spine like a giant centipede. I slowly turned in circles to get my bearings of the vault which was empty of everything except the candle resting on the floor next to me. It was the size of a squash court, but with a ceiling I could touch with my fingers and rub the soot between them. The muffled sound of the outside door closing isolated me completely. Suddenly the candle went out and a small hand closed its fingers over mine.

'Go! Now!' a boy's voice quivered.

'Stag, be…' The first punch crunched into my chin before I could call for back-up. I'd blown the first lesson Logan ever taught me: never to journey without your ally.

'Get out, fucker!' a man's voice spat into my ear. His hand thrust into my pocket and grabbed my phone, smashing it into the black hole before I could shed light on the exit. The small hand once holding mine had gone.

'Wait! I have only come to…'

'Too late, fucker. No escape now.' The man hawked a mouth full of phlegm from his crackling lungs and spat it at me. It trickled into my gasping mouth and tasted of roadkill. The second punch hit me square on the nose, knocking me flat on my back, bouncing my head on the concrete. All the fear I'd ever felt as a child from being stalked by phantom breathing and the ghost of a Victorian woman returned to me. I tried to scream, but I was paralysed by terror and unable to utter a sound.

'You think you had nightmares, fucker. Ha! I'm your worst one, all of your Four Horsemen wrapped into one. You think you were ill? You greedy little drinker. I'm about to make you sick to fucking death of me.' His face suddenly brushed the side of mine. His stubble scratched my cheek. My arms flailed, I was falling, spinning with horror at how he could read my mind, exposed to my demons all over again. I grabbed hold of his leg and tried to lift it from my chest, but my hands slipped over the leather of full-length boots which pressed firmly down on my ribcage. A stick snapped as it hit my knuckles.

'Strike one!' Mr Boots shouted.

'Crow! Crow!' I screamed.

'You're alone now. Nothing can find you here. Time to die and stay here with us all. You can call me Boots, no need for formalities down here.' He pressed his foot onto my throat. I heard him unwrap something and start chewing before lifting the boot to let me breathe briefly and then he cracked the heel into my ribcage. 'That one's for Terror!' Blood filled my mouth, more spit hit my face, dripping the taste of rancid tobacco into my mouth. I started to lose consciousness, but the agony of a wood-splinter being driven through my hand as I feebly fought off the monster brought me back to the present. 'That one's for Frustration. You liked that, didn't you? Not like your cigarettes burning though, eh! Bet you felt that one more.'

I writhed in pain, accidentally stabbing myself in the face with the wooden splinter sticking out of my hand. I wrenched it out, dripping blood into my eyes as Boots tapped into my story of despair and carnage.

'Crow!' I called hoarsely. No strength to scream. Nowhere to hide from the bogeyman who knew my darkest hours.

'Here's a new one for you. Ready, fucker? Here comes Despair.' His footsteps went away from me until the room went silent and I was left broken on the floor. I gathered myself for the charge out of the room in a random direction, praying it would lead me to the exit. I rolled onto my stomach and brought myself to one knee. Still just the ghostly silence. Then the sound came. A shrieking from the far reaches of my hell-cell which sounded strangely familiar. A woman's shrieking petered out to a sobbing interspersed with words made inaudible by the despair in her voice.

'You promised me, Aaron. You promised me. Why didn't you stop? You promised me.' I froze as the words my ex-wife had screamed a million times filled my head.

'Such a sweetie, what a shame,' Mr Boots hissed back at me.

'Crooow!' I screamed.

A match scraped and burst into life as his finger curled under my chin and lifted it, bringing me face-to-face with the bogeyman tinted red by blood in my eyes. His white face, hooked nose and septic red eyes were all I remember. 'Let's not forget Bewilderment, eh, laddie. You'll like this one.' He blew out the match and spat in my face one more time before dropping me. All strength to support myself sapped, leaving me a sitting duck for the stream of stinking ice-cold piss which sprayed up and down my body.

'Goodbye, fucker! Give our regards to hell.'

My ribs cracked as he kicked me one more time. I yelped like a dying puppy and freefell into the blackness as the lights behind my eyes went out.

#

I heard the soft sound of water trickling beneath me and felt my body rocked gently from side-to-side like a baby in a crib. I thought I'd died and found the afterlife, but then the stench of stale urine and the taste of roadkill laced with rancid tobacco greeted me. I managed to force one eye open a fraction as the other, swollen to the point of bursting, refused to move. Pleated ripples from the boat's movement shimmered on the stone above me as it moved through a narrow tunnel just wide enough for the small boat to drift past candles resting in small holes in a cave wall.

'Lie still,' a woman said in a velvet voice, calming my contorted body. Part of an oar came into view and slowly pulled away. I swallowed another mouthful of tobacco-flavoured phlegm and bitter blood. I flinched. Pain jabbed my chest. 'Lie still, we will be there soon,' she said, making a gentle blowing sound with her pursed lips. A fine mist of lavender fell on me, cooling my cheeks. I stuck out my tongue to cleanse my mouth of the foul taste.

I travelled along the tunnel, in and out of pain and sleep and flashes of violence, all time lost. I crawled my fingers onto the bottom of the boat where they sank into a deep soft blanket. The ceiling got lower every time I opened my eye, to the point where I could see how smoothly the water had shaped the channel in which we moved. I heard the mystery woman adjust her position, crouching lower; lavender-scented hair brushed my cheeks and lulled me, reminding me of being tickled as a child by my sister.

'He is here, come sisters.' I heard her say. The boat moved into a dome-like clearing and turned in circles giving me a three-sixty view of the ceiling which sparkled madly with quartz-glitter. The water moved all around me. I caught glimpses of women entering the pool by way of sloping banks surrounding the boat, before a tear of blood clouded my vision red. One, two… I lost count of them. Soft, excited whispers filled the cave. The water teemed with activity as the women encircled me. I heard the light tap of a ring on the edge of the boat, as a hand brought it to a standstill. I tried to wipe blood from my eye to get a better picture of the faces now standing around me, blocking out all but a circle of the star-studded ceiling. A hand gently held my arm down. I had no strength to challenge her touch which emptied my lungs. I exhaled endlessly, sinking into the deep mossy pile of the blanket. I forced my swollen eye to open and turned my head both sides to look at the women as my vision briefly improved. Some of their hands held the rim of the boat. I saw women of different heights and features. Long and short hair: some brown, some blonde, some red, some silver. I felt their closeness, heard their whispers and mutterings, but it was their breathing which I focused on. At first there was no order to it, but as more women entered the water and the air in the cave warmed with their presence, it gathered in unison and tempo. In, out, in, out, in out… they all breathed as one. A trickle of blood left my ear. I felt sick and distant. Pain hit my ribs and gripped my punctured hand. A pair of hands lifted my head and held it from beneath while they removed the crane bag Oka had given me. I tried to object, but couldn't utter a sound. A piece of cloth wiped the blood away.

'We must hurry,' someone said. She sounded like a teenager. 'He doesn't have long. Look, he has bones poking through his skin.'

The women bunched together, holding the boat solid, pressing against it. Hands grasped mine several at a time, spreading onto my wrists and forearm. Some rested on my cheeks and chest, others on my legs and bare feet. They buried me under their limbs. Fear hit me, a panic I'd never felt before as I heard them discuss the extent of my injuries – was I near death? I felt thirsty, so thirsty and tired. All I wanted to do was sleep. Their breathing got louder, longer and stronger. The heat from their hands came slowly at first, creeping onto my skin so as not to singe me. Yellow light flooded my eyes and turned a deeper shade of gold which glittered like the Reiki I knew so well. The heat increased to the poker-hot intensity I had felt in my own hands when I channelled the healing energy. Then the humming began: the final layer of an elemental healing symphony encased beneath the earth, floating on water, blinded by light, and cooled by the breathings of their lungs and hearts. All elements and voices harmonised perfectly, stirring something in my bruised body and releasing tears from my eyes. I lay wrapped in a womb of divine femininity which rocked me like a baby. I was good at surrendering and practising humility. For all the false courage drugs had given me, knowing when to surrender was what had saved me and now I let the anonymous women into my soul. The more I let go, the limper I felt and the deeper and slower my breathing became. Bright blasts of purple, green, red and blue shimmered across the golden sea in my mind's eye like northern lights. With each wave of colour, bursts of sheer terror left my body. I had never felt fear like it. Or perhaps I had, as after each horrific spasm I felt clearer and stronger and the colours got brighter. My body twisted, turned and flipped off the bottom of the boat like a hooked fish trying to make its escape. Mr Boots' face leered into me as the orgy of humming, swaying, flipping, twisting and gasping banished him, reaching a crescendo as if the energy now possessed the women. The boat began rocking in all directions and water splashed onto my bruised face as the terror and pain shot out of me.

'Stop, please!' I cried.

My ribs and spine cracked and popped with the sporadic sound of an excited child finding bubble wrap for the first time and jumping all over it. In one swift motion, several pairs of hands slid beneath me, injecting heat down my spine. Their gasping slowed, the splashing calmed and tears flowed from my eyes the like of which I hadn't felt since the early days of rehab when the counsellors brutally unlocked pain of another kind. As the water flowed down my cheeks, my swollen eye cleared and I caught sight of the ceiling of the cave where beams of colour still bounced off the curved recesses of a sandstone dome and slowly faded into a cosmic Underworld. The water lay still. I flexed my limbs and body, daring to sit up to acquaint myself with my hostesses. No pain nor hands kept me down. The women retreated slowly, removing their hands as I sat up in the boat. I touched my healed face, momentarily wondering if I was still alive and not suspended in purgatory, and a beautiful one at that. I looked at the faces gazing at me.

A woman stood behind a freckled teenage girl, holding

her close around the chest. Their identical blue eyes connected them as mother and daughter, both with the same quizzical expression seen on every other female face I looked at. There were wise faces which had stood the test of time and the elements, probably great-grandmothers to grandmothers of the younger women in front of them. Some preferred to keep their faces hidden under shawls.

'Thank you,' I said, pressing my hands over my ribcage to feel the perfectly formed bones. Even the rib I had broken two years earlier in a drunken fall was smooth and unblemished. My voice made the crowd flinch, disturbing the surface of the water which formed golden girdles around their waists.

'We haven't heard the sound of a man's voice for hundreds of years, let alone seen one. You must forgive our apprehension. What are you doing here?' said the woman steering the boat with a voice layered with a thousand female tones. The other women in the cave remained silent, looking at their captain and back at me. 'Yes, I speak for us all,' she said. 'We are a collective, or coven, to be true to our nature. We are all witches from this land and we all arrived here in the same manner – by fire. Some of us still bear the flames' marks.' She looked over her shoulder to where the shawled women bowed their heads. 'Why are you here?' she repeated.

I lost my hold on the boat and fell, rocking it to the point of capsize. The woman stretched out her arms, palms facing down, with all the poise of a tightrope artist and as she did, the water climbed up the sides of the boat to keep it still. She lowered her arms and sat on a small plank of wood at the end of the boat. I braced myself, expecting to hear their voices again, but she was still, just looking with her head cocked to one side. Her eyes were the first thing I saw. Black swirling opalescent pearls, peering at me from a long and slender face with a pure white complexion, and a small birthmark on her left cheek; an island, stranded in beauty, all framed by silver-tipped strands of long auburn hair cascading over one shoulder to her waist where it tied itself into a single complex Celtic knot. She wore a white tunic, bunched at the waist with strands of fishing net laced with limpet shells.

'I don't know why I'm here. I don't even know where I am, or how I got here.'

'Can't you see?' She leaned close to my face, prising her eye open with thumb and forefinger to show me the same flames as I saw burning in Crow's eyes. The smell of lavender made me lose my balance again, but the sight of her eye held me steady. 'The fires are still burning,' she whispered close enough for my face to feel her breath. 'We may be pristine on the outside, but within, we retain the element which killed us. Fire was the death of us, but now it sustains us.' She sat back, perturbed by something. 'But… you know this, don't you?' Her thousand voices raised their volume, irritated and confused. The water stirred chaotically.

I scampered to the back of the boat, crab-style. 'I've been to the castle and seen where they tortured and killed you all. I know where Mother Earth's voice used to speak; the volcanoes have led me here. Although I wouldn't have chosen this route had I known what waited for me in the vaults, I am honoured to be in your presence… presences.'

'Honoured!? A man, honoured to be in our company!' She slapped the water next to her hard and leered at me. The fire in her eyes flared angrily. She gritted her teeth and ground them, making a sound more terrible than the phobic touch of polystyrene. The circle of women closed around me, securing the boat. 'We are supposed to be safe from men here. Although we know you are not like the others.' All of the women looked at each other, nodding in agreement; heads bobbed up and down at the back of the crowd, trying to get a clearer view of me. The circle of hands released the boat and retreated, giving me space to breathe again.

'No, of course I'm not,' I said, trying to be assertive to hundreds of supernatural women somewhere in the Underworld.

'No, you have scars, much like us; you have felt a lot of pain, haven't you?' The coven nodded again. The woman grabbed hold of my hand to look at the palms and then softly traced her ice-cold fingers down the length of my cheeks. A static shock of electricity fired from her fingertips, making both of us jolt. 'You have been burnt, you did it yourself, here on your hands, and your face has felt it, and… what is on your back?' She tugged at my ripped clothes to reveal my most severe scars.

I was lost for words and looked for somewhere to retreat to, but the entrance to the tunnel had disappeared, replaced by smooth sandstone. My audience looked at me: the freak show. A childhood accident with fire temporarily blinded me and stripped the skin from my face and hands. Mental scars were healing, but the physical self-inflicted ones remained. Hands suddenly clutched at my jacket and shirt, lifting them up to view the marks from the lightning-strike on my back where wing-like scars remained from the calamitous LSD trip in the New England hills. The invasion made me angry. I couldn't control it and lashed out at the hands, losing my balance, falling head-first into the water. I sprang up, ready to fight. Since I'd found recovery and stopped physically abusing myself, any uninvited touch of my body felt instantly threatening and invasive, triggering a fight or flight response which I had little control over, but no one was near me. The women were sitting on the stone beach surrounding the water. The boat had vanished; only their spokeswoman remained before me with her hands outstretched, fingertips tickling the surface of the water, creating small snaps of static energy from her fingernails.

'You have our special attention, what is your name?' she said.

'Aaron. What's yours?'

'Madalane. What is it you seek from us, Aaron?' Some of the witches sniggered.

'I… I'm not entirely sure how you can help, but I know I need it. I met Saint George at an extinct volcano in Ardnamurchan. He told me he was responsible for the start of the witch hunts, by murdering the last dragon on earth, and that I was a key to help bring back King Arthur to restore the land to its former glory. That's the legend of his return.' Saying the words out loud instantly made me feel like a fool. I waited for the hyena laughter to begin, but silence remained. They looked at me blankly. Then the steady dripping of water echoed around the cave. Just one solitary drop after another. I looked above my head for the source, in the hope it would show me a way out, but the ceiling was dry. I looked at Madalane and found the source.

'I'm sorry, was it something I said?' I watched her tears blend with the cave's pool, each drop creating a small plume of fire which swirled around her.

'You descend on us without invitation, ask us to help a king and tell us that you are keeping counsel with this man-Saint who has sickened the spirit of the land and caused our disgusting demise,' Madalane said. The tone of her own, singular voice mesmerised me as the others stepped back into the encroaching shadows. Her anger rose again, teeth gritted and fire burned furiously in her eyes. 'It was a king who murdered us. King James oversaw some of our tortures personally before sending us to the stakes for burning.' The water whirl-pooled around me and the stone floor turned to mud and my feet were sucked into the softened bed of the pool, rooting me to the spot. The sparkling crystal ceiling turned to dark granite, transforming the atmosphere of the cavern into a foreboding cauldron of shadows and hatred – for me. Madalane outstretched her arms again and began muttering words in another language. A brisk wind gathered, skimming water from the surface and spitting it into my face. I sank knee-height into the silt until water tickled my chin.

'Wait!' I screamed. 'You asked me why I came here, well, why do you think that portal opened for me? That was the only way I could have come here. Yes, I know of the Underworld. I have travelled to other places down here to meet spirits, but I knew nothing of your existence down here. I haven't come to torment you. Please, ask yourselves, why would I have been given safe haven here? Just one more kick from Mr Boots up there would have killed me, but someone or something opened the portal and let me in.'

Madalane stopped her mutterings and lowered her arms. The water calmed. My feet remained sucked solidly into the mud. She walked towards me, untying the fishing net from around her waist; tears quickened and cascaded from her cheeks leaving a trail of floating fire in her wake. Her face passed close enough for me to kiss, and she glanced at me briefly before she turned, gracefully, ever so slightly dancing, to the melancholic sound of her heartstrings. She held the fishing net high above her head and then rested it over my shoulders, swaying, sighing, crying, circling me again and again. The water chilled; shivers crept over my skin.

'Do you know who these shells belong to?' Madalane said as a memory brought a smile to her troubled face. She stood still, facing me, holding a small conch to her ear, listening, remembering, loving. 'Shhh, can you hear them?' She offered the shell to me, gently placing it over my ear as her smile beamed wider and the fire in her eyes dwindled to a flicker. The familiar sound of the sea came to me, bringing visions of soaring gulls and the musty scent of salt and seaweed, but there was another sound, distant at first. I cupped my hand over Madalane's long slender fingers, pressing the shell firmly to my ear to hear the happy chatter of an infant playing, then came the first cries of a new-born baby, wailing for its first taste of mother's milk followed by the joyous cries of a man's deep voice. 'These are the shells my daughter collected from the beaches of Sanna Bay before I was taken to Edinburgh for questioning. I only wanted to share my healing gifts with others, to bring light into their lives and healing to the land in my own way. That's what we all wished for, but all we found was suspicion, darkness and death. I was dragged from my husband and children and thrown into fire by a man who called himself a king of his people; and you have the gall to speak to us about your desire to bring back another king! Look around you, Aaron, look at the women who have lost their children, their sons, brothers, fathers, grandfathers. Why would any of us want to help such a cause?'

Words failed me for what felt like an eternity. I couldn't tell her I understood, because I wasn't a father and hadn't felt the depth of love she knew so well, but I felt inspired to tell my audience all I knew about Arthur. It was all I had to offer as currency to convince them. 'Not all kings are the same, Madalane. Arthur was born of magic belonging to the alchemist Merlin, and they became great friends. He was known for his qualities of justice and fairness. Over his reign he rid this land of evil and dark powers. Like all of you, he has not died, but he sleeps somewhere in this land, waiting to be called, to return once more. He was one of the most benevolent rulers England has ever known. Arthur sat with his knights at a circular table, all on one level, no hierarchy. I can't tell you why you are needed, yet, but it will become clear to me the further I walk The Path.'

Madalane's blank expression reflected all of the other women's stone-cold faces. She cupped the shell to her ear, smiled, and pointed with her other hand to the wall behind me where the dark entrance to a tunnel big enough for a steam train to pass through emerged. 'Our minds and hearts are set in stone. We will not be moved. There is your way out, but remember, there is more healing waiting for you in there. Take this, for I have been told you may need what is inside it someday.' She reached to the back of her waist to retrieve my crane bag and looped it over my neck. Giving a slight bow of her head, she walked backwards, not willing to risk turning her back on me. She joined the other women who linked hands with her. They stood around me in their horseshoe shape with the tunnel being the only direction to go. No ceremony, no goodbyes, no sense that their will could be swayed. I turned slowly to look at them. Somehow, saying thank you felt inappropriate, so I placed a hand over my heavy heart and bowed back. I understood their decision, but the weight on my shoulders was unbearable.

Flames flared up behind me like a lighted match meeting a petrol slick. Their faces shone with the sudden burst of yellow light. Heat pressed against me, forcing me into the tunnel. I faced it, my hands raised to shield me from the heat. I peeked through my fingers to see Stag waiting for me. His antlers were on fire. He stood there in all his flaming magnificence like the most awesome beacon of hope I had ever seen. I'd learnt my lesson the hard way – never to journey without my ally – but now I knew that no matter how far down I went into the Underworld I would never be out of my depth as long as I kept him close.

As soon as I stepped onto the black stone of the tunnel the entrance closed kaleidoscopically behind me. Madalane's face was the last I saw of the coven.

Stag's feet tapped and ricocheted down the tunnel. There was no end in sight, just a long jet-black meandering wormhole. Something looked different about him; his antlers were taller; his eyes seemed bigger and darker, and his body broader. There was no sign of life in the tunnel, and yet I'd never seen Stag look more alive. He stood to one side and beckoned me to walk ahead of him with a low swooping arc of his head, which scraped his antlers on the stone.

My giant shadow loomed in front of me, curving around the walls as I gingerly made my way around the bends, disappointed that each turn revealed another stretch of darkness. Occasionally I'd have to pick my feet up to step over clumps of strange transparent foliage. Curiosity got the better of me, I stopped to pick up one clump of the material and felt sick. I was walking through piles of snake-skin.

'Make this end, Stag, please,' I said, turning to him in the hope he had the power to snap me out of this strange journey. 'I am back in the room!' I shouted, but the tunnel swallowed my voice; no echo returned. Stag shovelled his head forward, waving flame at me. I stumbled backwards, trying to keep my balance as he corralled me into the darkness. With each step, my feet became accustomed to the terrain, and my eyes to the thousands of firefly lights which swam in front of me. There was no evil here – only healing.

The penny dropped! Surely the witches wouldn't have saved my life, only to send me to my death? While my alliance with Stag was still in its early days, I knew his intentions were only to help me learn and acquire more knowledge of this fascinating world. We were both messengers: he of the spirit world and I of the world some called reality. Portals in the moon's craters, bamboo forests with eternal fires, ancient deserts inhabited by shapeshifting natives and giant supernatural birds: this was reality? As my nervous system was cleansed, my senses became more heightened and my trust in The Path of initiation grew stronger. If the architect of the tunnel was a giant snake, then I prepared myself to meet its maker.

Stag responded to my sureness of foot. He dimmed his flames. I walked into the underground firefly night with my arms held out and my palms facing ahead of me. I closed my eyes for a few paces and remembered how, years ago, the healing energy I saw glittering in front of me had induced a vision of my former life as a Native American boy, sprinting through tall green grass. Now, as I walked into the unknown, and wherever I seemed to turn, I could recall those days and realise that the past had not disappeared at all because my ancestors still walked beside me. I thought of Oka, and as I opened my eyes a transparent image of him filled the tunnel and faded, leaving his shape painted in dancing golden energy. My strides lengthened as we turned left and right following the curves of the giant underground tube. Stag slowed down and dropped back until his steps were a slow, distant rhythm, fading all sense of time. The skin disappeared. I saw small alcoves peppering the walls. I trawled memories of my conversations with Logan, searching for symbolism of animals in the spirit world, remembering his bizarre wall of artefacts and finding the perfectly preserved body of an anaconda. One word came to me: transmutation! The serpent was a symbol of growth and change. Logan had made it very clear that in shamanism the serpent was a symbol of transmutation, not transformation. There was an edginess about him when he was telling me, late into one night. His eyes had flitted back and forth from the Thunderbird mask and his knee had jigged nervously up and down. 'Transformation is change which is only skin-deep. Laddie, when you stopped drinking and drugging ya'self, you changed what you did; your actions, emotions and feelings were all different, eh? And because of that you changed on the outside, didn't you? You stopped burning yourself and started eating again! But with transmutation, you change at the deepest level, into a different being. Don't get me wrong, laddie, transformation is very useful! It's the first stage of transmutation, but still the old parts of you exist in your energy, to resurface one day, ready to be changed at the next, deeper level. That's why snake energy is such a powerful force for spiritual development; constantly shedding its skin to bring forward new growth and expansion. Its venom is deadly to everyone except those who are open to its power. Snake energy can teach us how to move through the various stages of transformation, into a full transmutation of Self!'

The madness in Logan's eyes that night was unforgettable.

His words shed light on the strange Underworld terrain I walked through. As I turned a ninety-degree bend the small pockets increased in number with every step. I traced my fingers around the silky smooth lips of the pockets which disappeared into the walls. The hard, fast beat of Stag's feet hammering away on the stone made me turn and throw myself against the wall as he charged past, his antlers at full blaze, disappearing into the darkness. I slid down the wall of the tunnel like a hamster exhausted on its wheel, with nothing but the sound of my crystal heart beating faster within the sudden solitude. I dropped to a sprinter's starting position and looked back as the distant sound of an ocean wave rolled towards me. Without Stag's fire I was plunged into darkness again; only the golden light kept me company this time. The wave roared, stopping close as the tunnel shut behind me, herding me forward. I pinched hard at my skin and bit my tongue to see if the pain would bring me back to my hotel bedroom and out of the dream. It would have been the easy way out.

The wall waited for my decision while the sound of hissing and slithering awoke around me. I could either run into the unknown or pin myself against the wall and be pushed out. 'The courage to change the things I can...' I whispered part of the Serenity Prayer, waited for the phantom starting gun and mustered all my courage. Springing to my feet, I powered into my stride, but gravity vanished. I had no speed or strength, and ran with all the grace of an astronaut getting to grips with his first moon-walk. I ran into the abyss constantly clambering for balance as the first black head struck my arm, hissing, cloaked by Earth's Underworld-night. Teeth hooked into my skin and tried to tug themselves free. I screamed as the pain of a thousand bee-stings flooded my veins. The second strike hit my neck from the other side: straight to the jugular. Excited slithering and hissing surrounded me as I tried desperately to find speed and make a hasty exit to who-knew-where. A force held me upright as I clutched at my neck and every part of my body. A barrage of strikes hit my legs, tearing away strips of skin through my wet trousers. One of my assailants hooked into my thigh, and I dragged it along for a few paces with it flapping in a frenzy, slapping its scaly skin against the stone as it flushed its venom into me. My yelps turned to screams as my blood boiled. My panic fuelled their attacks as they sprang at me from their holes in perfect synchronicity, each waiting its turn to strike me. One hit my cheek and recoiled, then several larger snakes focused on my torso. The wall pushed me down the tunnel of hell as the snakes hit me viciously, their bodies cracking like whips as they darted in and out of their layers. My screams turned to cries; my blood sizzled with the heat of a hundred chillies, but my strength didn't diminish; I grew stronger and more sure-footed with every strike of their needle-sharp teeth. Their venomous petrol fuelled my advance through the tunnel. If there was a demon still inside me, he owned me right now.

My eyes, nose, mouth and the soles of my feet were the only places they never bit, because there was somewhere I had to be, somewhere they needed me to get to, where all their venom and aggression would be put to use. There was a slight pause of a few seconds after several of them hacked into my back in quick succession, like the big-guns finale of a firework display. The last snakes carried extra anaconda-sized weight. My head whiplashed with the strikes. Venom and blood burnt my eyes as I fell out of the tunnel.

I dropped in silent relief for the respite, comforted by the sound of my rapid breathing, telling me I wasn't dead. I fell through the darkness and surrendered, holding out my arms and remembering the words of Scottish Joe, a veteran of recovery with over twenty years of sobriety under his belt who visited us in rehab to share his experience of strength and hope.

'I didn't make it all the way to the beach to drown in the sand,' he said.

I fell through the void with a presence I had felt close to me in Cape Town as I detoxed; it surrounded me now, but it didn't prepare me for the dull 'thud!' which knocked the wind out of my lungs. I gasped for breath, clawing at the plants and foot-high grasses which cushioned my fall. I turned my head to make sure my neck wasn't broken to see a neon-green beetle scamper away from the tip of my nose into its minute forest. Several layers of distant birdsong filled the air, disorientating me as I stared at a starlit sky framed by the opening in a tree canopy; it felt too late for the evening chorus. Bullfrogs and toads called out to each other and larger four-legged animals bayed like it was party time in a jungle: the last place I felt like being after leaving hundreds of reptiles behind. I touched my forearms and face, and winced as I found the cuts made by their teeth. The burning had left my skin and the bleeding had stopped, but the strange taste of their venom remained as I dabbed the end of my finger into a cut on my cheek and touched my tongue to sample the strange, peppery taste. The touch of my body on the ground made me want to sleep so badly. I succumbed to the lullaby of the natural world, trying to hide from the Underworld's next instalment.

'Ding!' tolled the deep tone of a bell. My eyes sprang open and triggered my racing heart, and the animals burst into a frenzy. I rose slowly to my feet expecting to see Tarzan swinging through the trees towards me, but the sight of my ripped body kept my head bowed low as I examined the gaping wounds on my arms and legs. My movements made the cuts breathe like goldfish. The snakes' teeth had pulled away perfect gaping ellipse-shaped patches of red-raw skin. I lifted what was left of my shipwrecked-shirt to find that every cut was exactly the same shape and size. There were too many to count, and the sight of them made whatever anaesthetic was keeping the pain at bay wear off fast.

'Dinggg!' tolled the bell again, louder, longer. I dropped my shirt and caught my trousers before they fell down as the last ripped thread on the fastenings gave way. The dull blue-black light took some adjusting to. I squinted madly at the top of the giant shape in front of me, eventually focusing on the largest oak tree I had ever seen. Its branches disappeared into a star-spangled sky with bark so thick, it formed deep crevasses in its trunk. Millions of dark green leaves rustled as a tropical wind flowed in from the darkened recesses of the landscape. I closed my eyes to savour every second of the wind's touch, momentarily losing my balance as its earthy scent intoxicated me. I was so deeply in love with the wind, having grown up with a fascination for it. To me, it was the most spiritual of all elements, touching my soul more than any other. The way it danced with trees and sculpted the sea mesmerised me, as did the games of hide-and-seek it played when I walked through hills and forests, suddenly charging through me, bursting every molecule of my being. We had an innate connection with each other. Sometimes I'd try to summon and wield it, unnerved by the times it arrived right on cue.

'Dinnnggg!!!' The loudest chime rudely awoke me from my hypnotic state. The wind dropped and the remaining reverberations faded away. The undergrowth bristled with life. Scampering rodents made the grass twitch in waves which encroached on me in the same horseshoe shape made by the witches who dwelled somewhere above my head. The birds fell silent. I heard the thudding steps of larger animals moving in the darkness. Somewhere in the distance a horse neighed loudly and the familiar bay of a stag quickly followed on its heels. Another audience gathered for a late-night supernatural show. Small clouds of light came out of the shadows and watched, hovering above the tips of the grass in clouds of chlorophyll. They just hung there like lanterns, waiting for the compere to arrive and shout, 'Animal spirits, ancestors and earthly gentleman, welcome!'

It was obvious where the main event was going to take place. At the base of the oak tree sat a huge silver cauldron, secured to the ground by roots which spread from the base of the tree and wrapped themselves around its ten-foot circumference in a mesh of Celtic weaves. Despite its apparent manmade shape, the cauldron looked part of the surrounding natural furniture. As the forest quietened, a subtle throbbing sound took over from the animals. The tree and the vines pulsated with energy, heating the simmering liquid. Its steam wafted the most earthen scent I had ever smelt towards me. It acted like a natural anaesthetic, numbing the soreness of my skin. The witches were the only logical owners of such a vessel; I sat down slowly, dizzied by the smell and my supernatural helter-skelter ride, and waited for them to appear again. The cauldron fizzed and spewed a thick cloud of steam. I squinted hard through the white veil as the shape of a green figure walked out of the tree and stood behind the cauldron. It waved its arms over the surface in slow swimming movements, humming deeply, like a bull-elephant standing its ground – or maybe it was getting ready to charge. The water calmed and the steam cleared with every wave of the figure's arms. I clutched my arms and dribbled in astonishment as the tips of thick green antlers poked through the dispersing cloud.

'Mmmmmm… mmmmm… mmmmm,' it hummed. Phantom hairs on the back of my shaved head stood on end as I clenched parts of myself I didn't know existed. The antlers sprouted from the unmistakable head of Cernunnos: Lord of the Underworld. I wasn't ready for such a meeting. Logan's fireside lectures had more than covered how royal this spirit was. In fact, royalty was not befitting of a being who gives birth to all power animals, including Stag. He looked at me with eyes of light beaming from a complexion the colour of the greenest lichen. He was an awesome sight. Instinctively, as if succumbing to the majesty of his huge eight-foot frame, I knelt like a lost knight asking for mercy. My movement made his humming stop and he stood there in silence with his arms frozen mid-swim over the dancing bubbles. I froze too, half squatting, not daring to do anything more to provoke him. I had no idea what to do. My legs started to shake, so I stood up with a slight bow of my head, which seemed to be agreeable to him. His arms beckoned. I was more than twenty feet away from him, a distance which suited me fine as his aura had all the power and turbulence of a thunderstorm. The first lightning strike felt imminent. As I shuffled my feet forward, though, flattening the grass to leave a snail's trail behind me, I was able to see the finer points of Cernunnos' body. A fine network of roots trailed from the stems of his dark green antlers down the back of his head and onto his shoulders, making a natural-weave cloak, fanning out and disappearing into the base of the tree. It wasn't clear if the roots fed Cernunnos, or he, them. Or maybe they were all one. His hand, the size of a road sign, slowly raised into a stop gesture. Somehow English seemed the most ridiculous language for this god to speak. I was under his spell. The laser-beam from his eyes marked the spot where he wanted me to stay. He looked over my body with great interest, and I, his.

He had all the usual facial features of a human, but they were accentuated by the forces of nature. Boulders for shoulders and massive gnarly branch-sized arms extending from a torso that would've put Arnold Schwarzenegger's to shame, all clothed in different shades of green. The animals moved in unison, hemming me in, unbalancing me. I was weakened by the pain with no reserves to stave it off. Cernunnos made a twirling motion with his hand, and I turned, lowering my shirt to show him the harrowed skin on my back. It was a hash of snake bites and lightning-strike scars the shape of a crow's wing. I didn't feel like boring him with the story and he didn't seem in the mood for conversation. Energy pressed against my back and held me, pulling me backwards. The smell coming off the cauldron made me retch.

'Mmmmm…' Cernunnos said. His magnet let me go and I turned to face him. He looked at me with a wry smile. I wondered if he were about to eat me. I tried to return the compliment, but I had nothing left. Had I journeyed too far below? Was I out of my depth, never to return to the surface?

Cernunnos reached behind the cauldron and raised a cup made from half a giant acorn. He cradled it in his open palm and circled it over the surface of the liquid which calmed, still, like glass blown with every tint of green and brown nature had ever intended. He curled his fingers around the bottom of the acorn and, in one swift motion, scooped up a full serving of the liquid and held it inches from my face. I felt consciousness leaving me; there was an urgency in his gesture, jerking forwards, spilling some of the acorn's mysterious potion onto my slashed feet. Years of compulsive drinking had primed my gullet to open like a seagull necking its silvery catch. Grabbing the acorn, I held my breath to mask the stench, and downed it in one. I didn't taste a thing, just vapour burning up my nose. The smell doubled me over, and I tried with all my might to keep it down. Offending the God of the Underworld didn't seem like a good idea at this juncture and I had no reason to be concerned for my safety since leaving the surface of the vaults. The liquid saturated my empty stomach as I fell to the ground.

'Timber… Stag, be with me,' I murmured from my grassy bed. His familiar footsteps came from no more than a few feet away, brushing through the undergrowth. I smiled as his long brown face stooped down to meet mine. He glanced over at Cernunnos and snorted through his nose, bellowing huge clouds of smoke over my cuts. Moments passed, and a strange buzz I could only associate with some kind of opiate, of which I had tried a few, affected my mind, but instead of relaxing my body, it made my muscles tighten. I clenched my fists and gritted my teeth moments before the shock of a thousand volts flicked through me. The burn-scar on my back heated up again. Someone else had control of me, and I didn't like it. There was no lightning in the sky, no sign of Oka, yet the surge of energy felt so familiar. I tried to lift my head to address Cernunnos, but the ground held me fast like a circus knife-thrower's assistant ready to be skewered. I turned my head to the side and found Stag standing sentry in the distance, framed by two blades of grass which wavered in front of my eyes. If Stag wasn't concerned for my safety, nor was I.

'Caw!' Crow called from high above me. His silhouette

darted repeatedly left and right across the canopy's opening with his usual supernatural speed. I smiled as I found the lightning-strike zig-zag again, remembering his dance along Cape Town's street lights as I took my early morning strolls to the gym. Maybe my intuition, sharpened by spirit, told me what was coming next, or perhaps it was the way Crow had been keeping his distance more than usual as I found my feet on The Path. He'd been there for me in my darkest unconscious hours and led me to the light. His work was done in some ways. I opened my heart to him with such abandon, and as the first tear escaped from my eyes Crow hovered and then dived straight through my chest. The impact sent shockwaves through the forest followed by a brief lull which had an air of expectation, like the pause a jet makes before it launches itself down the runaway. I braced myself.

The first black feather appeared on my left wrist from a snake-slit in my skin. Crow had posted me an invitation to a party – spirit style. I held my arm up to examine the spectacle as the feather kept growing until it was nearly a foot long, secured at its base to my skin by a thick quill which glistened with a thin film of blood. I felt lighter with the first token of flight, and I sat up to look at Cernunnos; there was nowhere to run, but I was enthralled with the idea of making my exit vertically. He stood with his massive arms outstretched either side of the cauldron and bashed both fists against it simultaneously. The vibration instantly excited the forest as it responded to the deep slow drum-beat with a chaotic outcry of noise as the rhythm of the Underworld came to life. Pressure built again; I held up my other wrist to greet another feather as it found its way out of my body. I sat there, hands in front of me, staring at two feathers poking out of my wrists with my burn-scar on fire and cosmic electricity coursing through my veins. I stared at Cernunnos with my eyes crazed wider than a rabbit caught in his head-lights.

'More, give me more!' I said. The craving for more feathers to appear from my snake bites was greater than any I'd had for cocaine or alcohol. There was no comparison. 'More!' I shouted, closing my eyes, jumping to my feet. The drumming quickened, and I felt my adrenals go into overdrive, but there was no fright or fight, only the impulse of flight as the hormone pumped more feathers from my arms and legs. I hit myself in the head and started jumping on the ground with both feet like a Zulu possessed by the blackest juju. Feather after feather sprouted from the snake-cuts all over my body as the mad initiation party reached a crescendo of drumming, primal screaming, and the undertone of Stag's deep baying filling the gaps in Cernunnos' drumming. With every feather I felt lighter, and every drumbeat brought the cosmic sky closer to me. I danced and flapped in circles, stooped low to sweep my wings over the tips of the grass, marvelling at the way the feathers felt as one with me as I jumped up and spun wildly; my toes barely touched the ground the faster I spun. As my plumage thickened and my desire to soar heightened, I kept perfect balance, eyes closed, revelling in the sounds around me and the energy of my movement. Forks of lightning pierced the darkness of my mind and Crow's caws were clearly audible, but I had no idea where they came from. I felt surrounded by him, yet he was nowhere to be seen. I'd always known we were tied together, even before Troy had opened my mind's eye to the idea as we sat and talked at Calloway House. Rehab was proving to be responsible for much more than helping me get clean and sober. It had made me face up to the psychic side of my life, a side I had been hiding from and numbing with any substance I could somehow cram into my bloodstream, but the reformed junkie was ready and now the masters were appearing.

Cernunnos stopped drumming. His fists hit the cauldron with such might, the soundwaves clattered off the trees, further widening the diameter of the canopy above me. I felt an impulse stir in my centre, like a million butterflies looking for a way out of my solar plexus. Despite my novice level of experience at surfing the spirit world, I was far from being a fish out of water. I felt primed for this moment – God and all. Instinctively, I knew what to do. Drawing energy from above my head into my crown, and from the earth below, up my legs, both streams of energy collided in my solar plexus setting the butterflies free. I jumped with all the supernatural energy bursting from within me. I found myself above the trees, no soundtrack, just the whisper of wind through my wings. Fright kicked in as I looked down at the ground. My arms outstretched, wings extended, with layers of feathers perfectly stacked on top of each other – I floated down. A hush befell the forest. Cernunnos faced me and grunted, nodding at the sky. I looked at myself in the cauldron as it reflected the blackness I'd carried inside me for too long. I cocooned myself inside my wings and listened to my breathing. Despite my new appearance, I sensed an oldness, a return of the ancient sleeping side to me I'd once associated with violence but now it was different. It was time to get acquainted with all of me. I sensed the wind again, but it wasn't whispering, it was running at me like a freight train from deep within the forest. I heard trees crashing to the ground; King Kong wasn't supposed to be in the Underworld. I knew this wind well, it had hit me in Cape Town, forcing memories back to me. I crouched and lifted my wings, holding them rigid, tilted slightly to catch the howling wind as it burst into the clearing.

'Aaaaaaaaaaa!' Cernunnos roared as I ascended, light-speed to the stars on the supernatural slipstream. There I remained, suspended for what felt like an eternity, basking in the ever-present moon and its gaping crater-portal. Time lost all definition. For those endless moments I forgot everything that had passed before me. I played dot-to-dot with the stars, making vivid images of Stag and Oka. Their shapes floated by like satellites reminding me they were there to communicate with me and guide the way, but I was in my element, flying solo, transforming, basking in the weightlessness with faraway stars, dreaming of Icarus and how I could teach him a few things. I dreamt of the eternal fire burning in the centre of the moon's bamboo forest and sat opposite a version of myself in human form, dressed in animal tattoos, stones and crystals. His crane bag glowed gold. I felt his confidence: his knowledge of magic and the supernatural. I felt the strength of his energy flow over me from the other side of the fire.

My sudden descent shattered my embodiment with Crow; darkness surrounded me whether my eyes were open or closed. The stars had disappeared and I hurtled towards the familiar sound of the tour guide's voice. I felt the contours of the clammy cobbled steps and looked up at the group I had been with in the vaults. Her voice stopped suddenly; I looked up at her and the group's astonished expressions as they looked at me. I checked myself for feathers, but there were none. Just the Robinson Crusoe outfit I was wearing. My clothes were shredded, but my skin was unblemished.

The group broke into a mad anxious chatter, swearing and gasping, some running away, convinced I had been ravaged by the malevolent spirits lurking behind me. I didn't entertain them with a full account of my journey; preferring to appear confused to match my dishevelled appearance.

'I… I don't know what happened. I was following the group when something grabbed my neck and dragged me to the floor,' I said, shaking.

'Here, you'd better take this for your way back to the hotel,' the guide said, placing her black cloak around me. Her eyes were wide with excitement for the future stories my misfortune had given her.

'Thank you,' I said, holding my head low to hide the smile which came as I saw myself cloaked in black again.

I crossed the South Bridge, craving and succumbing to the seduction of the spirit world luring me back. Mr Boots could have his way with me again if it was the only portal back to the witches or Cernunnos. A hint of the junkie insanity I'd escaped unbalanced me as I walked a tightrope, teetering on the brink of a relapse the counsellors wouldn't have known to warn me about.

I looked across to Holyrood Park where Arthur's Seat slept quietly in the darkness and wondered what I would awaken there tomorrow.

NINE

The next morning, I had vague memories of my return to the hotel and a night's sleep clouded by twisted dreams and flashbacks to the vaults and lower landscapes when contorted images of witches, snakes and nature gods swamped me. I'd always been too quick to accept offers of mind-altering substances, too eager to please, too weak to say 'no', but as I sat on the slope of Salisbury Crags wrapped in full rain-gear, watching the tourists on Arthur's Seat through a curtain of thick drizzle, I found an excuse for the madness. Occasionally, I lowered my hood to feel the reviving cool shower on my scalp before hiding again to neck coffee from the small lid of my trusty bullet-shaped flask. The skin on my arms and face looked as if I was recovering from an argument with a combine harvester, with countless faint inch-long scars being the only trace of my encounter with the snakes. I drifted between excitement and confusion, not knowing for certain which world I belonged to, but craving more contact with my new drug, the world of spirit. For years I had searched for spirits in a bottle, and now they were everywhere. I was prepared to wait all day for the extinct volcano to be empty of people before making the short but steep nine-hundred-feet ascent to the summit. The coffee kicked in, triggering a weird catalytic reaction with whatever otherworldly substances swam through my bloodstream, conjuring images of what the volcano looked like in all its eruptive glory: spewing rivers of magma, flooding the terrain below me. I could almost hear Mother's dragons screaming in ecstasy.

No one could explain why it was called Arthur's Seat. Even with the gradual sharpening of my senses, I had no idea why I had to visit a place so aptly named.

It remained steeped in mystery and magnetism: a place people visited on pilgrimage every day and where more spiritually inclined folk would maraud around the hillside with skulls and antlers on their heads during any one of the Celtic festivals when the veil between the worlds is at its thinnest. It had an energy which possessed its visitors, and I was next in the queue. Some say it was named after a dragon which wreaked havoc on the land, feeding on its livestock. Others preferred the idea that Camelot Castle occupied the site, but it was the discovery of seventeen miniature coffins buried on three different levels inside the hill which was most bizarre. Each coffin contained wooden figures, dressed individually in full sets of clothes, with years separating the burials of the top and bottom rows of coffins.

I prodded the ground cautiously next to me to check for hidden portals about to swallow me whole and tinged the small silver bell I'd picked up from a souvenir shop, running my thumb over the engraved owl on the handle. It made a sweet, high-pitched ring sure to get the spirits' attention at the top of the Seat. I downed another shot of coffee, just for good measure, and watched more tourists make their way through the drizzle to the top of the hill, drawn by the magnetism through sodden, slippery ground.

'Come on, if you're going to rain, do it properly,' I said, looking skyward in the hope a serious downpour would change their minds. I checked my shoulder for bird-shit as the first heavy drops bounced off my coat, then, holding my cup out, I watched the rain bounce out of it as the sky turned on its taps. Logan had always told me to be careful what I asked for, and as the quest progressed I realised that he was a man of few, yet wise words. I watched the exodus of people from the hill as they slipped and scurried down the slopes for cover.

A giant spaceship-sized blanket of cloud lowered into position above me, consuming the city and its cathedral spire. The last rain-soaked visitor left Arthur's Seat as the rain reached full-pelt and greyness enveloped me. Streams formed next to my perch and found their own way down from the Crags. Then my worst enemy appeared: loneliness. I had all this support from the spirit world, but I had no one to share any of what was happening to me with. My heart still ached, even with Merlin's upgrade. Denial used to be my forte. I'd fooled everyone for years, hiding the slow self-mutilation I was indulging in, but all the speed dating in the world wouldn't take away the pain of yearning for someone to love with all the light of my crystal heart. I removed my hood and turned my face to the sky, knowing that until I knew who I really was, until I found where this journey was taking me, I wouldn't truly know myself and that when I fell in love with my soul, then I would find my soulmate.

I shook the rain from my skin, and with it, the feeling of self-pity. There was more of spirit's work to be done, but while Arthur's Seat was my prime focus, next to it sat Crow Hill with several of my half-brother's cousins playing in the rain. I closed my eyes and savoured every raindrop. Something about the rain felt different: cleansing, like the holy water I used to drink in Lourdes, but this water was blessed by weather spirits. I opened my mouth and drank it in, while an image of Merlin dancing his magic down on me from the moon floated by. Sleep-deprived and covered in lacerations, I courted the edge of insanity again, not knowing or caring what was real and what was imagined. Impulse took over and I hurriedly began removing my clothes to expose my cuts to the water, but a sound drew me to a shadowy figure stalking through the mist of Arthur's Seat, distracting me from my impromptu strip and bringing me back on track. He stood astride the highest boulder, held two weapons aloft in his hand and hit them together again.

'I'm coming, keep raining,' I said, ringing the bell. The mist thickened around me. I made my way once more into what used to be so unseen. With each step I sank inches deep into the sodden earth, trudging with more purpose than ever before, and a hint of the insanity I had courted in addiction, ringing the bell and whispering, 'I'm coming, keep raining. Mist keep falling.' The steps were steep, slippery black, and crunched into the hillside. I climbed the back of the serpent onto the shrouded peak, and waited in the swirling cloud. I gave a long ring of the owl-bell and called him in. 'Stag, be with me.' He breathed heavily once behind me and scraped his foot along the stone to mark his arrival. I didn't need to turn around and look. I felt him. As Crow felt like part of me now, so Stag's energy was blending with mine. There was no intoxication, only an enhancement of my own energy and strength every time he appeared.

I saw the horns on a man's head peep over the brow of Arthur's Seat first; they were the length of my thumbs, and lulled me into a false sense of security with their resemblance to the nature god, Pan. He leapt onto a boulder holding a short sword and cross-bow tightly in his fists, soon putting that idea to rest. The weird light shining behind him made it challenging to see more than a silhouette, but as he turned to look back and signal something to others by raising his sword, I saw the half-wolf, half-human features of his face, set in a fine crew-cut-length fur. His eyes cut through me, staring, snake-like. I warmed to him instantly, reminiscing about the snakes, running my fingers over fresh scar tissue. He wore a kilt and filled it with muscle so thick, it looked as if his joints shouldn't have been able to bend.

'I have come to ask for your blessing to visit Arthur's Seat. I wish to visit you in a sacred way,' I said.

He stood there looking down on me from the highest boulder, remaining silent for minutes, reminding me I did not have right-of-passage to go wherever I wanted and that if I did want to get the most out my time, I should do it with respect for the ancestors still living there. The thought of being refused permission made me slip and cut my hand on a jagged stone. I sucked on a droplet of blood; somehow it didn't taste as I'd remembered and I'd had many wounds to lick. Suddenly he jumped down from the boulder and disappeared below the brow of the hill again where I heard the sound of a large committee meeting. The low murmur of voices ebbed and flowed with emotion and volume, as some of the meeting's members fought to have their words heard. Metal clanked on stone and bursts of laughter belittled me. Doubt seeped into my mind again; of course, the idea that my presence was needed to bring back Arthur was such a joke. Then silence, as though the warrior had made a cutting motion with his hand to his throat.

'But he has asked us for permission! A rarity, wouldn't you say?' a prickling Scottish voice said.

'Raaaaaaaaa!' the crowd cheered.

The horned warrior pounced back onto the top of the hill. 'Come! Come!' he shouted, and jumped back down to more elated cheers which sounded like a homecoming.

'Clang!' The ear-splitting sound of iron clanking on rock startled me and made me lose my footing again. The bell slipped out of my hands and tumbled out of sight. I could see nothing in the grey mist surrounding me. 'Clang!' Another loud clash of metal answered the random call of the falling bell. 'Clang clang!' The rock-chimes came thick and fast. I spun around to see if the spirits had advanced, but only the faint outline of Stag's antlers remained, slowly swallowed by the mist as he did his customary bowing-out.

'I have come to visit you in a sacred way; please give me a teaching about why I am here.'

'Clang! Clang!!!' A trail of sparks marched towards me as the horned warrior walked out of the grey onto the jagged black rock. Raindrops cascaded from the dark-green fur on his face. The sound of the sword grated on me like the coarsest side of a cheese-grater being dragged across my forehead. I pushed my hood back to show him my face. He lifted the sword where he stood, and speared it into the stone with arms which would have beaten a gorilla in an arm wrestle. He wore sandals secured with latticed leather straps stretching over rugby-ball-shaped calf muscles to the crook of his knees, where a plain brown leather kilt fronted with a thick fur sporran covered the rest of his legs. He stood in front of me, shirtless, all Silverback-like, bending his knees slightly as though about to challenge me. He examined me from head to foot, sniffing, then stepped close enough to smell my breath. He closed his brown-green eyes and inhaled deeply. When he opened them again, they were glazed with tears and his mouth was tight and quivering.

'Lavender! Where did you get that smell, and where did you get those cuts?' he said in a low gruff voice. Madalane's hair was the first thing which came to mind. I couldn't smell anything, my crane bag was hidden under three layers of clothing, but his heightened sense of smell was more animal than human. 'I am Beorn, who are you?' He drew his sword from the stone with all the ease of the king I was searching for, and held its tip to my throat. The cold steel pressed into my skin.

'Stag!' I shouted.

He walked out of the cloud before another breath was taken, with his head bowed, antlers poised for the charge with one front leg staggered forward, expelling huge blasts of air from his nostrils with all the rage of a bull about to spear its matador meat.

'Ha! Indeed, laddie, it was wise not to come alone.' Beorn waved his sword once and rested its tip on my shoulder, his head half-cocked, listening for the advance of hundreds of footsteps squelching in the drenched grass as his army climbed to join him at the top of the mist-shrouded hill. Men of all shapes and sizes surrounded us like a crown on the king's hill. They were muddied, bloodied, and dressed in the same simple uniform as Beorn. Their faces held the same scowling expression, as if they were wondering at my audacity to come here and challenge their chief's authority on the very land they watched over and called their home.

'I was in the South Bridge vaults on a ghost tour, it went a bit wrong. Something… someone attacked, no… nearly killed me actually. I fell through the earth and woke up in a boat steered by a woman, a witch. She said her name is Madalane. That might be her hair. I'm not sure. There were hundreds of them down there,' I said, nodding toward the city. Beorn didn't move. I thought he had turned to stone; he froze, staring into space. The only sign of life was the way his heart moved his chest as it pounded fiercely. There was an uneasiness to the stand-off. Beorn's hand squeaked as it tightened around the sword's handle, but he remained statue-still. I took one step back, deciding distance from his sword when such tension held it was a wise idea. The cut from its blade nicked the skin behind my ear, swift and clean, like a shaving nick.

'You'll need to stand still, laddie. This is no time to leave. What did she look like, this Madalane?'

'She's tall, slender… beautiful, there's a birth mark on her cheek. She has black eyes that swim with colours and burn with fire. Her gown was tied with a belt made of fishing net, laced with shells and sea urchins.'

Beorn's feet slipped on the rock as his legs buckled. He used his sword to stop his fall as he was overcome by grief. 'My dear, where is Mother keeping you?' he said, pressing knuckles hard into his creased brow, then he thumped the earth repeatedly until fur wore away, exposing the hard brown hide of his hand. 'What is *your* name?' He flashed his sword at me, tears streaming from his wild eyes.

'Aaron.'

'Hmm, an interesting name for someone so keen to blend into the Celtic spirit world, yet you don't look like you've a drop of Celtic blood in you anymore, not after those bites begin to take their hold. The journey isn't always easy, is it, Aaron?'

'No, sir.' I hadn't called anyone sir since my school days. Beorn's manner rekindled my inferiority complex, but then I remembered my animal instincts lay just beneath the surface of my human skin, and something told me he knew it. 'You know Madalane?'

'Aye. She was, is, my wife. I watched her burn at the castle. She was the last woman to be killed before King James ended the trials. Her fire burned for three days. No amount of water could put it out. In the end they tipped a cart of earth over her to put out the flames – her touch had more light than the sun. She was blessed with the most beautiful magic from the seas of Sanna Bay. I watched her soul disappear below the castle. Years of searching in the Underworld left me this way. We have both made sacrifices, haven't we? Those are the scars of snake bites from the doorways, aren't they? Hmmm, they look fresh.' Beorn growled with pleasure as he looked at the scars, remembering his own encounters with the snakes. 'All of the men who lost their loved ones joined forces and hid out, waiting for a chance to fight King James and his armies. We were never trained as warriors, our grief and anger made us fighters; that's what fuelled us. I walked many a tunnel searching for her. I could feel her below me, but I lost sight of daylight and succumbed to the seductive night of the Underworld. With every failed search I lost myself further to the spirit world, preferring to fight and kill as many of the King's men as possible. Murder sapped my love. The venom stirred that primal instinct in me. I chose the wolf – what did you choose?'

'My brother, Crow,' I said, looking for the quickest way down the hill, be it tumbling or a vertical fall, I didn't care. The witches had made it clear they would play no part in bringing Arthur back, but my limited knowledge of what the hell I was bringing him back for did me no favours in trying to convince them.

'You aren't going anywhere just yet, Aaron.' Beorn's

sword touched my throat. Death seemed a ridiculous idea, but for a split unbalanced second, I saw a way to immortality as a spirit and wondered how the steel would feel inside my throat as I walked onto it. 'Can't you see how similar we are? What were you doing scurrying around in the unseen?' He twisted the blade.

I pushed the sword away and confronted him. 'A year ago I was trying to find my way out of the darkest time of my life. At one point suicide seemed like the best way to leave, but I heard something calling me back from the edge: the sound of Mother Earth's beating heart. If it weren't for that sound I don't know where, or *if*, I'd be today. I've known about the world of spirit for as long as I can remember, as a child, and especially during my sickness. Its malice tried to end me and it also called me back, presenting me with this new path, one which I have accepted, knowing that at any time there may be a fork in the road leading me back to the insanity. It's everywhere, all our cities are crawling with the smell of addiction, its epidemic. My quest is to find a man I know little about, a man who was once a king; his name is Arthur,' I said, bracing myself.

Beorn stepped close enough for a small misted cloud of his animal breath to make me cough. He slipped into wolf-mode and sniffed quickly around my head in silence, honing in on my neck. He kept his head low, as if he was walking on all fours, following the tracks of his dinner. I felt the coarse fur of his fingers reach under my shirt and removed the crane bag. He tipped a small lock of Madalane's hair onto his hand and threw the bag at me, inhaling the smell of her hair as he fell deeply into prayer.

'Go now,' he said, hushed.

'But…'

'Go! You are not welcome here. I will find her now.'

I picked up the crane bag and walked through the cloud to where I thought Crow Hill was. I turned back to catch one last glimpse of the army filing in behind him as they wandered, lamenting silently down the back of Arthur's Seat. I gripped Stag's fur, partly for guidance and also to vent my frustration at the impossible situation I found myself in.

The witches had no idea their loved ones were held suspended in this time and place, and neither of them were able to see past their hate for any king. Their disdain sapped my enthusiasm for the quest and The Path as the adrenalin and dopamine flooding my veins during the last twenty-four hours dissipated, leaving me with an all too familiar come-down.

The walk to Crow Hill was a few minutes down a small dip between the two peaks. With no secret meeting to hide, the rain eased and the cloud lifted swiftly, thinned by the rising sun as it took its midday position. I sat and faced the ball of fire, watching Mother draw a halo around it. She stared at me with her bright beady eye. My quest was dwindling, but she may've had other plans. I was disenchanted with Edinburgh, choosing to forget the personal spiritual processes which were all part of the awakening triggered by my decision to visit a Cape Town rehab. I rested an elbow on the crook of one of Stag's antlers as he bent his flagpole legs and rested his chin on the ground next to me. I removed my rain-gear and exposed my arms to the sun's heat and light. The snake bites disappeared before my jaded eyes. I cupped my hands and held them in front of me as though I was about to blow a feather to the wind. I don't remember the words that came from my lips, but the power of déjà vu told me I had said them hundreds of years ago growing up with my feathered friend. I was no stranger to magic, I just had trouble remembering that sometimes it was no further away than the end of my fingertips. I watched my hands turn black as the skin softened to the texture of the finest pillow. Crow's head peeked out from the bowl my hands made, he paused, like a mole checking the coast was clear, and then with a 'CAW!' he burst out of me. My hands remained glued together. Another crow darted from my hands, and another, in quick succession. Three crows flew every which way their feathers could take them, shouting boisterously with their long deep cawing, set free for the very first time. I took a deep breath and exhaled steadily on my hands to tease three more into the daylight from the still darkened depths of my soul. They joined their companions in the sky. Another breath brought more forth then three more, and three more. The sky was alive – with me.

The weather cleared, uncovering the old volcanoes and bringing the incessant, meaningless chatter of a group of tourists my way. Something about their quick-fire lingo grated on me. Unable to speak quietly or with any awareness of my need for sanctity, I felt consequences coming their way. I zeroed my sights on a tall fellow with the collars of his glossy puffer jacket turned up, carefully flicking a few droplets of rain from his slick black hair and Ray-Ban Aviators. He struggled to keep his footing on the wet ground with his immaculate leather loafers, the kind that had the name of the tailor embossed in gold leaf on the inside. I had bought a pair myself from the town I looked down upon. He spoke as though he were a confused opera singer, half singing, half talking.

I tucked my blackened hands inside the sleeves of my jacket, uncertain about who could see what had happened to me. The crows were definitely making their presence known as the first arrivals on Arthur's Seat's summit stood and watched the loud black cloud of feathers in the sky. With the slightest intention, I sent the crows after the group of tourists as they foolishly chose Crow Hill as their destination. I just wanted to be left alone. Solitude was always the easier option, but here was a chance for some entertainment. My head buzzed with energy, my hands prickled with heat. Mother's beady eye got brighter, scrutinising my psychic tomfoolery. What did I care? The quest had hit a dead-end anyway. I aligned the crows into a flying V formation and sent them for the tourists. They cawed loudly with excitement for their new mission and swooped for the attack and within seconds they were shitting all over their leader. I'd never seen so much bird-shit on one person. The group deteriorated into a horrible mess of screams and more bird-shit as the crows returned for a second pass-by to exterminate the rest of them. Laughter erupted from the top of the once extinct volcano and Mother closed her beady eye, unimpressed.

The strange sound of rusted farm machinery and jangling glass bottles distracted me. It was only then that I realised how inappropriate my magic was as it played out on the hillside below. The nonchalance I felt was unfamiliar to me. Who was I to ruin people's experiences with a gift which, twenty-four hours earlier, I had not been graced with? Black magic was never to be my path, yet here I was embodied with avian allies of that very colour, mocking others. It wasn't the first time I'd seen the crows' aerial bombardment. Before Crow introduced himself to me properly in Cape Town, he'd attacked one of the counsellors in the same way. The dark side still beckoned. I'd been willingly sucked in by the spirit world, which spun me round and spewed me out: snake bites and all. Lack of sleep and appetite had left me searching for sustenance of a different kind. I was wielding my new magic like a loose cannon, mocking people who hadn't been where I had. The quest to bring back Arthur seemed arduous all of a sudden.

The awful noise got louder. I turned around expecting to see Tin Man pleading for his oil, and I wasn't far off. George climbed up the side of Crow Hill on his hands and knees looking worse for wear, if that were possible. He sat next to me, trying to catch his breath; the world was suddenly muted. Crows flew, clouds drifted, people walked, traffic glided, all in silence as a cloak of invisibility covered us and the strong smell of whisky perked me up like a dose of smelling salts.

'You look like shit,' he said, pushing his visor up with two clenched fists, gasping for breath. 'Why can't you sit on flat ground for a change?'

'So do you, as always. Please tell me you haven't been drinking?'

'Well, you know, when in Rome and all that,' George said, grinning. 'The whisky shops here are astounding, never had anything like that in my day, mostly mead… hic!' He reached into the neck of his armour and pulled out a miniature bottle of Talisker single malt. 'You don't partake anymore, do you?'

'No. How the hell did you get hold of whisky? I thought I was the one losing the plot, up here, making crows shit on tourists. You're supposed to be guiding me,' I said, gobsmacked.

'Shame, it's not much fun drinking on your own, although you'd know all about that, wouldn't you? Don't worry, I can take it or leave it… hic! So far, you're the only one who can see me, remember?' He tilted his head back and poured most of the whisky into his mouth, although some spilled down his chin into the cesspit of his armour. God only knew what lurked in the ancient recesses of his armpits.

'If I had a match, I'd see how flammable you are.'

'Ha! I'd welcome any heat you can send in my direction, I've been cold for a thousand years. If I still had my lance I would kill for a cigarette right now, ha ha!' He slapped me on the shoulder making a dragon scream in my head. For all his ridiculousness, I didn't feel angry. Being cast aside by heaven and hell had consequences I knew only too well, after trying unsuccessfully to end my life with a series of massive overdoses.

'If you're going to drink, at least do it properly. Those

tiddly little bottles are pathetic,' I said.

'Believe me, this little baby goes a long way after centuries of sobriety. Wow, the world looks rather beautiful through whisky-eyes, doesn't it? What a view. Cheers to you, Mother.' George sucked the last drop of whisky out of the bottle and hurled it down the hill.

'I know a good rehab in Cape Town, George.'

'Ha! Sure, maybe we'll go there one day. I think I need to lie down.'

'No you don't, not until you've told me what's going on down there.' I showed George the snake bites on my forearm and told him about my journey through the vaults to meet the witches and Cernunnos. 'I don't regret these experiences – in fact, I crave more of them now – but they're changing me, down to the core, and I need to understand where...' I stopped mid-sentence, immediately answering my own question, just as I'd done before. 'I know, just let it unfold and see where it goes.'

'You're catching on fast, laddie!' George said, spooking me with an excellent impersonation of Logan. 'There are vortices all over this city. We're sitting next to one of them.' He nodded at Arthur's Seat, tipping his visor shut. 'You found another in the South Bridge Vaults. Look over there, and let your vision go a little blurred.' He pointed to the south of the city where the faint shape of a glass tornado wobbled like a spinning-top about to topple. 'They were all positive once, most of the earth was full of positive energy, but some places have been traumatised and flooded with negativity from human emotion or tragedy. Be it by rape, massacre, suicide, a battle, or natural events that created widespread human despair such as earthquakes or the giant waves you call tsunamis. A huge amount of life force can be held up in trauma, and you seem to have encountered many spirits of the damned or those who've experienced such trauma. That army on Arthur's Seat? They all lost someone they loved to violence, and they carry the weight of that perpetration against them on their shoulders. They think they seek vengeance, but all they really seek, deep down in their broken hearts, is to go to heaven and be reunited with their soulmates. That hill has seen so much over the years, some good, and more recently bad. It is not as clean as it used to be; people have used its energy for conjuring wrong doing and the hundreds of visitors traipsing over such sacred land has changed its polarity. Positive vortices still exist; they travel up, to heaven, and exist mainly in the wilderness like Ardnamurchan. That one is almighty!'

I remembered Logan telling me what his grandmother said: to get to Ardnamurchan if anything ever went wrong in the world. George was making sense. If some awful cloud of negativity covered part of the earth, through war or whatever, surely people would gravitate towards areas of positive energy? The problem as I saw it was that not everyone had woken up to their other senses.

'If you know all this, why do you need me to get involved? And how do you know what a tsunami is? That word can't have been invented in your heyday.' I prodded his shoulder and examined the mud-like texture of dragon blood on my fingertip.

'Don't forget, Aaron, I have heard many a geologist's conversation while shackled to that barren piece of land and have learnt more than you give me credit for, but I can only see further into what you find. Remember, I was cast aside, waiting for you to arrive. I have known Mother in a different way to you. She is both my jailor and my teacher. Look at the rust constantly eating away at me.' George found one of the small areas of armour where the blood had missed him and scraped a flake of rust from his arm. He crumbled it with his hand and then presented his open palm to the breeze, which carried it away. The small patch glowed with light. I couldn't tell if the sun was reflecting an under-layer of pristine armour, or whether George's saintly soul was streaming through for all to see, desperately trying to reclaim the grandeur he once knew. But it was short-lived; the light was extinguished by a freshly grown patch of rust. 'Hmm, always my jailor, Mother.' George patted the ground gently. 'You are becoming who you are supposed to be, Aaron, and I remain who I am supposed to be. Stay true to your heart and you will find a way – do not doubt. This rust may be my destiny, regardless of whether I can redeem myself by helping you find a way to bring back Arthur, but there is always hope that if you succeed, I may find peace instead of this degradation.'

'So, where to next, navigator?'

'You can't leave Edinburgh until you've journeyed below the castle's volcano.' George pushed his mud-matted fringe away from his eyes to look at the city.

'Shit, I was blocking that one out. God knows what's

beneath it if the witches were burnt there.'

'Have you ever thought that your work is not just to bring Arthur back, but to reunite lost souls in the process of doing so?'

'Right now I think I'm feeling too self-obsessed to think about the bigger picture. Look at me – what's happening?' I touched the few remaining scars on my face and arms. They were healing fast.

'Progress, that's what's happening. Look at it as progress, not perfection.'

I snapped my neck to look at George as he repeated one of the classic recovery slogans I'd heard countless times in rehab. I knew he was right, though. I was sitting on Crow Hill looking at pieces of my soul flying around me, talking to the patron saint of England, purely because I had chosen this strange path; this is what I had asked the Universe for – adventure! Granted, the message that one of the counsellors, Troy, had given me in Cape Town hadn't sounded like I had much of a choice, but I was willing to take the first step.

'You don't get the next destination until you've visited the castle,' George said. 'Quests are all about perseverance and trust. The end will never be obvious.' He held out his shield and ran his finger around the outline of the British Isles. 'Round and round she goes, where she stops, nobody knows… TAP!' He crashed the shield like a cymbal, sat on his shield, smiled at me, and surfed it down Crow Hill, right through several Italians. 'See you in the Underworld, dude!' he shouted.

I admired his ability to smile under such lurid circumstances, but remained a little concerned about his state of mind and whether he was actually sending me on a random goose chase which just happened to visit some of the finest distilleries in the land.

'Don't second guess, laddie. Trust your first instinct.' Logan's voice was never far away. I wondered – no, hoped – that he might already be talking to me from the other side and that there'd be no need to kill him.

#

My last night in the Waterloo Hotel was a restless one. Dreams as vivid as the ones with George rapping his knuckles on the shield hadn't occurred for months. I dreamt all night of my doppelganger staring at me across the fire, and of stone circles first bathed in moonlight before golden sunlight flashed onto the stones. I woke momentarily before tumbling back to sleep and being whisked off to another dimension where warped images of church bells and giant stone megaliths spun around in my mind. An atom bomb flash of light woke me suddenly. I felt the puddle of sweat in my bed which flashed me back to the last incontinent days of active addiction. I fell out of bed with sun spots in my eyes, careering into furniture and smashing a table lamp, scrambling for the shower like a blind man searching for his cane. Images of Crow and Stag flashed like strobe lights in my head as the hot water cascaded over me. I watched the water swirl around the plughole and held grimly onto the wet walls to stop myself being sucked down to join Madalane in her weird wonderland. I towelled dry, trying to think of a good excuse for the broken bedside lamp. I was beginning to wonder if I'd ever sleep through the night. Haunted as a child, and stoned on cannabis, or wired from cocaine for most of my adult life, drugs had left me screaming for help in my nightmares during rehab. Sleep deprivation woke my bastard inner critic.

'You're preposterous, you know that, don't you?' my head blurted at me. 'Running away to Scotland won't change anything. You think you're important enough to bring back King Arthur! Think again, fucker.' It was Mr Boots' voice hissing at me. I sat on the edge of the bed and thumped my forehead hard with my fist. Then there was this silence, as if the whole world was holding its breath in the most comfortable black satin darkness, and out of it, for just a few precious seconds, I saw her eyes. I had no idea who she was, but she was looking right at me. No face, just the bluest circles framed by the most perfect eyelashes: a stranger, suspended in space.

I left my room and walked to Edinburgh Castle shrouded by the woman's eyes which served as welcome protection against the city's attack on my senses. Something had changed since Arthur's Seat. I felt overloaded: people and traffic destroying me with their chatter and tyres, blocking my path, forcing me to find a quieter alternative route to the volcano. My detours took me to a residential area at the wrong end of the city. I walked past massive waste bins belonging to apartment blocks, stepping over puddles of vomit and takeaway food. With no mobile signal to GPS my way out of there, I looked for the first street sign and found exactly what

I was looking for. The small piece of white metal shone brightly down on me: 'New King Arthur Street'. The sign looked at me, and I at it. Time stopped. I wondered if…

'Don't be stupid!' Mr Boots shouted.

I shook my head, walked up the Royal Mile and soon found myself on the cobbled streets approaching the castle's square esplanade. Its dark stone slabs glistened after a brief shower. A bronze bust of a stag stood proudly on a pillar flanking one of the entrances, prompting me to call him to me. 'Stag, be with me.' His energy surrounded me, his breath whispered in my ear, poised, ready.

The right side of the esplanade was lined with a large cloaked statue, turned a light jade green by years of weather. It stood next to a white stone Cleopatra's Needle. Next to that was the grey, raised tomb, the size of a small car with the eagle engraved on its end. The unobstructed views of the city's surroundings were on the other side of the courtyard, which attracted more visitors, leaving me to find some space next to the tomb. I smiled as I read the main inscription on it, 'Here lies Ensign Ewart of the Royal North British Dragoons', and looked over to the low cloud rolling over the top of Arthur's Seat, wondering if I would ever meet a dragon, the likes of which legend said used to torment this ancient land.

I stamped on the ground, expecting a small trapdoor to open and let me descend to the Underworld by way of a glass staircase; nothing happened. I reached for my iPod and headphones, pulling out a small stalk of sage. I lit it and let the small strands of smoke cleanse me, bringing me to the here and now. I telegraphed my intention to visit whichever spirits were waiting in the ancient magma below. The sage smoke rose, mingling with an overhanging branch of a tree which tried to make its way over the thick castle walls. I stilled myself with the tree, our connection strengthened since I had last walked through the Sitka spruce trees to Singing Sands. The stillness helped to block out the possibility that journeying through the negative vortex formed by the witches' agony could hold worse in store for me than Mr Boots' abuse.

Stag stood next to me as I pushed the headphones firmly into my ears to mute the outside world and help me hone in on the rhythm. I rubbed my fingertip gently on the start button, waiting patiently for a small group of tourists, probably Greek in origin, to finish their impromptu photos next to the tomb. 'Click.' I pressed the launch button. 'Boom boom boom boom.' The rhythm kicked in and I plummeted through the stone, synchronising perfectly with the beat which faded into the background as I acquainted myself with the strange room I found myself in. Years of listening and playing rhythms on my African drums had prepared me for these moments. Nothing had happened to me by accident, not even the carnage of drug addiction which had taken me to Cape Town to heed Mother Earth's call as she pounded Table Mountain's drum-skin. Stag stepped back through the fine brown dust which hung in the air, his retreat signifying respect for whoever or whatever was coming to take his place. My feet shuffled over the loose earth which covered the floor of a huge round arena. I turned three-sixty, tracking the wooden posts which lined the outer circle of the space, big enough to support a circus big-top, but instead of being painted clown red, they were blackened, not by paint, but charcoal. I'd seen such marks before on trees struck by lightning. It was more than the charred wood, though. The electricity still hung in the air, suspending the dust in its static aura. I was edgy, expecting the bogey-man to jump out from the dark recesses between the posts and shout 'booga booga booga!' at me. Then there was the animal smell, as if I'd landed in the middle of a dairy farm.

'Stag?' I called. He responded with a soft blast through his nostrils to help me locate him behind me.

A familiar voice spoke from beyond the posts. 'You are welcome to this place, Aaron. Don't be afraid. Lower your guard and he may come to meet you.'

'Madalane?' My heartbeat slowed, reassured as I watched her tall slender figure walk out of the darkness. She looked magnificent. Platted tassels of hair furled around her forehead, and anklets of cowrie shells tinkled as she stepped her bare feet, toe-heel, towards me. Her figure oscillated like the surface of a pristine millpond disturbed by large carp.

'Your presence has caused many ripples through the Underworld, Aaron,' she said, turning her head to listen to the sound of heavy hooves scratching through the dirt behind her. Two thick clouds of an animal's breath bellowed out of the shadows into the centre of the circle. The aroma couldn't be hidden by any amount of Madalane's heavenly lavender.

'Why are you here, Madalane?'

She looked up. 'Because I knew you would come here. I have learnt much about this king you mentioned and I am curious to know more. Arthur was no stranger to witches. Mother tells us that he was rescued by three of my sisters after being gravely injured and his soul was preserved by the one named Nimue, the Lady of the Lake.'

'Do you know, then, where I have been and who I have met at Arthur's Seat? There was a spirit, once a man, now more animal; he knew your lavender scent. Beorn.'

Madalane stared, her eyes, fixed and glazed as they looked beyond me into the past.

'Madalane, can you hear me?' I waited.

Her eyes overflowed, raining tears onto the parched ground. 'He said he would find me one day. That he would never rest until we were together again. I heard him shouting my name through the roar of the flames as they melted me away… Were there others with him, other men?'

'I heard others. Beorn said he had an army of men all related to your sisters. He took the lock of hair from my crane bag; he was disturbed by my quest's association with a king, as you were. There was no reasoning with him. He intends to find you himself.'

'He will not find us where you did. That place no longer exists since you opened the doorway. Mother has moved us.'

I sensed movement again, farther back, and all around me, then heard the faint brushing of material.

'Taranis,' Madalane said, holding out her hand. 'Do not move, Aaron.'

The points of his horns emerged first, firing sparks of

electricity which lit up the broad plate of bone between his horns. A white bull approached, driven by stocky legs thumping a ton of beast onto the floor of the arena. There was a honeycomb hollowness to the terrain which boomed as he walked between two posts and began his tour of the circle. His head faced into the centre while his massive body, rippling with muscle, flanked me, proudly exhibiting swinging testicles, each the size of a boxer's punch bag. His tail arched high in the air over his back and then smacked down on his legs. The whole display clearly said, 'do not mess with me'. The sound of short sniffs and snorts from his nose and a steady bass drum-beat encircled me. More rhythm, forming a layer over the faster and more distant drumming from my iPod which kept me submerged in their domain – a world I longed to be more a part of.

Taranis returned to Madalane's side, shaking his head violently as though he were trying to stave off a sneeze that would've sent us all to hell, charred and smoking. Stag walked into the centre of the circle mimicking Taranis' rhythm perfectly, making the fine rust-coloured gravel jump an inch above the ground. Stag stood by my side and drew a straight line in front of my feet with his antlers. I didn't like the way this was shaping up. The animal spirits had their common language, Madalane and I had ours, but her heritage and prolonged residence in the Underworld opened a direct channel to all spirits.

'The bull mediates for Taranis, the Druid god of thunder and lightning; for pagans, he indicates power, fertility and prosperity.' Madalane courteously waved her hand in his direction. I didn't have to ask why the posts were charred, having had such a close encounter with lightning myself. 'Do you know what pagan means, Aaron?'

'No,' I said, preparing to take evasive action in the event Taranis felt like sending either himself or a bolt of lightning my way.

'It means farmer. Most of the magic witches used was to make the land more fertile. Food and cattle were all we had to trade with, so the land we lived on became more than just our home. We worshipped it, and the lines of dragon energy running beneath its surface. It defined everything about us, even myself and Beorn living on the coastline, so close to water. I learnt ways of communicating with earth energies and weather, which made our land yield more than any other farms for miles around. Most witches, male and female alike, celebrate untamed nature and the wilderness – just as you seem to do, is that not true, Aaron?'

I paused before answering. Madalane's supernatural beauty slowed me down, but so did her insight. She was right. All I had wanted since rehab was to be alone with the land and the weather. During the last days of my four months of treatment, I sat next to Maclear's Beacon on top of Table Mountain and dreamt of starting a new life in the distant mountains where no one knew me. Was I so different from a witch? I had been burnt too, but had lived to tell the convoluted LSD tale and bare the marks. 'You're right, I crave a connection with nature which is so much more than a mundane walk in the park. For me, nature is full of doorways into the unseen, even if it's as simple as leaning against a tree to become acquainted with it.'

Madalane smiled. 'Of course, our success with farming the land brought jealousy and unwanted attention from King James' men. Witchcraft was the only way they could explain how our land still produced food in a drought when all others' remained parched or damaged after a storm. The fools! After all, witchcraft is what a witch *does*! To avoid droughts or floods, those of us who believed reached out to Taranis for help and in return he made our land fertile again. Food and livestock were what we traded in, they were our currency.' She turned and curtseyed to the bull-god next to her. Taranis stood straight, puffing his chest out like a sergeant major, then slumping and bowing his head to acknowledge Madalane's attention as his steaming slobber splatted on the floor. She stepped forwards, removing a necklace of cowrie shells. The smell of lavender made me teeter back and forth. 'Take these, you may need them soon. I have asked Mother what she intends for you and this Arthur you seek, but she was not forthcoming. She will only speak directly to you.'

'What do they do?' I opened my hand, caught the shiny white shells, and placed them in my empty crane bag.

'Cowrie shells are the symbol of the feminine, they signify everything my sisters and I stood for. They encourage fertility. Mother told me to give them to you. It is not for me to know – only for you to realise. This is your quest. I will say this, though – do not think of fertility only in human terms; remember the fertility of the land. Without it, no one would survive.'

I looked up, and then at each space between the posts,

expecting another snake-ridden tunnel to open. The air became uncomfortably charged with energy and a heavy weight pressed down on my shoulders as if gravity was increasing. I looked down, expecting the ground to swallow my feet. 'How do I leave this place?' I said, my eyes widened with anxiety brought on by the last beat of my iPod's drumming track and the realisation that my body and soul were still submerged beneath the castle's esplanade.

'There is something Mother has asked me to teach you before you go,' Madalane said. The tone of her voice hardened to that of a school teacher.

'Okay,' I said uncertainly. 'Whatever it is can't be any worse than the snakes.' Stag walked past, brushing the full length of his two-metre torso firmly against me as he took his place next to Taranis and Madalane. He turned and faced me with the bull-god and the queen of the Scottish witches. I felt slightly outnumbered. But Stag's brown pools of wisdom calmed me.

'This place, Aaron, is used for a ritual.' She held her hands aloft and walked to one of the charred posts. 'All great acts of magic are defined by either ceremony or ritual. It's where we place belief and purpose for the healing intention. Of course, not all witches used their magic for good, which is why King James ordered the Berwick Witch Trials after his boat was sunk by supernatural storms. But the magic you are seeking, some of which you have already found, is for the good of others. I know that now. I don't know the exact reason you need Arthur to return, and neither do you, but it relates to healing, doesn't it?'

'Yes, I believe so. There is a man, George, he was once a saint of this land and its people. He committed the worst crime against Mother by killing her last dragon-child. I met him in Ardnamurchan and he sent me to Edinburgh to explore its ancient volcanic lands and learn how to bring Arthur back; only then would George be healed and released from his prison.'

'Do you think there is more than just this man, George, to be healed?' Madalane pressed her palm against the charred wood and felt the fine black powder between her thumb and finger, raising it to her nose to smell its mustiness, clearly remembering how she once burnt. 'Think, Aaron, what heals all things? There is one emotion which unites us all.' She looked at me and blew the cloud of charcoal from her hand. It swirled with twisting black twines of Celtic knots and figure-of-eights towards me; black magic approached.

'Corvus,' I whispered, turning the dust into a miniature murder of crows. The small birds flew around me; their presence ignited my skin like the first burst of a hot shower. Then the lightbulb turned on, and inspiration found me. 'Love, we need to find love again.'

'Who does?' she said.

'Your sisterhood, you and Beorn, his so-called army… and me. I need love and so does Mother, she needs it now more than ever.' Maybe it was the isolation beneath the earth which gave me the quiet space to think about all that had happened over the past few months, or perhaps Madalane had used a spell on me? I didn't care which.

'You learn very quickly, Aaron. Don't forget yourself.

You will grow mad with loneliness if you stay down here too long.' She walked to the centre of the circle and faced me, drawing a straight line between us with her big toe. 'Aside from all the spells, potions, herbs and other very strange goings-on you would expect a witch to be involved in to effect change, the most powerful healing force is love. We found that by blessing everything with love; be it water, land, sky or seeds, our yield would always increase. No magic compares to the power of love.' She placed her hand inches from my heart and closed her eyes for a moment. 'Hmm, it is true,' she whispered, turning away to join her four-legged companions. 'Aaron, Mother chose you because you were an empty vessel. Your body was worn out, your spirit broken, your heart learning, no, yearning to love again, and you found the energy most fundamental to personal growth: the energy of self-love. How can you love anything or anyone else if you don't know how to love yourself?'

'Such love is false, even if the person doesn't realise it. That love will never last,' I said.

'Indeed.' Madalane said, standing between Taranis and Stag, placing her hands on them. I prepared myself for sentencing by Taranis before he blasted me to oblivion with a bolt from his horns; although I had no idea what I had done. My head still had a strong tendency to think of the worse-case scenario in any situation.

'Stag, is this goodbye? What's happening?'

'Can't you see, Aaron? You're not standing before *us* – no, we stand before *you*.'

Boom! Stag and Taranis stamped their front feet, firing

an echo which hit all of the cave's hidden walls and ceiling. Madalane curtseyed again, but this time she directed the greeting at me. The sound of rustling linen rose briefly from beyond the posts. 'All animals represent something, Aaron. Your Crow signifies the same to us as it does you - initiation, and the deepest form of healing; the death of one way of life, giving way to the birth of another. Your personal prophecy is ours too. Mother has shown that we were moved here to meet you again, and that you would return with a messenger from the Otherworld, a Stag, to take us to heaven, and in doing so, we release Arthur from his resting place to…'

'To restore the land to its former glory?' I interrupted, but I already knew the answer. I'd been running away from the toxic reality above my head instead of using my spiritual awakening to find a way to help others. I replayed my counsellor's words, ingrained on my psyche. 'It isn't all about you, Aaron.' It used to be, though; my last quest had been all about self-destruction and now the table had turned.

'Yes, do you know what that means, Aaron?'

'No idea, it's just what I've read about Arthur. I am not a scholar, king, politician or farmer, nor do I want to be. I'm Aaron, a recovering drug addict with a Crow and Stag chaperoning me as I journey through the Otherworld.' I heard how ridiculous I sounded to most of the population above me. 'What does Arthur do if, or when, I manage to find him and bring him back?'

'That is your prophecy, Aaron, not ours. You will have to succeed to find out. Your fate is tied with his.'

'And if I fail?'

'Then we will stay here happily in Mother's womb, but tell me, does it look like you are failing?' Madalane looked at Taranis and Stag. 'See how far you have already come. Mother has put her faith in you for a reason. It could take lifetimes for someone like you to arrive again. Someone who has been emptied of all life as you were; someone who has your vision, gifts and abilities, and is ready for such a quest.'

'Why don't your sisters come out? It's them I can hear, isn't it?' I said.

'Not all of us trust you,' voices shouted from the shadows.

'We may be a collective, but our will is not always united,' Madalane said.

I crouched down and grabbed a handful of the strange rust-coloured gravel, realising that I'd seen it years before, touring the active volcanic areas of Lanzarote.

'Nothing grows here, Aaron, this is the most negative vortex of energy you will find in Scotland. Taranis has tried to change the charge of the energy to positive, but no amount of lightning can reverse it. The earth here is infertile, drenched in death, forever dead to the world.'

I pressed my palm flat against the ground and listened, to nothing. 'Where is Arthur?'

Madalane placed both hands on her abdomen and closed her eyes. 'Like the journey of the oldest animal, the salmon, Arthur returned to the place of his birth. You will need to find that place yourself.'

'Then what?' I snapped in agitation.

'Ritual, you bring him back through ritual and grand

ceremony. That is the only way to effect a change in reality. You, for example, have been in the midst of one for more than this lifetime; your Native American ancestors knew about the power of ritual. They understood the significance of conviction and of being totally absorbed in concentration while speaking straight from the heart. You are no stranger to magic, Aaron, it follows wherever you go. Mark my words, you will be master of the ceremony which tries to call him back, but you cannot do it alone, you need to learn to embody Stag's energy. You and he must be one when you call the king.'

I had felt the moment coming in my bones ever since Crow introduced me to the concept of embodying Stag. Calling for Crow's trickster presence could've been disastrous. Even if I'd learnt to control his movements at Glen Coe, his cavalier tongue risked unsettling my hosts and ruining the atmosphere of a place which felt like a cross between a gladiator's auditorium and volcanic tomb. This was a massive hike upwards in my learning curve. Until now, Stag had been there for me in transit. Our chaperone style of relationship was simplistic yet powerful, with his energy creating a force-field around me whenever I journeyed by land or spirit world.

He made the first move to the line, bowed his head down to the rust-coloured soil and dug the highest tine of his antler into it, marking the place where he wanted me to stand. We shared no words, no telepathy, just a powerful sense of connection, tied together not by our souls, but by another precious part of anatomy – our hearts. He stood statue-still and looked at me. I moved closer, inhaling the sage-scented clouds of his misted breath, and placed the palms of my hands on the spikes of the lowest tines. I pressed harder into the antlers, remembering the pain again. Stag's eyes remained fixed on me like caves holding answers to all the questions I was yet to ask, and as I gazed, hypnotised, his eyes returned the reflection of my supernatural doppelganger staring at me across the fire, fully transmuted.

'Stag, how do I stop the embodiment?' I lowered a hand to feel his heart, resting the other on mine. We closed our eyes, our heartbeats, mistimed, then synchronising until they beat as one. Spirit and human entwined as one, our skins coated in dew from the moisture in the air evoked by Madalane as she swayed from side to side. I found my answer in his beating heart.

Taranis brought down the storm energy from its heavenly abodes, charging the crackling atmosphere with his beast cathode and then, from the shadows, the low eerie hum started.

'Mmmm… mmmm… mmmm.' The reluctant witches remained hidden, yet contributed to the alchemy with their song. Layer upon layer of harmonies covered us.

Our heartbeats made a deafening blast just like cannons firing Cape Town's Noon Day Gun. Our feet dug into the earth. I gripped Stag's antlers, white-knuckled. I knew exactly what to do, I'd been born for it: pressing the crown of my head against his skull and rubbing it hard into the bristles, our breath, hearts, life force, as one, rocking back and forth to get a feel for each other's weight. Stag could have steamrolled me through the walls, but neither of us competed, and his power flowed through me. We pulled our heads apart and paused; I stared into his dark crystal-ball eyes and we both grunted as our heads smashed together. *Crack!* The sound of two giant pool balls smashing together startled a colony of bats roosting in the eves.

'One,' I said, shaking a graphic image of Stag's bloody beating heart from my mind.

'Mmmm… mmmm,' the witches hummed, in perfect time to our rocking. I gritted my teeth and threw myself into Stag again. *Crack!*

'Two.' I drew blood from my hands as they twisted around his antlers. The witches stopped humming, Stag and I held our breaths, freezing time. His power hit me like a bullet. *Crack!* I prepared to lose my body and adopt Stag's, but sudden vertigo made me grapple thin air, and my arms flailed, with my hands eventually grasping the familiar rough bone of Stag's antlers. My legs straddled his bare back. I was confused, mistakenly prepared for an embodiment that would move my body and spirit into his, but here I was sitting six feet off the ground with nothing except his antlers for reins. I felt different, though. Steady and safe on his back, releasing my grip, I sensed a magnetic bond cementing us together. I couldn't fall. Then the sound of his heartbeat and mine drumming the same exhilarating rhythm filled my head, pounding away inside the Otherworld. I was restless and bursting for fresh air! I grabbed the lower stalks of antler in front of me. 'Grow!' I said. Poison ivy vines sprouted and wrapped themselves around my wrists. I'd consumed every plant-based toxin known to man. Now the ivy's poison gave me strength and security. Mother's poisonous protective instinct was keeping me safe. The restlessness and energy surged and I understood what a bull felt like in a china shop. Stag thrashed his head and stamped his feet. Taranis and Madalane moved apart and we burst through the circle's outer darkness into an abyss of blinding light.

TEN

'My name's Dawn, I'm an alcoholic,' she said, opening the first AA meeting I'd been to for months. I'd never gone longer than a few days without sitting in one of the rooms. Having distanced myself from one fellowship in exchange for a more supernatural alternative, it wasn't until I left Scotland that I realised how complacent I'd become about meetings and my recovery. There wasn't anyone I knew in England who I could talk to about what was happening. Troy was thousands of miles away in Cape Town, and I needed someone closer at hand to be able to process the task I'd been given. Every spirit's face, voice, body and mannerisms were as fresh as a daisy. Every scent and atmosphere of the landscapes I'd visited remained with me. I sat in South London's Kings Road Community Centre half-heartedly listening to Dawn's share, my mind a melting pot; I drifted in and out of my meditation mantra, trying to piece together the initiations and encounters. Everything had felt and looked different since I'd returned to my parents' house to ground myself in Mum's home cooking and to reassure them I was doing okay, regardless of the crazy shamanic shit-storm I had just weathered.

I was changing, and I didn't know how I presented to the rest of the human race. The alien-like feeling was uncannily similar to my homecoming after four months of traumatic, yet healing and life-changing rehab. It was a feeling which could only be caused by an overdue detox, a year backpacking around the world for the first time, or making descents and ascents to the spirit worlds for quantum leaps in personal transformation. Not forgetting the weight of Arthur's return resting squarely on my shoulders. Most people would've gone insane with the pressure and outlandishness of the situation, but I'd already dealt with drug-induced insanity and when I thought about it, when I *really* thought about it, I'd been waiting for this quest all my life. I was the perfect candidate – a space-cadet in recovery looking for the meaning of life; a way to spread his spiritual wings for the first time, to soar and make a difference.

It was good to see my family again, to take stock and sleep in a familiar bed, but I couldn't get away from the niggling pecks of Crow's beak inside my head, telling me to stop stalling and get myself to Arthur's birthplace – Tintagel.

As soon as Madalane had told me about the salmon, I'd replayed snippets of memories from a childhood family holiday to North Cornwall. I didn't even have to ask myself where his birthplace was. My mind just fed me the information as though it had been stored, just waiting for the moment I needed to remember it. My memories showed me steep steps, walking on huge flagstones and looking out to sea. Internet trawling had shown me much more, and it was Merlin's cave, nestling in the rocks next to the tidal beach below Tintagel Island, which loomed largest. I had stared at endless photos and read various accounts of people being trapped in the cave by freak waves and having to spend the night clinging to the inner shelves of quartz-veined rock until the cave emptied. The castle had a long history dating back to the Dark Ages, before Earl Richard took residence there in the thirteenth century. Tintagel Island had once been connected to the mainland, but a massive landslip sometime in the thirteen or fourteen hundreds had isolated it from the mainland. Cornish royalty kept a small group of staff in place, including a priest, but the castle soon fell into disrepair at the mercy of the elements. It was the gap between the end of the Dark Age settlement in the seventh century and the arrival of Earl Richard of Cornwall which intrigued me. Ancient legend existed for a reason. It came from somewhere, and was going nowhere for now. Something told me a pause would do me good, regardless of what Crow thought. My initiations tied us even closer together. The night-times were vacant spaces where my mind and body settled, allowing the venom to work its magic. A new recurring dream began as soon as I got home. It was the simplest but most powerful vision. I danced to drumming in the middle of a fire, raging in total blackness. Its roar and light faded into the distance as I zoomed out to see the scene held within one of Crow's eyes. The black magic was getting blacker.

The AA meeting's creaking plastic chairs and bright

fluorescent lighting did nothing to enhance the mood of a room I felt uncomfortable in. As always, I sat as close to an open window as possible to satisfy my now obsessive need for fresh air. If the windows were shut, you could be sure I was going to open them, and to hell with anyone who felt the cold; I needed my fresh air, even if it did let in the traffic rumble and the occasional jerk on their way to a bar shouting, 'Give me some whisky!' through the window. The wall heater next to me rattled away as I stared through the window at Crow's silhouette, reflecting on the glass from – where, though? I cocked my head sideways an inch and watched his reflection mirror my movement. Just his jet-black shape, and the intermittent glint of the flames in his eyes. We both knew very well I'd rather be somewhere else than listen to someone talk about how shit everything had been. I hadn't craved alcohol since leaving for rehab, but I did what I knew was best for me, through gritted teeth, to spend an hour soaking in the healing energy which accompanied every meeting.

Crack! Crow tapped his beak on the window, leaving his trademark Zorro lightning strike, and flew away with his 'caws' fading into the night. I let him go. We hadn't spoken since my journey to meet Cernunnos, but I felt his presence more than ever, deep within me. The sound of the window cracking distracted Dawn. She looked at me, as though she knew what had hit the window. I waited for her to continue, expecting to hear a familiar list of personal damages.

'I won't bore you with the specifics of what happened. Let's just say it was bad enough for me to go to rehab and a few secure units before I got it. I thought I came to Alcoholics Anonymous just to get sober, but nothing prepared me for the spiritual awakening which happened as a result of the Twelve Steps.' My ears pricked up. She was talking my language. I stopped slouching and moved to the edge of my seat, leaning forward in trepidation, suddenly eager to learn more about what this woman with punky rainbow-dyed hair had to say. 'Nothing made me as powerless as alcohol and coming from someone who cured themselves of multiple sclerosis; that's saying something. I found something in these rooms that I haven't found anywhere else. A fellowship which taught me that I don't have to do it alone, and a programme which came from a man, Bill Wilson, who knew that we're all spiritual beings, living in a material world. You know...' She paused, leaned forward and rested her elbows on the table, looking at me with the feathers hanging from her dream-catcher earrings ticking back and forth. 'I spent enough time cooped up in my attic drinking, away from the world. Now I spend my time in nature – with people, helping the land through prayer, pilgrimage and ceremony.'

Her words were music to my ears, except the 'people' bit. Speed dating was the only fleeting contact with people I was comfortable with. Making pleasant conversation with other recovering alcoholics after meetings just wasn't a skill I had mastered, nor did I want to. I'd only chosen this meeting because it was near another tapas bar running an event later. The secretary opened up the meeting for general sharing, which always entailed the same anxiety for me. Whenever I did manage to share, the feeling of liberation was followed by a surge of spiritual energy through my every being.

'I'm Aaron, I'm an alcoholic.' Bam! The words which were usually stunted shot out of my mouth, helping me to avoid the torrent of self-criticism for not having the guts to say anything. 'Thanks for your share, Dawn. I loved what you said about connecting with nature. It's something I've been doing a lot of recently. In fact, sometimes I feel like the sole reason I became an addict and went to rehab was to get on the path I'm now on.' There it was, short, but sweet and honest. Ever since I laid eyes on Table Mountain, I'd always seen my recovery as something much deeper, bigger and more meaningful than my life before addiction, if there ever was one. The shackles had come off for a reason. I closed my eyes as the energy flooded my body. When I opened them, Dawn was looking at and around me while she said the closing Serenity Prayer. I thought there'd be a queue of people waiting to speak to her afterwards, but she immediately made a beeline for me. The combination of her large bright orange shawl, permanently wide smile and sparkling eyes made her look saintly. I couldn't help but beam back at her.

'Lots going on around you, Aaron,' she said, greeting me with a gentle shake of my hand.

'Yes, you could say that.' I exchanged a psychic smile with her.

'Have you been away? You've got colour,' she said.

'It's mostly windburn from gallivanting around Scotland.'

'Oh… ha!' She laughed. 'I didn't mean that kind of

colour. I see people's life colours, and it's incredibly vivid around you. You are a purple life colour with an aurora sheen energy moving through the purple. Very beautiful. The first purple life colours were born around the time of King Arthur, and the last were born at the end of the seventies, so those still alive today are the oldest and only purples there will ever be. What's really interesting is that purples are on their own quest. Where were you in Scotland – anywhere near Orkney?'

I'd glazed over, synchronicity-stunned, missing most of what she had said after you-know-who. 'Erm… no, mostly the far west coast, and Edinburgh… something happened to me while I was in rehab in Cape Town about a year ago. Long story short, I realised I had to go to this extinct volcano in Ardnamurchan. I met someone who taught me about shamanism and how to journey, but it went beyond that, way beyond.' I looked left and right, spy-like. 'I've been connecting with the land and learning, first-hand, you could say, about how the dragon Saint George killed triggered the witch hunts of the fifteen and sixteen hundreds.' I saw Dawn's smile suddenly harden. 'Umm, I'm on some kind of quest which involves restoring the divine feminine earth energies.' I kept Arthur's name locked deep inside me.

'Of course!' she whispered. 'Don't forget the masculine, Aaron. There needs to be balance. The women haven't been the only ones persecuted by life. Listen, this is part of a separate conversation we will have another time. I am taking a group of men on a walk along The Ridgeway, from the Uffington White Horse to Avebury in a couple of weeks' time, starting on the eve of the Summer Solstice. You're very welcome to come. I think it makes perfect sense, but have a think about it. There's something interesting about what you said, though. Dragon Hill is one of the places we're visiting, fabled for being the place Saint George killed the dragon.'

'Wow!' I didn't know what else to say. Any dregs of doubt I had in coincidences disappeared in that moment. I'd been guided to this moment in time, again. 'The answer's yes.'

'Splendid, splendid. Here's my card. Send me your email. I'll be in touch with the details.'

She left before I could say thank you. I looked through the cracked window. 'He's coming, Crow, isn't he? Arthur, he's really coming.' Fate was getting closer by the day; with every new introduction and whichever way I turned, something or someone was there to guide me.

#

The last time I had celebrated the Summer Solstice was a year earlier, just a few months after rehab. Then, my nervous system could barely cope with a cup of coffee, but my trusted flask of caffeine was the only way I managed to drive a carload of Spanish friends to Stonehenge for a sunrise shrouded by cloud. They were some of the few remaining friends in my life who didn't take drugs and so hadn't tailed off like the rest of them. That clean and sober all-nighter took its toll on me for days, bringing back memories of cocaine and tequila-infused benders and the awful, jaded feeling of dread which goes with such sleep deprivation and the first birdsong of dawn. I had never gotten over the rave-like atmosphere with a presence of police sniffer dogs and people on ecstasy drumming themselves into a frenzy inside such a sacred stone circle, but I still managed to find a small patch of stone to lean against and drum until my hands went numb. That hour or so of my life made the journey worthwhile, and here I was one year later in the miniscule hamlet of Uffington in Oxfordshire, about to celebrate the longest day again. But this time, I understood more about the times of year when the veils between the worlds were thinnest and when some of the other ninety-six percent of the Universe showed itself to those aware enough to connect, learn and grow.

I walked out of my accommodation at the White Horse Inn, groggy-eyed, adrenaline waking me. Dawn had welcomed me to the group via email shortly after we'd met, and from the responses of the five other men coming on the walk, we were all of similar spiritual persuasion. Their emails were brief but full of flower-power. 'Peace, love and light friend', 'many blessings brother', and 'looking forward to enlivening the spirit of The Ridgeway with you': that was the general flavour. Fundamentally, that's what we had all gathered to do – enliven the spirit of the oldest road in Britain. Used since prehistoric times by travellers, herdsmen and soldiers, The Ridgeway followed ninety miles of track through areas of outstanding natural beauty marked by several ancient sites. One route ran from Avebury's stone circle in Wiltshire to Ivinghoe Beacon in Buckinghamshire.

We were joining the path at The Vale of the White Horse in Uffington, to where we were about to walk, and observe the solstice sunrise in ceremony. Although we met and walked as a group, Dawn had made it clear this was a personal pilgrimage with several purposes.

The intention was to use our primarily male group energy and yang life-force to pray for healing of the motherly, yin Earth energy and consecrate the route by entering a spiritual state of mind to consciously connect with where we were.

After my wild experiences of the Earth energies in the north, I relished the opportunity to walk simply and silently through fertile farmland and rolling hills with less sudden and dramatic personal transformation. Our silence was for personal reflection, to retreat into ourselves in a walking meditation at a time of year when a rare astrological event made the potential for change even greater, and which had the signature of a Universe which was saying 'Get on that walk!'

My journeys created a deepening relationship with Mother Earth and, by comparison, my meeting with Merlin through the moon's interdimensional portal had developed a new curiosity in me for what was happening beyond the skies above. My research confirmed that I was in alignment with more than just being at the right AA meeting at the right time. The moon which rose on the night of our walk was the second consecutive full moon in the Gemini constellation, my star sign, and the fourth full moon in one season – a blue moon, my favourite colour. The difference between this full moon and the others was that it formed at the twenty-ninth degree, the last degree before it moved into the next sign of the zodiac. The twenty-ninth degree defines the spiritual principle of movement and the eternal dance of light happening inside everyone, and right now there was a rave like no other kicking off inside me, opening the realm of infinite possibilities and offering me the chance to realise my highest potential. This solstice was cosmically designed to challenge any limiting beliefs I had both of the world and of myself, but with the light of unity, the darkness of duality was also to be revealed, illuminating where healing and transformation was still needed. I found the idea that my healing path would be a lifelong event quite agreeable. The full moon offered me a special opportunity to take a big step forward, highlighting spiritual goals as well as the shadow side of my sign, and the solstice full moon peaked only twelve hours before the Cancer Solstice, a rare occurrence greatly magnifying its transformative potential. There hadn't been a full moon on the same day as the Cancer Solstice for sixty-seven years.

Hundreds of my ancestors' arrows pointed to this time and place: a powerful energetic gateway lasting three days, causing a reduction in Earth's magnetic field, allowing a greater influx of cosmic radiation to penetrate our atmosphere, with the potential to affect my psyche, body and DNA. This was an extra potent time to participate in ceremony, ritual and prayer with huge potential for inner and outward growth.

We left our bedrooms in the old converted stables next

to the Inn and gathered in the country lane at three a.m., greeting each other groggy-eyed and with quietly spoken good-mornings. I sat on a large boulder which flanked the steps to the entrance of the Inn, observing how we were all preparing ourselves before walking to the Vale. I listened to the complete stillness of the night while we waited for Dawn to lead us. I smiled at the irony and she stepped out of her room with her arms folded across her midriff, dressed in standard hiking waterproofs, with feathers in her hair and small strands of plants she'd picked from the hedgerow threaded through her rings. Then there was the quartz-crystal cluster the size of a dinner plate she cradled in her arms wherever we walked as a group. Some of the group swirled their arms high above their heads and low to the ground in a movement I'd only seen once before in a video of a Siberian shaman bringing in the energies of Heaven and Earth. Others yawned and stretched while they stood with their hands occasionally resting affectionately on a near-by oak tree. I patted the boulder I sat on, feeling very at home with where I was and who I was with. There was a relaxed atmosphere between us and a common understanding that each of us wanted to be part of this special solstice event, at both a group and a personal level. We respected each other's space as modern-day pilgrims. The night before we met, Dawn had asked us all to connect wherever we were, in whatever way felt right to us, at nine p.m. My drumming-journey took me to fertile fields of lush waist-high grass blowing in the wind. The image of lighting striking the earth all around me as I walked through the green sea lingered as

I felt Taranis' presence high above me; Stag's energy surrounding me, and Crow's within me.

After a short, steep walk to the site of the old hill fort plateau directly above the White Horse, we gathered in prayer around Dawn's crystal and pondered what the walk meant for us individually. Thanks to Step Eleven of the Twelve Steps, I'd become quite adept at prayer and meditation and treasured any opportunities like this to connect with myself and the energy of the moment. I'd also learnt to ask for help. Recovery hadn't come to me any other way. Be it through acceptance of the counsellors' support or spirit's unseen guidance, it didn't matter to me, and as we held hands around the altar we'd made with crystals, wooden totems, herbs and my stones from the Singings Sands beach, I prayed with all my heart to be given the strength, courage and wisdom to succeed in returning Arthur.

I looked down at Dragon Hill, unable or unwilling to imagine the carnage, as I embraced the quest George was responsible for. He was nowhere in sight to ask and somehow it never seemed as if he would arrive. His soul was tormented enough; no need to return to the murder scene, and there was no room on the flattened top of the small ten-metre-high mound. A pagan priest dressed in white gowns blasted a curled ox horn in front of twenty people. His hailing voice carried to us on the wind intermittently as my eyes scanned the horizon for the ever-increasing glow of the solstice sun as it rose and changed from pink to orange and then yellow.

'Look at the moon,' one of our group said, pointing behind him at the huge silver disc behind us – and there it was, the full moon falling to one horizon and the sun rising above the other: a moment I'd only dreamed of experiencing since studying Yeats at college. Of the few pieces of literature I retained from my weed-infused days studying English, 'A Vision' had had a lasting effect on me. I was fascinated by Yeats' love of the esoteric and his discerning appetite for translating his wife's automatic writing, especially on the phases of the moon. He compared the growth and life curve of an individual to the cycle of the moon which starts dark, the primary situation, where I lived without definition, trying to find some sense of identity and belonging, in a world which confused me and made me nervous. I'd followed the wrong crowd. Unable to carve out my own unique path, I descended into the darkest phase of my life.

Then there was the first glint of light, shining on the seed within me containing an ancient, pre-science clairvoyant consciousness with limitless potentiality. At the eighth night of moon, the first quarter, the light of the moon began to dominate, like the awakening of my own potential as it rose from the Earth's base chakra – Table Mountain. Up until now, my life had been akin to the lunar world of darkness and light, constantly struggling to find out who I was and where I was supposed to be going. Yes, there were those stark moments of clarity, when I knew I was killing myself, but the strength to commit and return from the edge was nowhere to be seen. Now, though, as I sat between two planets, fate presented me with the opportunity to leap into the solar world of everlasting light.

I turned my face to the rising sun and let the moon go

down. The darkness no longer defined me. It was now just a place which showed me how brightly I should be shining. A skylark ascended vertically out of the grass next to us, its ecstatic song piercing my soul, lifting me, and I surrendered to the rising sun as its rays etched new beginnings on me.

ELEVEN

Wayland's Smithy was our next destination on Midsummer's Day. The five-thousand-year-old Neolithic long-barrow tomb lay a mile from The White Horse, and was reached by walking our first stretch of The Ridgeway. Dawn gathered us in a circle to open the ceremonial walk before we visited the tomb and then Dragon Hill at the end of the day. We would spend another night at the White Horse Inn before starting our walk to the hamlet of Ogbourne St George to visit the church named after my forsaken friend and where the Michael ley line passed through.

'The Ridgeway is still here today because people like us have kept it alive by walking its path,' Dawn said as we held hands, heads bowed. 'This is a sacred route, walked by contemplative pilgrims, warmongering soldiers, praying monks and trading farmers, but it hasn't been kept alive just by their footsteps – The Ridgeway is here because of the collective memory of everyone who has walked it. There is a resonance here. Just as ants follow an unmarked route to and from their home, or migratory birds fly thousands of miles to warmer climates, or whales return to their feeding grounds on the other side of the world, or the salmon remembers its birthplace: this path has its own consciousness, and its own light. We are walking in the energetic slipstream of all those who have come here before us.'

I knew I'd heard something important because a crow cawed twice. The whole world slowed down for me to listen to Dawn and in the stillness that followed, as I closed my eyes, I saw Stag's feet running hard on the Earth, with his breath powering through every stride like a storm's wind. I had no idea what I'd find at Tintagel, or whether Arthur's body was encased in another impenetrable tomb waiting for me to perform an act of necromancy to return him. What was certain, though, was the constant stream of supporting signs I received from the people I met, the places I visited and the situations the Universe put me in. All I had to be was willing and trusting.

We walked west in silence from the crossroads where we'd stood together, eventually ducking into the forest to the left only to be awe-inspired by a green tunnel of beech trees lining a clear path running parallel with The Ridgeway. The canopy blocked direct sunlight, leaving us surrounded by green on all sides. Light emerald green above us, descending to dark green on the trees coated in ivy and to the foliage growing on the forest floor where bushes and branches danced together. The trees lining the path were as tall and straight as telegraph poles, creating a processional feel for the group as we prepared to take this ceremonial way to Wayland's Smithy.

'Sit or lie down; prepare yourselves in any way that feels right for you before we enter this sacred space,' Dawn said, lighting several sticks of incense around us.

I rested my head on the forest floor and folded my arms across my chest before calling Stag to be with me. Our union was effortless. Sometimes the faint outline of his antlers loomed into view, and at others, his eyes looked over me. Then occasionally there was no visible evidence of him: just the sense of his strong primal presence. Closing my eyes, I remembered Logan had told me that drumming wasn't always necessary to journey and that, with practice and perseverance, it would be possible to simply close my eyes, and go. So I used the sound of the wind in the trees to journey and take me to meet the spirits of the forest.

'I am journeying to meet the spirits of this place, to ask for your blessing and a teaching,' I whispered.

The first snake appeared on the ground beside me. Its size surprised me. I hadn't seen any of them clearly when I was in the Underworld tunnel after meeting Madalane and the other witches for the first time, just the fleeting departure of their tails, but these snakes were clearly adults, some several feet long and all gloss-black. I stood between two trees at the entrance to the path. The patterns of burrs, cracks and lines in the bark formed faces which stared at the snakes grouping around me. I soon lost count of their numbers. There was no fear, no fanged lunges at my skin, just the sound of their skins slithering over the foliage and through the trees towards me. They moved onto my arms and legs, excited by the sense of my warm blood, but there wasn't one bite from the fifty or so snakes which engulfed me. Within seconds I was swarmed by them. Only my head remained free to breathe and see the event. The writhing reptilian knot lifted me several feet off the ground and led me down the path with a high-pitched hiss which excited every living thing in the forest. It was deafening, like the sound of a jungle gone mad. There was nothing else to the journey, just a mass of giant black snakes writhing around me at high speed, before the tickle of insects exploring the route from my ankles up my trouser legs brought me back to the present, where all that remained was the forest and a slight breeze. There wasn't any hint of bird feathers about to explode through my skin, only the usual pressure on my third-eye and crown chakra which followed soul-flight. The snakes had come to continue the process of transformation. I had no idea what happened while they'd been swarming me, so I looked for an opportune moment to ask Dawn as we moved onto the Smithy.

'Ha! Very interesting you ask, Aaron, because the snakes were all around you when the sun was rising this morning. There's so much snake, water-serpent and dragon energy around you. I could see it at the AA meeting in London before you told me about your quest. The transformation happening to you is prolific. There will either be a sudden leap, or a gradual transition; to what, I cannot say, but the one thing I am hearing is that you have no reason to be afraid of the past anymore. It can't touch you. You will not be going back,' she said, sliding a leaf into one of her rings.

We walked half a mile of the tree-lined path in silence. I

was so grateful to receive such an affirmation. Logan was the only other person I wanted to ask for a progress report, but I was grateful he hadn't shown up on the walk as I didn't feel like killing anyone today, and the only person I'd ever wanted to kill was myself. As my legs moved and the soles of my feet touched the earth again, I saw myself, sitting across from the same fire, looking through the flames. My skin had browned from the sun; tribal amulets and animal claws hung around my neck and wrists. I recognised the physical presence of myself, but the look in my eyes had changed. I saw someone who had travelled far; someone who knew the flames burning in front of him as well as his own breath, but more than anything – I knew he was waiting for someone – me.

Dawn led the group through the hedgerow back to the wider track again, where a small information plaque about Wayland's Smithy told of the fourteen bodies found buried in the second of two large tombs which had been built on top of the first one, in four hundred BC. My brief pre-walk research told of how the site was named after the Saxon God of Metal Working. Legend told of horsemen who would leave their steed tied to a post with some silver, and return later to find the horse freshly shod. What was more coincidental, though, was the limited available literature naming the site as the place Merlin had visited to ask Wayland to forge Excalibur. I couldn't be so bold as to expect my visit to be as productive, but one thought was going around in my head repeatedly – Arthur would need his sword back when he returned, wouldn't he?

Nothing had prepared me for the atmosphere of the twenty-metre-long tomb. It was the perfect picture-frame scene. Old beech trees bursting with summer leaves lined the site's outer rectangle. Grass had been left to grow tall around the freshly mowed roof of the tomb. Whoever tended to the area did so with utmost care and respect for the Neolithic chamber which rose from the Earth at one end, sloping upwards to the two-metre-high entrance where we stood. Four tall flat stones were parted in the centre to mark the blocked entrance to the chamber. It was only possible to enter a small hole in the stone, where Dawn rested her crystal cluster while we explored. The surface of the giant grave called to me. It bore an uncanny resemblance to the surface of the underground basilica in Lourdes where I'd wished my life away consumed by absinthe. This grass was celestially perfect; not a blemishing weed in sight. Here I was on another pilgrimage, but sober, and meeting spirits who were perhaps not as holy as Jesus Christ, but still possessed miraculous healing powers.

I watched Dawn's husband climb the stone corner-steps onto the grass. He took a few strides, paused and fell to the ground in slow motion, as if something was catching him. Without the threat of Lourdes' truncheon-poking French policemen, I followed his lead, facing my palms downward, scanning the surface to detect any hint of a buzz or prickle of energy. I made my way past Dawn's sleeping husband and felt the energy as soon as I crossed the halfway mark. I lay down and rested on the soft grass. I made no effort to move, I was exhausted and welcomed the opportunity to rest without drumming, or any need to embark on a soul-flight. I drifted in the space between waking and sleep as sunlight flickered through random openings in the trees onto my face. The land claimed me and it felt so good. No sinking, no flying or strange tunnels to negotiate and no giant Saxon god bashing red-hot metal. I surrendered to nature and dreamed of an arrow.

At first I saw glimmers of its mirror-like colour as shapeless globules of mercury sliding over a black metal surface, finding each other, growing as two globules became one and the perfect rod formed. It rotated constantly, as if I were being asked for my approval on the quality of the workmanship. Then it stopped moving and stood vertically, hitting the black metal twice, sending a loud *ting!* into the dream-space between my ears. I approved of its solidity. Then the fletching grew from one end of the shaft and the arrowhead from the other before the arrow rotated again, showing me every angle. I gave my approval again and the arrow stopped on its tip, for a silver blade to descend to add the finishing touch, sliding back and forth, cutting the nock for the bow's string.

When I finally popped my head up from the grass, an hour had passed. Dawn's husband was walking down the steps to join the rest of the group at the entrance. I joined them, squinting my eyes to adjust to the sunlight whilst the faultless craftsmanship of the arrow impressed itself on me – beautiful, yet so deadly.

We walked on in silence, some of us walking in pairs, others choosing to walk in solitude, like me: not because I wanted to be alone, though. My crane bag was much heavier since leaving the Smithy, but there was nothing new to be felt inside and the drawstring was stuck for no apparent reason. I lagged behind the group as I fumbled with the small leather bag, unable to loosen it even enough to lift it over my head and take a good look at it. Eventually, after several frustrated tugs, trying to catch it unawares with the occasional yank out of the blue, I admitted defeat.

We were to spend a second night at the White Horse Inn before walking to Ogbourne Saint George. Our route from Wayland's Smithy back to our digs gave us a second chance to visit Dragon Hill.

'Remember; if you are drawn down and find yourself in another place – it's because someone else is calling you,' Dawn said, as we lay on the chalky plateau of Dragon Hill with our feet encircling an improvised design of the sun made by the pagan gathering who used the hill at sunrise. Its intricacy was astounding. Lines of grain and seed marked the outline of a sun. A spiral of white shells wrapped itself around the design which had flowers scattered as offerings all around and within it. Dawn reached into the small velvet sack where she kept her runes and handed each of us the rune we picked on our way to the Smithy. Mine was Uruz, a Norse word meaning Aurochs, a now extinct European wild ox, symbolising primal power and strength: a simple design, not unlike a crooked letter 'n'. 'Close your eyes and draw the rune on the surface of this hill. The rune will open the door to a portal.' She started a steady rhythm with her small rattle to send us into a trance.

I drew the rune in golden light on the dark easel behind my eyes and sank. I was met by brightness as I descended rapidly down a shining crystal water-slide which twisted and turned in every perceivable direction. Just when I got used to the movement and exhilaration, I was thrown upwards, into daylight, where I peered down on the unmistakable ancient remains of Maccu Piccu. I'd never been to Peru, let alone completed the steep hike to the city in the clouds which had always fascinated me. I zoomed into a natural rock formation shaped by the Inca, into the outspread wings of a condor, and sat on the stone with Stag, watching an eight-foot-tall male angel sweep the altar in front of me with a broomstick. His head, bowed, hid his face. There was nothing more to it, just the surreal scene of Heaven and Earth meeting each other. Dawn began the call-back with faster shakes of her rattle, prompting a return back to Dragon Hill. A turn of my fate was sealed that day – an angel in Peru was calling for me.

#

After nine miles of walking through stretches of poppy fields and grazing land where the only traffic was four-legged, we reached Ogbourne St George. The group's small Irish contingent remained at the local pub to see their football team defeat the Italians through a cloud of Guinness and black pudding, while I explored the local church named after the dragon-slaying saint. Dawn had led many a group through the same landmarks every summer, so she gave me approximate directions to the spot where the Michael ley line passed through the cemetery, briefly parting from the Mary line. I'd never knowingly sat in one of the famous lines before and was highly curious about what the energy would feel like. Ogbourne St George was a sleepy village. I felt grounded after so much time in nature and walked with my sandals flapping on the tarmac down the old shop-less High Street, past a school and collection of large houses with thatched roofs. Each had a large rusted metal weathervane crowned with the hollowed shape of an animal. I peered through the outline of a badger at the setting sun's bright pink rays and said a silent prayer of gratitude for my recovery.

The road forked right and turned from tarmac to gravel with rain-filled potholes, leading me to a dead-end where the church was nestled on the edge of the village with nothing but common land beyond it. A crooked and sinking paved path led me clockwise around the back of the church, through tombs and crooked lichen-covered gravestones. I slowed my pace, trying to sense the Michael line. Sudden pressure on the centre of my forehead energised my third-eye and stopped several feet later. I backtracked into the energy and sat down, letting it spread to the crown of my head and down to my ears. It was intense, and addictive. My head raced with images of the last few months. The faces of all the spirits I'd met in Scotland flickered in my mind like a movie played at double speed. Their voices overlapped each other until all I heard was a sound similar to a hundred Canada geese heading west back home.

The clanking of metal, drunken profanity and the

panicked bark of a small dog called time on the movie. 'Get lost, you mongrel!' George said, stumbling through the cemetery, propping himself up on the gravestones. A Jack Russell yapped at his heels, trying hopelessly to grip the steel between his tiny jaw. 'Aaron! How can something so small be so vicious?' George collapsed against a grave and pulled out a small hip-flask from his breastplate. 'These bastards have got it easy, six feet under, not a care in the world.'

The Jack Russell stopped barking for a few seconds and then hurled itself at George's crotch where he furrowed for his shrivelled sainthood, tugging at it like a badger on crack cocaine. The combination of intense ley energy and seeing George inebriated and persecuted by a puppy-sized dog made me lost for words, until he made the most inhuman scream and a thick, foot-long forked tongue darted out of his mouth to within inches of the dog's clamped teeth. It let go and ran off whimpering as it bounced off the gravestones.

'That's one hell of an entrance! What came out of your mouth?'

'Mother's sense of humour. She's turning me into a dragon, unless you return Arthur… you found him yet? He's not in there, I can give you that one for free.' George crawled under a sagging link chain suspended by spiked metal posts and onto the tomb it was trying to safeguard which had sunk into the ground in front of me. He sat on the only corner of stone not yet covered by the grass and moss and patted it with his hand, wobbling and wrecked. 'This tomb is just like me, Aaron, consumed by Mother, never to be released.' He reached inside his helmet, trying to wipe some of the tears away from his eyes, and shook out the last remaining drops of whisky from his hip flask into his gaping mouth before retrieving a fresh miniature with a different label from inside the crook of his knee. 'Aahh, I love Edinburgh. A whisky shop on every corner.' He forced a smile, but his shoulders slumped and his cheeks just squeezed more tears from his eyes. He was on the verge of a breakdown; I knew the signs all too well. 'Do you know what's absolutely fascinating, Aaron?' George necked the small bottle. His back quickly straightened as the whisky shot down his spine and shocked his nervous system. '… you're sitting right next to my lance, the one I killed the dragon with. Look how Mother's trying to reclaim every last drop of her daughter's blood! I couldn't have plotted a more perfect synchronicity. There isn't a body in here, it's Ascalon, my six-foot bronze-tipped steel spear… hic! The church was built around the bloody tomb. It was hidden in here hundreds of years before anyone thought about building anything.'

It took me a while to process the revelation. Synchronicities kept lining up, and not just the ones George accounted for. I was sitting in one of the most well-known 'dragon lines' in Britain, feet from the spear which had killed the last dragon Mother gave birth to, talking to the man who had killed it. 'You should try sobering up, she might give you another chance.'

'Whoohooo! There it is. Didn't take you long, did it? Spoken like a true recovering alcoholic… hic.' He fell backwards and rested on the tomb, falling silent and then turning onto his side as though he were about to talk to his lover on the next pillow.

'Did you kill her on Dragon Hill?' I wanted to know if the legend was true. His answer might forever erase the doubt from my mind.

'You've been below it, what do you think? Those channels had to come from somewhere, like her blood, for example. Dragons didn't roam the Earth, they were born of it! Ascalon, I miss you,' he whispered, stroking his drunken dribble into the moss, yearning for his weapon. 'You know, Aaron, I haven't always been a murderer. Ascalon saved more lives than it took; the mere threat of its point from the height of a horse was enough to ward off enemies. I've never seen it since Mother took it from me; but I know she leaves it unprotected sometimes, when the lines move.'

'What do you mean, move?'

'The dragon lines move… hic! That's when the force-field leaves this tomb unprotected. Even when imprisoned at Ardnamurchan I sense their movement and feel Ascalon rise. You'll need to ask someone else when it's going to happen again. Someone who knows about the sun, moon, stars and Earth – they're what makes the dragons move.' George closed his eyes and slept. I left him with his fated lance and returned to the guest house, deep in thought, glancing at Merlin in the moon.

#

The next morning we completed the remainder of our thirty-mile Ridgeway Walk through a giant patchwork of grass and blood-red poppy fields to Avebury and the remains of Britain's largest stone circle, which was another point intersected by the Michael and Mary lines. There was only so much spiritual ambience I could muster with the constant noise of motorbikes, cars and articulated lorries rumbling through the village. Even in the more secluded fields away from the road, the ant-like stream of people walking around the stones on a family day out felt invasive and distracting. Dawn gathered us by a massive standing stone for a group photo and what I thought was to be a closing prayer. She looked at us one by one and thanked us with a shining smile, before turning to the stone and placing her hands on it. Her aura prickled with energy and with a deep breath she opened her eyes and turned to us.

'These stones are amazing, they are a granite very high in quartz which makes them piezoelectric; they generate electricity when subjected to vibrations such as the dragon lines running through here. They're in a constant state of vibration, making them electromagnetically active. All sites like this are power-spots, and all cultures allude to them being interconnected and umbilically linked to the heavens by a hollow tube or reed. They were used by sensitives to communicate with each other and they offer a conduit for the spirit world to enter the Earth's domain. Someone standing here could tune into someone's thoughts where they stood in Stonehenge. NASA even proved the aliveness of these places with their investigations. The Earth is linked to the Sun by a network of magnetic portals which open every eight minutes. Sacred sites and temples are much more than the dead stones they appear to be. They condense and conduct the energy stored within them, sleeping at night, and waking at dawn. They are alive!'

I went deep into the quiet library of my mind, silently shuffling the jigsaw piece Dawn had just given me, wondering where it fitted as we hugged each other, went our separate ways, and I drew nearer to the king.

The Priest

The ghost of Father Francis looked down at the waves crashing against giant pebble-shaped boulders below the west side of Tintagel Island. His feet were bare to the earth, just as they'd been when his warm blood pulsed through them. He had never owned shoes, preferring to remain barefoot, to be closer to the king. The soles of his feet trapped years of the island's soil, grass and grit in the fine creases of callouses which formed their own shoes. The hardened lumps of skin were sacred to him; a way to feel and be with him, such as no other would ever be able to comprehend. Before mortality left him, Father Francis washed with the water from the well at the centre of the island as a daily baptism to remind him of why the spirit world insisted on his existence in the doldrums. Even now, with nothing more than ectoplasm to wash, he still visited the well to submerge himself in the king's essence, but never his feet, which pressed onto the most sacred piece of land he had ever known.

In the beginning, he'd never questioned why the earth didn't want to claim his coffin, instead throwing him back to haunt the living who visited the island. After the giant landslip, he was one of three people chosen to remain on the island. The chapel had been a small affair. Big enough for ten people and built on top of Dark Age ruins. The small patch of land was lit up by Father Francis' once unwavering faith in his ghostly purpose. He had broken free from the Christian ranks of the church; finding solace and new belief in the destructive power of the wind and waves as they relentlessly shaped the landscape. Time was taking its toll in more ways than one; shaking the foundations of his faith. Hundreds of years, waiting for the brief window in time when elements, spirits and stars would align to give him back his physical body just to ring the church bell one last time and ignite the most profound chain reaction the kingdoms of animals, humans and spirits had ever known.

He looked at the clouds as they circled around him and remembered the day of the storm, when the land fell away isolating the chapel and the Great Hall from the mainland. The way the black thundering clouds had rolled in, tracking the gold beam of light under the surface of the ocean as it sped towards the tip of the island like a sea monster searching for its haven. He recalled the screams of the castle's inhabitants as they hopelessly looked for refuge from the land as it shook beneath their panicked feet. Children were snatched up by their fraught parents; men clutched at their weapons, searching for an enemy that didn't exist. The light carried with it a wave of such speed, and tinged with Mother Earth's anger at how one of her favourite sons had been harmed, casualties were inevitable. He was placed to rest perfectly, in the place of his conception, where Merlin brought him into the world to be held in Mother's womb once more, until the time was right for his return.

'Today, I pray, please make it today,' Father Francis said, closing his eyes to search hopelessly for the sensation of the north wind on his skin as it blew down from Scotland. Nothing touched him. Determined to make sure, as he did every day, he walked into the waist-high ruins of the chapel entrance, to the bell where it hung invisible to all but himself. He held his hand next to the rope as it dangled in the breeze and tried to pull it; but all hope was lost in his phantom presence as the hand passed through the coarse braided twine. 'Tomorrow, I pray, please make it tomorrow.' He closed his eyes and bowed his head as a cloud of sleet attacked the island, keeping the king hidden for just a little while longer.

TWELVE

The air was laced with sea-salt and the sun dipped near the horizon when I crossed the Devon and Cornwall border. Rush hour doesn't exist in North Cornwall, mainly because there are so few jobs for people to do. A field of double-bladed wind-turbines looked down on me, all stopped with two of their blades horizontal. I counted eight giant letter 'T's' before taking evasive action to avoid an oncoming tractor and then pulling over to relieve myself in the company of sheep as I neared the end of a six-hour drive.

I tried to approach my visit to Tintagel with glass totally empty, hoping for anything of worth to fill it with inspiration, but that proved pointless as I battered off grandiose daydreams of Arthur leaping out of his ancient grave to embrace me and hold my arm aloft to the elated heavens.

I found a guest house in Boscastle a few miles away from Tintagel, and went for the cheapest room to preserve my savings in case I was called to some other far-flung corner of the British Isles, or Peru. I had a gut feeling that calling

Arthur back was only the first step in the larger scheme of things. After all, rehab was only supposed to sober me up and show me a new way to live. I hadn't bargained for any of this. Cogs turned everywhere for me, inside and out. The weather did the right thing at the right time; people, places and things synchronised, eerily at times, and I found myself trusting the way life unfolded more every day. I began to appreciate first-hand the true meaning of existing as a spiritual being: opening up to my psychic abilities and insights. There were times I felt so aligned with nature that I could almost wield it. If only I knew how, and for what purpose! The importance of clarity of intention when in the company of most spirits seemed to be the key. Where George fitted into that category, I didn't know. He was the most reluctant immortal. I felt sorrow for him, and at the same time I identified with everything he'd been through. I had also killed something: a marriage, and almost myself, welcoming consumption of the kind George was getting to know all too willingly. Like me, though, there was always hope for him and always the propensity for change, no matter how far down he had gone.

Boscastle was just my cuppa tea, with its affinity for witches making it an attractive base for my trip or trips to Tintagel. As chance, or fate as the case may've been, would have it, the town most famous for being flash-flooded by over four hundred million gallons of water in 2004 was also home to The Museum of Witchcraft.

I tugged on my crane bag as I walked a stone's throw from the guest house to the Nelson Inn for dinner, on the off-chance that it might open and let me examine its mysterious contents. I found it tighter than ever. Street lighting was minimal on the outskirts of a town nestled in a shallow valley cut in two by the tidal river which snaked its way out to sea. There was something ancient in the Cornish air that night, which wasn't unusual for the area, but whatever it was followed my every move.

#

On my first morning I chose a corner table in the breakfast room and ate at a faster than usual pace. I was eager both to get to Tintagel and to make a swift exit before the landlady tried to engage me in conversation. The main risk was that I'd tell her far more than was necessary about the importance of my visit. I didn't mind people telling me I was a space cadet with my head in the clouds, it came as a compliment. I didn't expect most people to understand. It was how I got the most out of life's experiences: to see more deeply into them, and maybe add a bit of my own history to the world's chronicles.

After a broken night's sleep, I arrived before the castle opened to secure as much undisturbed time in Merlin's Cave as possible. The castle café was a welcome sight. I willingly let my guard down and ordered a triple-espresso to add an edge to the excitement bubbling inside me, denying any relationship my impromptu coffee binge had to my past. I hadn't slept through the night for years. My mind was so used to being coshed by chemicals, it didn't know how to settle naturally. Herbal sleep aids proved useless and unused prescriptions for sleeping pills littered my car as just another addiction waiting to happen. At times, with my dreams and perpetually whirring mind, I lived in an exhausted awakened state.

All caves have something supernatural about them, being so embedded in the Earth, and most of them carved by centuries of the elements' energy. Merlin's was no exception. The bedrock above it had several blocked entrances to tunnels which marked the island's brief industrial history when men mined silver lode and wolfram. Some of the original Tintagel families still owned clear quartz crystals as big as fists that they'd retrieved from the cave. Psychic experiences were not unheard of in Merlin's dark and watery domain.

I timed my visit to perfection with the retreating tide. Or was it Mother timing the tide for my arrival? Walking down the steep path to the cove with the island towering above me, I recognised a growing trust in destiny and The Path. I peered over the fence at the cave on my left and the waterfall which flailed onto the beach to my right, with the sea taking a breather before its next rampage onto the small beach marked by truck-sized boulders. I made my way onto the sand, staring at the outline of a giant face hundreds of feet high, shaped by the artistic talents of the weather. It was embedded into the western face of the island. Since leaving Logan's cabin I was able to see faces in the natural forms of trees, bushes and stones more frequently. In my ever-expanding mind, these were no fluke of geometry, but nature spirits peering through the veil at me to check on my progress before reporting back to Mother.

Once on the beach I was suddenly stopped in my tracks by another stone face, but very manmade and sculpted into a boulder the size of a small house in an attempt to lure visitors to the area.

'Maybe one day we'll meet,' I said, standing at eye level with Merlin's sculpted interpretation for the tourists. I stroked his beard before entering the cave and walking as far as the saturated sand would take me. I crouched near the rear entrance where the sound of the sea gave way to the excited high-pitched song of tiny birds. I turned back to look at where I'd entered, tracing the shelves of smooth grey rock lined with veins of white quartz all the way to the high ceiling and back down to the flat wall on my left. I looked out of the stone whale's mouth at the waterfall on the other side of the beach and climbed onto one of the smooth grey-white shelves to meditate. I closed my eyes and managed several repetitions of the mantra before my eyes were repelled upwards to the back of their sockets, forced there by energy hitting the centre of my forehead. I knew in that instant that Arthur was in the very land, towering above my head. Not his body, but his energy; his soul.

Each repetition of the mantra brought me closer to him. I felt his soul's breath in the wind and sea as it danced and crashed around the island. 'He's here, everywhere… he's here, Aaron!' I kept hearing. My eyes remained rolled back as the force pushed with each burst of the mantra. I knew then not to expect to find any remains of his burial or body, because the male energy surrounding me was so strong.

The click of camera shutters and feet squelching into wet sand signalled the arrival of a man and woman, their voices hushed at seeing me high up on a ledge with my hood pulled up and my legs crossed. I let go of the mantra and opened my eyes; message received loud and clear. I climbed down from the ledge and walked out of the cave, eager to explore the rest of the island with my new awareness. There was no question, no doubt in my mind that I'd found him, but he wasn't hidden under an ancient tombstone reached by any treacherous labyrinth, he was cocooned within the very land he swore to protect. I entered the cave and there he was — waiting for me. I walked back to the steps, catching a tall dark figure out of the corner of my eye.

'Fecking terrible likeness, don't ya think, Aaron?' the man said in a thick Irish accent. He was shaking his head, facing the sculpture of Merlin's face. His long black hair was weaved into an intricate Celtic knot. I got drawn to and lost in its complex circles and swirls. A round clear quartz crystal bound in leather hung at the end of the weave, ticking back and forth like the pendulum on a grandfather clock. He wore a black leather biker's suit, with his arm poking through the strap of a matt-black open-faced helmet which sparkled, star-like. 'I mean, for starters the beard is all wrong and the eyes have no life in them. Maybe they've got the cheekbones right, yes, I think I like them… ha!' He laughed and turned to face me.

Waves of fear laced with a disorientating sense of déjà vu ran through me. My mind raced, flicking through scenes in my life to find where I'd seen the man before. His blue bedazzling eyes stared at me, amused at my confusion. He started twiddling a small crystal ball at the end of his beard and reached into his helmet to pull out a small green porcelain bowl with a gold Chinese dragon engraved on its circumference. 'Fancy some of this shit? It's lekker, ha!' he said, switching to a South African accent and pulling a stone chillum out of his breast pocket. He stubbed it into the bowl, packing it with bright green and orange flecked weed, and held it to his mouth. 'Don't have a light now do you, Aaron? Oh, no, you're clean now. Good show, sir.' He clicked his fingers over the end of the chillum as it spilled with weed, sparking a red ball of fire to life and inhaled with his mouth as wide as a groper's. Thick wisps of smoke tumbled into his lungs. His ring finger had a large amethyst dome crystal. It took him ten seconds to let out the massive smoke-plume, during which time I had dropped to my knees. 'Whoah! That's some good shit. Come up here and sit with me, out of harm's way, Aaron. You never know what those waves are gonna do. C'mon, boy.'

He climbed a short way onto the outcrop near the entrance of the cave and sat back on a boulder weathered into the shape of an armchair. He looked comfortable, as if he'd been sitting there for centuries. I dragged myself to my feet, dizzy, head aching. His brief use of the South African accent knocked the wind from my sails. It was the barber from Cape Town, or was it?

I put my hands on the rock, raised one foot off the sand and paused, looking at him billowing clouds of smoke from the chillum. 'Merlin?' I asked.

'Ha! Been a long time since I rock'n'rolled. You know I can't resist a bit of Zeppelin and weed now, don't ya? So… now you know where he is, what are you gonna do with him?'

'I… I've no idea. Why don't you bring him back? You brought him into the world.'

'Exactly. I sparked the light which gave birth to him, but you of all people should realise that sometimes you only get one chance at something, like your recovery. Someone else has to bring him back; I did my bit hundreds of years ago.'

I finished the short climb and sat next to his stone chair. The smell of weed was pungent and enticing. My nervous system would fray the instant I took a drag, but it didn't stop me enjoying the heady smell. I took a closer look at his amethyst ring and the swirling cosmos inside it, and then at the weathered hand which wore it. His knuckles looked like tree burrs on fingers of oak. He just sat there, stoned, eyes staring out to sea with an air of profound sadness about him. I looked at his thick-hooped gold earrings which would've suited any swashbuckling pirate and at the jowls flanking his pouting mouth.

'Can you see how lost everything is, Aaron? How this beautiful Earth is being torn apart by the idiocy of humankind? There are those, like you, who know it and who shy away from what's going on because you know how polluted our thinking has become and how that stinkin' thinkin' is polluting the Earth. Getting high seems to take the edge off, doesn't it? I'm a man who lives by the light and dark of the moon, Aaron. Up there, where I did your heart surgery, that's where I'm bright, like light! But down here I'm happy to succumb to earthly pleasures.' He drew hot smoke down into his lungs and sucked it into his nose as it trickled out of his mouth. 'I'd offer you some, but we both know you're not going back there, don't we? If you were going to relapse, it would've happened in Cape Town.'

'What were you doing there?' I said.

'To see if you were worth it. If you'd actually had enough and wanted to change. I wasn't going to chuck my faith at you only to see it squandered. See, I needed someone who was ready to tread a new path, but they're not easy to come by. That barber's was the perfect place to meet people looking for redemption of sorts, but it wasn't just your most recent history I was interested in. It's your connection with other pasts which is your trump card – your Native American ancestors.' He blew a heart-shaped smoke ring and sent it out to sea. 'They know about the heart and its power, and you carry that power. Even more so with that shiny new ticker you've got in your chest. But there's more to it than that, and much more to you than meets the eye. How's your feathered friend doing?'

'Crow?' I said.

'Of course. I don't see him. He was with you at Logan's, eh?'

'Yes. Where were you then – the moon?'

'Not far away. I'd made a deal with Cernunnos. He released Stag for you. Tell me where Crow is.' Merlin sucked on the chillum and shut one eye, Popeye-style.

'He's more within me. You might say we've blended.' I said.

'How fascinating.' Merlin tapped the chillum on the edge of the green bowl, rested it on the stone armrest and put his arm on my shoulder. 'There are signs and symbols everywhere, Aaron, and sometimes they appear as people, like you. Logan told me many a yarn while I visited him over the years. Every single object on his wall symbolised something, either to him or to the tribe it came from. The story of the crow was one which always stuck with me. So when I met you in Cape Town and saw that big black bird going berserk outside, I thought I was onto a winner with you. See, all the Native American and Northwest Coast nations told the same story about the crow's trickster or shape-shifting abilities, or blending, you might say.' Merlin released my shoulder and sat sideways in his armchair, hugging his knees to his chest, and slipped into storyteller mode as a cloud scudded over the sun, dimming the lights. 'Long ago, so they say, before time and light had graced the Universe, everything lived in darkness because an old man named Lucifer had stolen the sun, moon and stars away from humanity. He kept them for himself in his cabin where he lived with his daughter. One day a crow was flying by a river and saw his daughter washing there, so he changed himself into a spruce needle and dropped into the girl's drinking water which she drank, swallowing the needle. When the girl became pregnant the crow possessed the baby. She eventually gave birth to a baby boy. When he was old enough to crawl around, he began to take great interest in the things the man kept on his shelves, crying incessantly to see them. When the man gave in and let him see the bag with sun, moon and stars in it, the boy changed into a huge crow and took them up the chimney where he released them into the sky.' He paused as the cloud released the sun back to the sky and the sea sparkled in its light. 'The crow is known to all Native nations as the bringer of light. I do believe history is repeating itself right here in ancient Cornwall. Tell me what you've gleaned from your travels so far… laddie!' He leaned closer, giving me a good view of a quartz crystal tooth and a glint of the madness I'd seen in someone else's eyes: Logan's.

'How well do you know Logan?' I said.

'You could say we're well acquainted. As you are with him.' Merlin looked at the couple leaving the cave. He stretched an arm and curled his index finger. 'Come, sea,' he said, bringing a freak wave onto the beach and swamping them knee-height. 'He just took a piss in my cave. I'm not havin' that.'

'Fair play. Well, I know the spirits of the witches killed in the Berwick witch trials are in Edinburgh, as are the spirits of their loved ones.'

'Noted… *loved* ones. Okay, go on,' Merlin said.

'I know that Mother Earth's last dragon daughter was murdered by Saint George, and that he is a lost soul, perpetually tortured by immortality and locked inside his armour, slowly being devoured by Mother, to become one of her dragons unless I can succeed in returning Arthur.'

'Not bad. What else? Tell me more about the dragons.' Merlin released his finger, sending the sea back and stopping the incessant shrieks of the half-drowning couple.

'The dragons haven't existed in their physical form for centuries, but they are still there, in the Earth, as lines of life-force. They flow like any wave of energy does, up and down, so they emerge out of the Earth and then dive below it like sea serpents. There are also other areas of energy, vortices, made positive or negative depending on what happened there. The wild areas of untouched land are the most positive ones; they reach up to the heavens while the negative vortices attract malevolence and traumatised spirits.' I stopped, surprised at what I'd retained from my bizarre collection of experiences. Telling someone for the first time gave the jigsaw a different dimension. It began to piece together. 'You know about the sun, moon and stars, don't you, Merlin?'

'For sure.' He sat on the edge of his seat and gave me his full attention.

'Do the lines really move?' I said.

Merlin sat back in his stone throne, while I reclined on the rock behind me, gazing at the castle ruins above the cave. 'Can someone direct the dragon lines? You know, steer them?'

'Yes, Aaron.' Merlin closed his eyes and smiled as though he were listening to classical music for the first time.

'So, Tintagel Island is imbued with Arthur's soul, his life-force; it's all around us, in the air, sea, and in this stone, right?'

'Right.' Merlin's hand moved like a conductor's again.

'So, if we found a way…'

'There's no *we*, remember, just you,' Merlin interrupted.

'So, if I found a way to move his soul into the ley line, if

I'm still alive when it happens, and move him to the positive vortex of the Ardnamurchan volcano – can he return there, through the land?'

'Bravo, bravo!' Merlin clapped. 'You'll be alive. I wouldn't have stayed in Cape Town otherwise, but if you don't get him to Ardnamurchan once he's moved and on his way, he'll be lost, dissipated, roaming the ley lines forever. The only reason Arthur's still here is because it's his birthplace. It's where his power came from.'

'What power?' I said.

'So many legends about a man people knew so little about. He's probably the most misunderstood king there ever was. Sure, he was a ruler for the people, not of the people. He had a heart as big and bountiful as that ocean, but he was more than the warrior and ruler he so rightly claimed to be; he knew the land and its creatures so well, because he came from the land. All that quartz in there was the perfect epicentre to bring him into the world. He was a man who knew nature's magic – not without a little help from yours truly. You could've tried to bring him back here, but they've mined the land of its jewels and the tourists have muddied the energy up there. It's no longer clean. Not many places left like the one you found in Ardnamurchan, that's quite a find... quite a drum, eh?' Merlin picked a twig of marijuana from between his teeth and flicked it into the breeze.

'How do I get the drum to play?' I didn't need an answer, and Merlin didn't give me one, but his voice rang loud and true in my head.

'You know the answers, Aaron.'

'People… people play drums, don't they?' I said.

'Ha… I told you so. You'd be wise to remember that drums are also protective. Just as the ear-drum protects the ear, so the drum of the Earth protects its people, or king, while he's moving in the leys. Up there you might get a feeling for what he was like as a boy. Remember, we all possess different gifts; some can pull swords from stone, others can hear what the stone has to say.' Merlin winked at me. 'You need to get to know him a little better, so he'll trust you. Use your heart and he'll know you're coming with honourable intentions.'

'Why *am* I bringing him back? I need to know what the intention is… don't I? All journeys need an intention.'

'When he was here last, he brought people together, that was his forte – unity. If there's one thing he could do again, that'd be it, but Mother Earth also chose you, so there's something the two of you need to do together. He won't be the same Arthur, though. This isn't about bringing back the king of old. He'll be coming out of a new land, in a new time, as a new Arthur. If you manage to succeed, I'm certainly not expecting the same man I knew back then.' Merlin loaded his chillum again and paused his fingers a few inches from the mouth of the cannon-shaped tube dripping with weed. 'You know, Aaron, the best piece of advice I can give you is to just get on with it. You're on your own now. I've done all I can to help you along the way, perhaps more than I should've, but I'm glad I did. Something tells me you've been worth it.'

He lit the chillum and inhaled its crackling contents, summoning a gust of wind with the inhalation before looking at me as nature flooded his bloodstream and with another mischievous wink and a loud click of his fingers; he disappeared into a vast cloud of smoke.

I sat, alone again, with sea spray washing the smell of dope from my recovered skin and my heart yearning for someone to shine its light on.

#

The steps to the island were worn out from the constant stream of visitors making a climb not for the faint-hearted. They looked fluid and organic. Glossed by the damp air, no two steps were the same size or shape. It was an intense climb, needing slow and steady strides with the utmost concentration to avoid falling. I stepped through a small arched door at the top and into the crumbling ruins of a series of great halls and rooms. The now steady flow of tourists made the area devoid of any atmosphere. I stood still at various spots trying, in vain, to connect with any kind of atmosphere. A thousand years of salt-blasting was reclaiming the walls. The smooth neatly paved path running through the main entrance was out of sorts with the crumbling surroundings. I manoeuvred my head carefully into one of the small windows, avoiding the jagged teeth-like rocks which framed the opening. I looked north, far out to sea, where Ardnamurchan waited. I touched one of the rocks near my head, making it dissolve like papier-mâché under my fingers. I quickly left the courtyard to explore the rest of the island, wondering how long Arthur's tenancy would last in such a busy and deteriorating exhibition, with its energy tainted by tourism. I had no idea where I was going, or what I was looking for. I walked slowly, hoping my spiritual radar would hone in on something, or someone. There were hundreds of ruins remaining below the turf and those which were visible were mostly knee-high footprints of walls which marked where gardens, store rooms and accommodation once stood. Some of the older Dark Age ruins could only be reached by earthen paths no wider than my feet, down steep banks to small plateaus. Bright green grass grew inside the ruins, making ideal places to settle for a picnic or coffee, but I chose to use any vacant lots for meditation. The presence of Arthur's energy grew stronger with each period of mantra-infused stillness, causing energy to press urgently on the brow and crown of my head.

It wasn't until I reached the remains of the tiny roofless chapel of St Julitta, built long before the castle, that something different happened, and the energy pressed harder. I walked through the imaginary door and stood facing the altar where the low wall formed a small bottlenecked enclave. Cold gusts of wind charged across the island, pressing me further into the ruin. The sensation of a sheet of freezing ice passing through my back freaked me out almost as much as the ghost I saw walking through me and into the enclave. The man wore a cassock and held a rosary in his left hand. He stood with his back to me, looking upwards.

'Hello,' I said. The priest did nothing. 'Hello, can you hear me?' I raised my voice, but he didn't respond. I was surprised and slightly offended that a spirit had ignored me, raising old insecurities I thought I'd dealt with in rehab. His obliviousness to my presence was grounding as I'd become accustomed to conversing and being beaten by so many other spirits – or was he different? He was the first spirit to actually appear transparent. He reached above his head and waved an open palm through the air. At first I couldn't see the rope hanging there, but as I relaxed into the encounter it emerged out of the air, hanging from a large bell as faint as his body. He made three failed attempts to catch the rope and then his shoulders dropped and he held his head in both hands. I thought he was going to collapse in a heap on the grass, but he turned and trudged towards me, briefly stopping inches from my face, frowning.

'Hello?' I said again. He cocked his head to one side, shook it, and walked his freezing presence through me, disappearing as soon as he left the chapel boundary.

I sat on the wall and bowed my head, overcome with nausea and on the verge of fainting. He hadn't seen me, but I wasn't immune to the priest's company. With the sudden feeling of incapacitation came the most depressing sense of weariness and desperation. His hopelessness engulfed me. I hadn't felt anything like it since looking at my skeletal reflection in the mirror after my last blackout. I looked back at the rope and bell hanging in mid-air and prayed for serenity. Then I remembered the golden lesson of recovery, the most reassuring piece of advice the counsellors had given me – my higher power would never give me anything I couldn't handle. I just happened to put all my faith in the great outdoors, nature, and right there, on the fragmented walls of an ancient chapel, I realised I was working in partnership with the forces which kept everything alive. I flicked through the pages of my mind to find the prayer Logan said on the porch of his cabin every morning.

'Blessed be the Earth which sustains us. Blessed be the air by which we are given life. Blessed be the water which cleanses. Blessed be the Sun, by which we are warmed. Blessed be spirit, which is within and all around us, and blessed be our ancestors, now, then, and to come.'

The nausea passed and I ventured a little further along the island, curiosity getting the better of me. A small tunnel lay midpoint, dipping and snaking below the land for twenty feet and then surfacing again. Its interior stone was smooth and clearly manmade. The guide plaque couldn't define its use, suggesting purposes from food storage to the home of ceremonial gateways to the other world. It was big enough to walk through, if one crouched low, and there were no snakes in sight, so I entered. The sound of the world stopped as I crossed its threshold. I was getting used to making such an entrance. I stepped back to check whether tourists were approaching, and tried to tune in to the whispering voices I could hear. The coast was clear. Once back in the tunnel I sat and listened to the voice again; it was Merlin, but with a younger voice and a hushed tone of secrecy hiding his words. I closed my eyes.

'Please show me,' I asked, my eyes clamped shut, wishing for clarity in my mind's eye or my ears.

'Arthur, all the mysteries of this world and the powers

you seek are hidden in the winds,' the invisible Merlin said.

'What winds?' a boy said.

'The coloured winds, but there is one you must find if you are to truly fulfil your destiny – the wind which blew on the day you were born,' Merlin replied.

'Hey! Over here, check out this hole, Dad! Oh, sorry,' a teenager shouted, quickly apologising on seeing me, and killing the psychic recall of whatever residual Arthurian energy I had picked up on.

The wind rose and with its touch and white noise in my ears, it brought clarity. I stared at St Materiana's church on the mainland where the font from the chapel I had sat in now stood, and pictured the congregation arriving for worship to the sound of the Sunday bells.

'A king for the people, not of the people,' I murmured. Cogs turned in my head, drawing images of everywhere the quest had taken me. A quest which started with Mother's distant South African drumbeat, banging on the skin of Earth's base chakra to draw me near and show me Ardnamurchan's earth-drum. Rhythm threaded my journey to Cornwall where the ghost of Father Francis tried in vain to ring the bell and call his congregation for one of the biggest gatherings the island had ever witnessed. Yes, I saw it now. No, I heard it! Drums talking to each other. My Native American ancestors knew all about that sacred call. Could the spirits of all who had ever lived on Tintagel since the Dark Ages rouse Arthur and send him to Ardnamurchan's drumming vortex of positive energy? Two protective drumbeats covering the land and sea while he made his journey north. I looked up and wondered when the stars would align to allow the Michael and Mary lines to move again. What if it was tomorrow? I returned to the car park, realising I needed to find Dawn again. If she knew about the alignment of the planets for the solstice, she might also know the timing. I slowed my pace as I came within eyesight of the four-by-four, freezing when I saw that it had moved from a space near the entrance of the car park to the furthest corner, backing onto a field. Music blared out of the vehicle and clouds of smoke hid the occupants who were only visible by their heads which banged in time to the music as their strained voices screamed wildly, trying to match Robert Plant's rock'n'roll sex-tone. I pushed the ignition key through the knuckles of my clenched fist, ready to confront whoever had found my Led Zeppelin playlist. Their choice of songs was a good one, though. 'When the Levee Breaks' – one of my favourite tracks. The slow, steady drumbeat made the windows vibrate. I cocked my arm back, ready to stab the intruder with my key, and opened the door. An atom-bomb cloud of marijuana smoke blinded me as it exploded from the car, and George made his trademark clattering entrance, or should I say exit, to the sound of electric guitar and John Bonham's pounding base-drum. Through the smoke I saw Merlin's hand turn off the stereo. George collapsed in stoned hysterics, blubbering something about rain.

Merlin's red eyes peered out of the smoke, grinning. He flashed his quartz tooth at me. 'Ah yes, I forgot to tell you about the rain. You'll need lots of it – biblical amounts!'

George grabbed both my ankles, barely managing to control his hysterics. His touch forced scenes of the dragon's murder into my mind with sounds of reptilian squealing as a blade cut through its flesh. The more I saw the scenes, the more just I felt Mother's sentencing of him was.

'Please help me, Aaron. I'm turning into a dragon!' He tried to laugh again, but vomited, stretching his forked tongue out of his mouth as he retched, and then he looked at me with eyes that no longer reflected his soul. They were dragon eyes. 'Skye!… you've still got the Isle of Skye, The Black Cuillin, that's the last one… see you in Ardnamurchan!'

Merlin launched himself out of the truck onto George and dragged him along the tarmac, making an awful motorbike-crash scraping sound as they flung themselves randomly forward and vanished down a plughole in the air. It was the weirdest scene from a pantomime I'd ever seen. I smiled as the marijuana cloud oozed its way into my bloodstream and drove the familiarly scented truck away, blaring Zeppelin as I went.

THIRTEEN

I'd had no response from Dawn during the measly thirty minutes I'd given her. The need for instant gratification took over. I hit the road, preferring to make the nine-hour drive to Skye fuelled by triple espressos and Zeppelin's Greatest Hits, on repeat. 'When the Levee Breaks' got special treatment. I thought the music might hold subliminal messages which my brain would decipher, presenting me with the keys to Arthur's kingdom. By the time I arrived at the Skye Bridge I was none the wiser and peered through the windows at the emerging stars to check for – what? I had no idea.

The bridge's long rolling curves and slick modern concrete carried my tyres silently away from the mainland towards the unique landscapes formed by giant landslips and lochs secluded high in perpetually singing mountains. I'd been upbeat for most of the drive, smiling about the reminder George had given me of what chaos marijuana and alcohol were capable of bringing. The smell of burning ganja and tobacco roused something uncomfortable within me.

Memories of past terror leered into view, but I pulled the gates to hell shut.

I approached the end of the bridge and watched the streetlights turn off at the end of their night shifts. Then a wave of dread hit me. I hadn't felt anything like it since my crashes from cocaine. Palpitations messed with my heartbeat. Instead of excitement and intrigue about my arrival, nothing but the most powerful sense of foreboding greeted me and with it – Logan loomed large. He was so near, and responsible for Mr Doom hitching a lift with me. I'd done well to block out thoughts of killing him, until now. I told myself he'd never show himself again, and that even if he did, he'd have had a change of heart. But if not, would I really be a murderer if he'd asked me to kill him? Or perhaps just a facilitator of euthanasia? I was no closer to establishing his reason for wanting me to do such a deed, but as I crossed the bridge his presence weighed heavy on my mind.

The guest house was ideally situated for exploring the island. Surrounded by some of Skye's most dramatic peaks, it was set at a midpoint on the island between the peak of Bla Bheinn and the Red and Back Cuillin ranges and close to the main road which travelled the circumference of the island. Time to sightsee was not on my side, though. I floated on trust. The Black Cuillin were the remains of a massive supervolcano which would've blown Ardnamurchan apart if they'd had a lava-shootout back in the days when Mother's furious chimneys and molten red roads ruled the world.

As luck, or destiny would have it, the landlady's husband

was a volunteer for the Mountain Rescue Team and an expert on walking and climbing routes. My only request was to get as close to the Black Cuillin as possible. He chose what he referred to as a 'nice walk', giving the impression that it was more of a Sunday stroll than anything set to test me. The destination was a small loch at the foot of Sgurr Alasdair, Skye's highest peak. The return route would take a left fork down the mountain and back to Glen Brittle campsite where I'd park my car. The triangle shape he pencilled on the map looked achievable for a solo novice like me. I feasted on fresh homemade Scottish sausage and local eggs and collapsed fully clothed on my bed, only to be woken two hours later by a dream of Logan speaking gibberish as he danced around my sleeping body wearing the Thunderbird mask, and throwing green dust over me. 'Wake up, laddie!' he shouted. I fell off the bed, patting my body to brush off the non-existent green dust.

After stuffing my bag with the leftovers from breakfast, along with maps, water and my trusted flask filled to the rim with coffee, I paused for a weird moment before leaving a bedroom I'd barely spent any time in. I wondered if I'd ever see the room again. 'Idiot, get a move on,' I said to myself. Merlin's voice seemed to be layered over mine.

The Glen Brittle road took me past signs for the Talisker whisky distillery, a place I'd always wanted to visit when I drank, but which faded away like any other road sign. I made the drive in silence, giving Led Zeppelin a day off. Some journeys were a pilgrimage. The silence was sacred and respectful to my intention to connect with whatever was waiting beyond the veil, and the grand purpose of my presence in Scotland. The more miles I travelled and the further my feet stepped on unchartered earth, the more sacred the quest became. I hadn't believed in anything so much since rehab. Back then I believed in finding myself and saying goodbye to a stranger who had taken over my life; now, I believed in spirit, once so unseen, but now so present and tangible.

The crane bag's cord pressed into the back of my neck as it got heavier the closer I got to the car park. I'd grown so used to having the cowrie shells lightly rattling on my chest that I'd almost forgotten the way it had shut after Wayland's Smithy, forbidding me access. By the time I parked the car, the bag was so heavy I had to loop the cord over my fleece's collar to stop it cutting into my skin. Logan's presence loomed, and the ancient volcanic mountains dwarfed me as I left the marijuana-infused truck and began the first leg of the walk up five hundred metres of steep incline to a small lochan where I planned to take a breather. I'd underestimated what the Scottish meant by steep, or perhaps it was the damage years of smoking and snorting had done to my lungs. My legs were strong, but my breathing was laboured.

I hadn't gone far from the road when I crossed a small recently made footbridge which crossed a stream. The paths were well tended, making the route up the mountain easy to follow over endless brows of hills hiding what lay ahead. I found my stride and breathing rhythm, picturing the old parts of my lungs giving way to new blood-filled flesh, brought back to life by the clean Scottish air. I was at least three hours' walk from the large cairn I was aiming for. The recovered me didn't give up on myself and I wasn't about to start now. The weight around my neck grew heavier, but my spirit grew stronger.

After half an hour the distant sound of the waterfall which fed the stream invigorated my step. I stood at the edge of a huge cavern and looked across the void to where the meltwater sprinted out of the rocks into the lagoon below. It was a welcome landmark with company from the elements as I took respite from carrying the heavy bag. I held it in the palm of my hand and tried to walk carrying it, but the weight threw me off balance and the effort made my biceps burn after a hundred metres of trudging. The heavier the bag got, the more my heart pounded; louder and stronger with every step. For all the unpredictability of Skye's Hebridean weather, it decided to bless me with clear blue skies and a cooling mountain breeze. I paused to remove my waterproof and closed my eyes, bringing Stag and Crow close. Their physical presences were unnecessary for a path I had to walk alone, but their soul-energy was essential. It recharged mine like a back-up generator when my mind became cluttered with negative thoughts of 'what if all this is in vain?' and 'you fool, Aaron, who do you think you are?' But I had a new power inside me, one which came from courageously throwing myself into the abandon of spirit's arms and Mother's will. My desire to meet my destiny burned more brightly than ever, and all the while, my crane bag got heavier and heavier.

I reached the lochan hunchbacked from the strain and

sat on a thick cushion of grass. The tear-drop-shaped pool of black water lay on a plateau with a beautiful view of the valley where wind combed the surface back and forth. The dark bottomless water looked lifeless, but ripples from a breeze brought it to life. I sat there, enjoying the view and total solitude. When I removed my backpack, the crane bag's cord slipped onto my skin and drew a single line of blood around the back of my neck. I looked up the mountain, daunted by the huge task in hand. I drew a full quota of mountain air into my lungs and shouted at the top of my voice.

'Give me some inspiration!'

I mistook the first drops of rain for spray from the surface of the lochan. The plateau was suddenly engulfed by clouds, all memory of a sunny blue-sky day washed away. Rain driven by the strengthening wind pelted me, forcing me to retreat to the nearest boulder and ride out the bombardment. I peeked out from the hood at the ballistic downpour, and then, as suddenly as it had started, it stopped. Minutes later the valley was floating in blue skies. When Mother delivered a telegram, she didn't mess about.

Rain's purification was needed somewhere in the ritual to return Arthur. My ancestors had used water to purify before ritual, in a sweat lodge, but the land also needed it to grow, and electricity travelled in it faster than any other medium. Water was the most conductive element I could think of and there were hundreds of miles of it between Tintagel and Ardnamurchan. I needed the mother of all storms to activate Ardnamurchan's earth-drum and I prayed the answers waited above me inside the mountain.

The crane bag gave a sudden tug as its weight increased. I unzipped my coat and crawled to the edge of the lochan to wash the blood from my neck and gave it the hardest yank with both hands to break the cord, furious at the lack of support from something which was supposed to give me power.

'It's not all about you, Aaron. Bring the bag,' the wind whispered in my ear. I looked around and saw no one, but knew I was being watched. The skin on my back crawled.

I looked at my reflection in the water and saw Stag standing behind me. His antlers rose behind my head. Crow's wings spread wide to either side, stretching every feather-tip on the surface of the black pool. A knot of black snakes appeared over my heart, then broke apart and disappeared, swimming over my reflection. Their energy lifted me. I pushed on to the cairn at double pace, spurred by the instant response to my request for inspiration from Mother and my guides' company.

The cairn stood at the bottom of a steep scree slope. At the top lay another lochan: Coirr Lachan. That was as far as my moderate route took me before turning into terrain only seasoned climbers attempted. I unwrapped the piece of the morning's breakfast sausage and wedged the mixture of meat, rusk and spices into a nook of the cairn with some coins as a gift for whatever spirit was guardian to the Black Cuillin. It was half the height of the cairn at Maclear's Beacon, standing no more than five feet high, but with a smoother dome shape. Maclear's was clearly the work of hundreds of Table Mountain visitors who'd left a memory encased in the random shaped rocks piled under the searing South African sun. I picked a rock from the ground to cover my gift, but no matter which way I tried, it didn't fit. My rock was the same colour as all others in the cairn, but its shape was natural and rounder than the cairn rocks which looked like they'd been cut. I stood back and looked at the dome of stones and their edges which could only have been made by a stonemason's hammer or chisel. I walked around the dome, scanning the rocks, picturing hands moulding the symmetrically perfect shape with the precision and pride of an artist. I glanced back down the mountain at the return route and the silvery sea resting on Glen Brittle beach, then pushed on through to the ledge and into the domain of whoever or whatever had made the cairn.

The scramble up scree to the ridge was a case of one step forward, five steps back. I might as well have been on loose sand in the desert with nothing to secure my grip and the crane bag dragging me down. With the constant struggle, the bag's cord slipped onto my skin as I lay flat on the slope with my arms and legs splayed like a frog splatted on a window. I edged myself to the side where a few fixed rocks offered the only chance I had to reach the lochan before I was spent.

'Stag, be with me,' I groaned, as blood and sweat dripped down my back. I launched myself with arms and legs pumping frantically until I rolled over the top ledge and lay prostrate looking at the sky. The sight that greeted me was worth all the effort. I looked at the most beautiful natural cathedral made of scree and rock. The lochan was shallow with one aquamarine hollow in the centre, emphasised by the solemn grey of gabbro rock encasing it. I wasn't alone, though. A man in a bright red quilted mountain jacket sat at the far end of the lochan.

'Welcome, laddie!' Logan shouted. He stood up and skimmed a stone across the water. It bounced several times before nutmegging me between the legs, hitting a small boulder. The sound echoed around the towering stone walls. 'Isn't it a beauty?' Logan proclaimed, turning with his arms aloft as he marvelled at the undeniable splendour of the spot.

'Good to see you, Logan. I think.' I walked over to meet him, extending my hand to shake his.

'None of that, give us a hug, laddie.' He swatted my hand away and embraced me with a bear hug. 'Damn fine to see you, well done!' he said quietly in my ear before releasing me. 'Here, sit, rest.'

I fell to the ground, exhausted and full of apprehension. 'Where have you been? What did you do to me after the storm? I was covered in green powder, everything went crazy after that…' I paused, refusing to dance around the main question burning a hole inside me. 'Is this where I kill you?'

'Not quite. In there, that's where.' Logan threw a stone into the aquamarine hollow. I watched his face closely. There was an unfamiliar serenity about him. Gone was the leaping-leprechaun mentality I remembered so well. I saw a man at peace with himself, the likes of which I hadn't seen since meeting Troy in Cape Town. A thin glaze of tears made his eyes shine. Their blue matched the crystal colour of the lochan's hollow. His happiness surrounded me like a bubble. 'See that stone I just threw, Aaron? It's like you, about to send ripples throughout the world and, who knows, maybe even further. You're feeling my happiness, aren't you?'

'Yes, enlighten me. What's going on? Why are you here?'

'I've been here for weeks, forging a deal with spirit. I'm so glad you've arrived. It's you who've enlightened *me*, laddie. I wasn't going to throw away my life if you didn't make it this far. I had to be sure Arthur's return was possible first, and anyways, I'm not going to die, just transform, or should I say transmute. You'd know all about that, eh? Those snakes won't leave you alone, will they?'

'You can see them too?'

'I see everything now. I'm so ready to leave. I've been coming to this place since I was a child, with my father. Now there was a man with a heart of gold. That's the key to all this – the heart. It's the reason you can feel my happiness right now. We're sitting inside the magnetic fields of each other's heart. It extends several feet around us. The heart is an amazing thing, Aaron. I bet you've wondered about the craziness of this whole quest shenanigans, eh?'

'Occasionally, yes.'

'Merlin saved your heart for a very good reason – because you've got Native American DNA. The genetic mode of thought, given at birth, is essentially our default mode. We are born operating in heart-mode. Our head-mode view of reality is simply based on concepts we learn to carry in our heads through parenting and education. We invented cars, space travel, land deeds, computers and other such concepts foreign to Native Americans that go to form the worldview of industrial nations. All of these new discoveries and laws that are passed are accompanied by changes in our behaviour. Children play outside much less these days because of computer games, television and the internet. They're all head-mode behaviours which rapidly change the content of any culture. However, laddie…' Logan nudged me with his elbow. 'In Native American cultures, where life was based on hunting and gathering, all the while using the heart-mode of thinking, there was very little change in their behaviour because theirs is a way of being, not a particular philosophical point of view. I'm not talking about their cultural habits, rather their mode of conscious operation which underlies their lifestyle. Even though there are hundreds of linguistically distinct Native American cultures, they all march to the sound of the same drummer – the heart. Native Americans approach reality in the same manner, with their respect for nature and their deep spiritual understanding of it. Sound familiar to you?' He nudged me again. I nodded, enthralled. 'That's because thinking from the heart behaviour transcends cultural boundaries for the simple reason it is programmed into everyone's DNA. We were all born into this mode. Young children worldwide all show the same characteristics by being humble, innocent, trusting, loving and, most importantly, being naturally happy all the time. They all march to the same drummer, the same inner beat of the heart.'

'What's all this got to do with Arthur's return?'

'Because you are at the core of the ceremony, Aaron! You're sitting here with me because your heart told you this was all worthwhile. If you'd listened to your head, we'd never have met. You would've talked yourself out of it and found another desk job, relapsing on sadness, but there's so much more. The heart is an astounding organ, its magnetic field is so powerful. When someone's intention or emotion arises from the heart, it's accompanied by consciousness, a power – love. That frequency of love is the Golden Ratio, Aaron, the most healing frequency known to man and spirit. It is all encompassing.'

Cogs turned in my head. Pieces of the quest's jigsaw floated around and I began slotting them together. 'The witches and their families, the men and children. This is about them, isn't it, I need to bring them to Ardnamurchan!'

'Yes, laddie. You need to call them, but there's more to it than that. Do you know what else I've learnt? The heart's main ventricle is a muscle which, when unravelled, forms a double-helix, the same shape as the DNA molecule. What's really cool is what they found when they put electrodes on a twelve-year-old boy and his dog, and then asked the boy to walk into the room and radiate feelings of love towards his dog. The data showed that both their heart rates and rhythms began to beat in synchronicity as a transfer of energy took place. Do you know how they measured the size of the heart's magnetic field? They put electrodes in a glass of water and found that the heartbeat of someone sitting nearby could be detected… in water!'

The cogs kept turning. 'Rain!' I said.

'Yes, biblical amounts.' His eyes twinkled. 'That's where I come in.' He looked to the sky, closed his eyes, smiled and swayed. 'Would you mind if I have a look in your crane bag?'

'Be my guest. It won't budge an inch, though. Not since Wayland's Smithy. It nearly cut my head off.'

'Marvellous.' Logan rested his hand on my shoulder and looked straight at me with eyes which reminded me of my dad. He reached across and pinched the crane bag with his finger and thumb, lengthened the cord, and looped it over my neck.

'H… how did you do that?'

Logan held the bag in the palm of his hand and juggled it from one to the other, grinning at me. 'Light as a feather!' He caught it in his right hand and delicately opened the bag with all the precision of a bomb-disposal expert. My heart played a drum-roll. I shuffled away from him, worried that something was going to engulf us. 'Beautiful!' he said, tipping out the cowrie shells and passing them to me. 'Look after these for a minute, laddie. Don't drop even one. They might come in handy tomorrow night.'

'Why then?' I said, holding the shells at eye level to examine them for the first time in natural light: all identical sizes, and perfect conical shapes with their small serrated ivory coloured mouths, constantly exhaling Sanna Bay air.

'That's your chance, that's *it*. The only time for the next eleven years that the Michael and Mary lines can be summoned and when a drop of the North Star's light has a wee window to contribute to the magic show below. It's part of the Great Bear constellation, or Arth Fawr, as the Druids call it. Uncanny eh? On a clear moonless night you can see the bear pointing its nose straight at Tintagel. This is going to be one almighty coming together of cosmic, Earth, human and spirit energy. It's never been done before, nor has it ever been needed so much. Every eleven years there is a period of waxing and waning of intense solar activity as vortices of concentrated magnetic fields, known as sun spots, create and hurl solar flares out into the solar system. These massive gaseous explosions contain the energy of forty billion atomic bombs and this energy careers towards Earth with very definite effects on the planet, its weather and all living organisms. Normally, when the solar winds hit the Earth's atmosphere, they create what's known as the Schumann resonance of a steady seven point eight three hertz – the Earth's aura. The flares cause a spike in that frequency. Last time it happened the Schumann resonance accelerated as fast as sixteen-point-five hertz. What does that mean for us? Well, when people meditate and calm their brain chatter, their brains emit alpha and theta frequencies close to the Schumann resonance. The human brain in a relaxed state then has the same frequency of vibration as the energy field of the Earth. When we live close to nature, their energy fields are in synchrony with the energy field of the Earth, so we experience more balance and better health. A shift towards sixteen hertz moves one out of the alpha theta range and into a fuller calmer alpha state, with faster, more alert beta frequencies which create an ideal state of awakened calm. With this frequency, thought processes are clearer and more focused, yet we are also connecting emotionally via the heart, with a greater knowledge and therefore more power. A la Buddha – with our thoughts we create the world. Imagine the power of that love when the witches and their families see each other for the first time in centuries; then magnify that power with the cosmic surge of energy about to enter the Earth's atmosphere, and then magnify that again with the power of the Ardnamurchan vortex beating its rhythm. All that power will call Arthur to you, but if you want to hear Mother's heartbeat, you'll need to get that drum playing. Nothing happens until you do. There's lots of magic in that North Cornwall land and not just on the island. You'd do well to return there once… if it's done.' Logan furled the cord into a neat spiral, cupped the crane bag in both hands and raised it to his ears, listening.

'How long have you known?' I sprang to my uncoordinated feet and tripped. My head raced with a zillion thoughts of science and panic.

'Shush. Calm down, remember,' he whispered. 'You're not the only one who's met Merlin. Sit down, laddie. There's nothing to be done today. You'll be there. Everything is divinely timed. The flare isn't happening until tomorrow and your taxi is here waiting.' He nodded to where the land fell away beyond the lochan. I heard a landslide from below the horizon and then Stag's antlers rose up. He stood there and bowed. 'I must say, laddie, you've got an impressive scaffolding of support around you from the spirit world. Stag was a gift form Cernunnos himself. He owed Merlin a few favours, ya see – oh the stories I could tell you about those two. One of the favours was that green dust.

Ancient moss from the bark of the Tree of Life. Precious stuff. Only walkers are given some, like you, Aaron. You're a walker.'

'A walker?'

'Aye! A walker between the worlds. You journey so well, so naturally. Not many take to it like a duck to water, but like I said, it's in your DNA; you've got an innately high level of what's known as the spirit-molecule that I knew you'd commit to the cause. I wouldn't have wasted such a precious gift on you, a gift which makes you real in the spirit world, all of you – mind, body and soul. So, have you figured it out yet? What the cause is – why we have to bring him back?'

'No, I was hoping you'd know.'

'Ha ha ha! That's funny.' Logan fell back in hysterics. 'Neither of us know then! Sometimes the answers lie in raw experience.'

'I thought he was supposed to help return the land to its former glory, wasn't that the legend?'

'Sure it was, and still is, but to restore the land, you need to have a word with the billions of people who live on it first. We're the ones who were entrusted to look after it… fine mess we made of that.' Logan shuffled a large stone behind his head and stared at the sky in silent contemplation for a few minutes. I joined him, reclining and resting a hand on my heart. I felt its beat and heard my breath. Nothing else. We were away from the billions of people Arthur was supposed to come and talk to. In those moments I forgot about killing the man lying next to me, as he breathed calmly and held his hands linked by the thumbs up to the sky, fluttering his fingers like a bird. I wondered what Arthur would look like and imagined a long-haired bearded warrior bursting out of the Scottish earth with Excalibur held aloft as he rocketed into the sky, propelled by new-born volcanic fires. Then the questions lined up in my head. What would I say to him? Where would we go? Would he be angry with me for waking him? Would he be hungry? What would he like to eat?

'All I've ever wanted was to be free as a bird, laddie,' Logan said, stopping the rampage in my head. 'Just to be an observer from beyond the veil, where my spirit can soar eternally. That's why I need your help, please, friend.'

His hand rested on mine. Teacher and student – one heart. He stood up, walked to the water's edge cupping the crane bag in his hands and whispered prayers into them, throwing the bag high into the air. He followed it down as it hit the shallow water and knelt, watching intently as it sank. I moved to join him, but something pushed me back: an invisible wall of cosmic energy I hadn't felt since my first Reiki attunement. I sat and waited, listening to his prayers again and to the soft simmering of water, which rose to the boil, disturbing sediment at the bottom of the crystal-clear water. Logan's voice rose with the water's activity, speaking what sounded like a Gaelic dialect. His hands extended over the water which spat back at him and as his voice began to quieten, so did the water. Finally his whispers conjured only the smallest strand of bubbles.

Logan knelt on both knees, delved his arms far into the

lochan and fished something out. He stood up and turned around, holding an arrow in his hands. The shaft, arrowhead, nock and fletching were all made from a single piece of silver. 'This is what weighed you down. Its energy was getting restless to be born into this fine, deadly thing. This is what you need to use on me, Aaron.'

'I can't fire an arrow. You'll need to find someone else, an archer, there must be at least one on Skye.' Panic set in.

'There's no way out, laddie; if you don't do it, there's no storm tomorrow, and no Arthur. Remember? I'm the storm-bringer. Come over here.'

Logan walked to the side of the lochan next to the aquamarine hollow. He stepped straight into the freezing water with the arrow grasped firmly between his fists, muttering profanities as he adjusted to the temperature. 'Come here, quick!'

I walked over and joined him in the freezing circle of angelic blueness, choosing to shout my profanity as the water bit into me. 'Hug me, and close your eyes, don't think twice, just do it.' Logan's eyes looked wildly at me; I'd never seen him so energised. 'Let's hope her highness is in today,' he said, stamping three times. 'Knock, knock!'

I knew what was coming, but not who or what we were going to meet. The familiar descent into the Underworld began as we plummeted through the hollow. All sensation of water was replaced by a warm envelope of white light, followed by sudden stillness and darkness lit only by the soft white glow of a moon, suspended somewhere above us in the cosmic skies. A journey of seconds to another world.

'Logan, you there?' I said, waiting for my eyes to adjust to the lack of light.

'Yes, right here.' He lit a match and appeared sitting on a boulder with his face surrounded by a halo of yellow light from the small flame.

'Where are we?' All I saw was dark wet rock and another larger round boulder behind Logan with a flattened top. 'Looks like a massive chimney,' I said, looking at the small dot of moonlight through the distant opening above our heads. The stone walls had a familiar cut look, almost manmade, like the cairn's stones, but there was nothing made by man anywhere in the Underworld.

'Shhh, listen. You're about to meet the queen of the Black Cuillin.'

I strained to listen in between the high and low-pitched dripping sounds as moisture formed vertical streams down the walls and fell into ponds of different shapes and sizes around us. A sound approached from behind Logan where only darkness lay. Something dragged against the rock with long sweeping strokes, juddering my teeth. Brief intermissions from the painful sound were filled with the smashing and splintering of rocks which flew out of the darkness, narrowly missing Logan's head.

'Here she comes. Don't ask any questions. Just watch and wait.' Logan lay on his boulder face-down with his hands covering his head as the rock exploded everywhere with the advancing mystery occupant of the chimney. I retreated to the wall behind me, crouching low enough to see veins of gold shining in the rock which lined the musical pools on either side of me.

The rock stopped exploding. Something large waited behind the black veil and took two long inhalations. A brief lull followed before an eagle the size of a mechanical digger jumped onto the large pedestal of granite, glaring at Logan. Her head moved with a flash and she hacked into the base of Logan's pedestal, dislodging a basketball-sized chunk of stone. She hit the stone again, breaking it up to eat the fragments, tipping her head backwards to swallow and then squawking at the moon with such force that her feathers spread like finely carved blades of wood. Everything was perfect about her royal appearance, from her jewel-like eyes and stone-sharpened beak to the deadly talons which tapped and scraped on the royal podium as she waited for her human-court to make the presentation. She peered over Logan at me and gave a hushed squawk before darting her attention back to Logan.

Logan stood up with his head bowed respectfully in her direction, holding the arrow out with both hands to show her his gift – or so I thought.

'Catch, laddie!' He spun around and threw it to me.

Not being adept at catching razor-sharp arrows, I made a pathetic attempt to show I was trying to catch it with one arm held out as I ran for cover, tripping into one of the bath-sized pools. The arrow clanked against the stone. The queen looked at Logan quizzically; Logan shrugged his shoulders

'I know,' Logan said to the queen. 'But believe me, he's the right choice.'

I lay in the pool with my feet up and my arms hanging over the side. I was surprised by its warmth and marvelled at the way gold leaf clung to the back of my hands.

'Aaron,' Logan said, his voice lowered. 'The Thunderbird isn't indigenous to the Native American and Northwest Coast tribes. It can be called by anyone, anywhere, with the right tools, even in the Celtic lands where it takes its own form and where it needs a human's body and soul, entwined by magic with the spirit of an eagle. This is where I leave you. I will bring the rain to you tomorrow, but she will not take me alive; it's forbidden. You're my ticket to the next life. I will miss you. Please don't fail me now.'

My mouth was too dry to utter a response. I looked at my reflection in the silver fletching, twisting the shaft back and forth to see the moon and my face, wondering whether Merlin was watching me, even now, to make sure I'd adhere to the contract I signed, somehow, somewhen, long ago in one of my many existences. Fate had dealt a cruel card, but I knew I had killed before, many times, as a Native American. I looked at Logan's smiling face and then back down at the reflection of the silvery moon cloaked by something descending down the shaft, forcing air into the cavern.

The owl was the same size as the Cuillin Queen, and very familiar. Its four claws dug into the granite as it landed and changed instantly to human feet – Oka had arrived with the bow. He walked straight toward me with the huge face-cracking smile he always had for me, and with his feet pounding on the ground with all the weight of the giant supernatural bird he had just metamorphosed from.

'I hope you're taking all this in, Crow,' I said, not

wanting to call on him in case his foolery fractured the ceremonial atmosphere.

Oka looked down on me and placed his palm over my head, closing my eyes; his other hand planted the bow into mine and he pressed his forehead briefly against mine before kissing it. He stepped away, smiling, and soared up towards the moon, giving me no chance to hitch a lift and avoid the task in hand.

All eyes were on me as I stood with a silver arrow in one hand and an ancient bow in the other, covered in specks of gold leaf from head to toe. My archery skills in this life were limited to a few pot shots at a holiday park as a teenager. The grip was thickened with animal skin twine. It had a sweatiness from Oka's years of use. Minute animal carvings lined the inside and outside of the bow's feather-light wood, tallying each sacred kill. There was no more room for Logan's death, but this wasn't a hunt for food; it was sacrificial.

The queen looked eagerly at Logan who was looking at me circling an index finger around his heart to show me the target. 'It's okay, laddie,' he mouthed silently. The pools twinkled their soft water music, sending melodic vibrations tinged with gold into the air, perfectly priming it for what was about to take place. The arrow was well balanced, teetering at its midpoint on my finger, just as you'd expect a weapon made by Excalibur's smithy to be. I listened to my heart beating, calmly. Adrenaline didn't course my veins; I felt so centred, remembering, as though it were only yesterday, the young Native American boy I'd seen in a vision years ago, running through tall green grass. The longer the quest continued, the more jigsaw pieces fitted together with sublime precision. 'Native American is a way of being,' I whispered to myself. I pressed the arrow's nocking point into the bow's thick string and pulled it back to test its tension. Everything moved with such familiarity as my DNA recalled the thousands of times I'd fired a bow a lifetime ago. My feet moved without thought, shifting diagonally to direct my leading shoulder towards Logan who began humming an eerie tune which oozed his Celtic roots. I envisaged my heart's energy spreading out towards him, expecting to find fear in need of calming, but instead I felt pride from this mysterious and passionate man. I'd never been so humbled. I pulled the bow's string to my chin, centred the arrow in one swift movement and waited for Logan's song to reach its finale and be sent rippling through the Universe for eternity. Gold flicked from my fingers as the arrow left me. It flew in silence, like an owl hunting at night, towards Logan's outstretched body and drilled into his heart. A burst of his human life-force hit me as he bit his tongue and blood escaped from his mouth.

'Goodbye,' I said, pressing my heart.

Logan's eyes closed and his body was engulfed by the queen in one swift peck of her gaping beak. She stepped off the pedestal and back into the darkness.

The pools stopped playing their music and the moon beckoned me upwards. The cavern was ghostly quiet, with just the sound of a cloud of dust brushing the floor as the bow dissolved in my hand. I looked up, waiting for a sign or something to happen. Nothing, but the shadow of grief and jealousy enveloping me and the sound of my head turning against me from the inside, stirring the rot I'd fought with all my might to leave behind in Cape Town.

I slumped to the ground, hungry, angry, lonely and tired. Full of all the things the counsellors told us to avoid. I listened to the self-sabotaging head which had such a low opinion of me. Whether it was the shock caused by the ease with which I'd killed him, or the way he'd arrived at Coirrie Laghan only to desert me somewhere deep within the Otherworld, I didn't know. I stood there, abandoned, bathed in the moon's searchlight, centre stage before the biggest show of my life, but so alone, and wishing for a way out like Logan's. Poor me. I looked for a sharpened edge of rock to bludgeon my head on, or a pool deep enough to drown myself in. The head was willing to kill, but I knew my body didn't have the guts. It had taken enough of a battering. I sat self-defeatedly against a silent pool and stared into space, wishing for everlasting sleep to arrive. My eyes closed and a woman's eyes appeared again, briefly, their crystal-blue shining long enough to wake me and remind me of where I was.

'Crow, where are you?' I reached out to the black hole, facing my palm towards the opening in a high-five gesture, praying for his company again. It had been so long. I tried to make his feathers appear from my skin, but the emptiness sapped my power. I was running out of ideas, and time. My head bowed in defeat towards my hand again, but it didn't make it.

'Caw!' the black hole said. 'Caw! Caw!' I stood and

squinted through the mirk as his jet-black shape and fiery eyes hit me straight through the heart. My spirit stirred again.

I cupped my hands around my mouth. 'Stag, be with me!' I yelled. The train approached from the tunnel again, its four legs pummelling the granite at a hundred miles an hour. He burst into the cavern with vines flaring from his antlers and abdomen and bawled up at the chimney. Then he looked over me, huffing, grunting and scraping his front foot. His eyes glowed lava-orange; fire was brewing in everything that night. The ivy's tentacles lowered from Stag's head, sniffing, searching for me. I offered my arm and it wrapped around my wrists, pulling me onto his back as he sprang effortlessly up the gaping chimney.

We waited on Skye's highest peak, for what, I'll never truly know, but I never forgot the unusual tightness with which the ivy vines held me on the eve of Arthur's return. Stag usually held just firmly enough to keep me from falling, but that night I felt an urgency in his grip. The risk of his rider falling bore too great a consequence: much more than I knew. Stag faced west, fixated on the horizon, waiting for the first glow of sunrise. I stared at the ivy, transfixed by its duality: a poisonous plant, akin to the essence of the myriad of plants I'd once smoked, drank and snorted, yet they spoke to me of the mysteries of death and rebirth and of my soul's journey through the labyrinth from this world to the next and back again.

The slightest tint of yellow rose beyond the Atlantic, making Stag shoot from the starting-blocks; stone splintered in our wake. There was only one way to Ardnamurchan that day – as the Crow flies.

FOURTEEN

The ride was a blur of land and sea. My eyes stung and streamed with tears from sea-salt blasting. As we arrived into Sanna Bay, the sun took its place in the sky, raising the curtain on the biggest performance of my life. He moved me to the dunes at the back of the fine coral beach for cover where we watched a school of dolphin idling its way across the dark blue water. The colour was so vibrant it looked supernatural as the changing angle of the sun's rays altered its hues. There was no wind or swell to stir the short slow waves. Nature had never looked so beautiful to me. Stag had found a fitting place to allow me to collect myself before the ceremony. I could see why Madalane and her family had settled here, where the outer rings of the volcano sloped toward the sea. A wilderness-witch in her element. I traced the last dolphin's fin as it swam out of sight, making way for the fear and nausea which gripped my stomach as the answers to so many questions arrived. Clarity always arrived in lulls or the calm before and after the storms of my life. Twice before I'd stood at personal precipices, deciding whether to leap or scurry away. The end of drug addiction and the beginning of a new clean life: these were things I was ready for. I knew I never wanted to go back to that sickness. Then, stepping onto the plane to visit Ardnamurchan, I'd felt the fear return as the plane left Heathrow's runway, taking me towards the third precipice here on Sanna Beach where memories that had evaded me all my life projected onto my mind's eye. I saw my mother holding me as a baby and her passing me to my proud father. I heard children playing all around me in kindergarten and saw myself stranded amongst them in a playground, unable to speak out and make friends, paralysed by shyness and alienation. Then I saw my ten-year-old sprawling body pressed close to the ground to hear Mother's heartbeat which travelled to the present moment, filling the silence after each caressing wave had had its say.

'Boom! Boom!' she called.

I held the crane bag with Madalane's cowrie shells in my hand. They were warm; her spirit was near and so were the words she'd spoken to me beneath Edinburgh Castle.

The stillness of the low dunes gave no shelter from the grief rising in me. I cried, loving every inch of my tears' touch. The freedom to feel, to let go of the emotion and taste my tears as they found the corner of my parched mouth was one of the most liberating moments of my life. And while quests were known to be notoriously challenging by definition, I hadn't expected to have another man's blood on my hands. Even if his death wasn't to be in vain, I still needed proof of the just cause he died for. That could come later when we arrived at Ardnamurchan. I felt a deeper grief, though, one that my subconscious insisted on me facing, but which I repeatedly pushed back down with my weakened capacity for denial. A grieving similar to the one I'd dealt with during rehab as I said goodbye to the old sick me. Never a day in recovery went by that I wasn't grateful to be alive. But I still didn't know who I was or where my destiny lay. So where was the melancholy coming from?

I leant against Stag, resting a hand on the crook of his antler. Ivy vines spread over my fingers, sensing my fear. There was nowhere to run, though; I was bound to the Earth and a part of me liked the confinement, away from the outward struggles of the world. He had taken me far, as high as the moon and deeper than I knew this world could ever go. His big eye stared at me, but I couldn't face him; I wanted to stall and sit there all day rather than face the magnitude of who or what waited for me a mile away beyond the small hamlet of Achnaha. To add to the weight on my shoulders, George's fate lay in my hands and every inch the sun moved in the sky, I was a minute closer to mine. Part of me, the dark shadow-side, prayed I was wrong about what was to come, but the new, emerging Aaron wanted it with all my heart. I looked for people anywhere on the beach or along the coast with whom to start meaningless banter about the weather, but Mother was keeping the area unnaturally quiet for the last weeks of summer.

Stag walked the single-track road with me on his back and the vines missing from my hands. I surrendered again; I was good at that. He surprised me with the route he took, passing through a crofting community where people lived who knew and tended to the land they lived on so well. Cars and trucks remained in driveways; everyone was home. A flurry of blinds rolled down and curtains closed as Stag sauntered through the small hamlet rapping his feet audaciously on the road, proclaiming our arrival. Who did he think I was? I expected tumbleweed to roll across this mysterious stranger's path as Stag paraded me through the Celtic ghost-town to meet the king.

He avoided the cross-country route which would've been quicker, but unceremonious, keeping instead to the road and through the quarry car-park over the brow of the hill to the path I'd walked on my first visit to the ancient volcano. I'd never seen his head held so high and proud.

Stag brought me to George who was sitting in the centre of a grass oval next to the small hill. There was no wind in the crater this time, just the blazing sun and layer upon layer of excited insect chatter, all jostling for front row seats. I scanned the vast crater walls rising ahead of me and jerked my head back to see George holding something in his hand.

'How the hell did you get that?' I said.

George lowered his lance and looked down its length to survey its straightness. 'The lines have started moving, Aaron. Only a few feet, but enough for me to retrieve it and fly down the Dragon Hill portal to get here.' He stroked his filthy blood-stained hand down its pristine silver surface and tested the razor-sharp point with his finger. 'Mother even cleaned it for me. If I'm going to be given my freedom today, I'll need everything I came with. How about you? Are you ready to die?'

Flies and midges feasted on the rancidness coating his armour. George could barely see out of his eyes as dragon scales crept over his forehead onto his eyelids.

'I haven't come here to die.'

'Part of you has,' he said, pointing the lance at me.

I stepped into the oval. Its grass was as hot as a bath, run for me by my Earth Mother.

'How long have you known,' George asked, his forked tongue snapping at a fly.

'Known what?'

'Ha! You're in denial again! Hahaha!' George roared with laughter and did his impression of an upturned beetle, realising he couldn't sit back up again. 'Stag! Please.' He raised an arm to request an antler, which promptly arrived and sat him up by the crook of the neck. 'That's what I've always liked about you, Aaron, your naivety.'

I remained silent, vulnerable, and yes, in total denial of what my heart was telling me. George waited, allowing me time to process and speak. I took a deep breath. 'What's really going to happen this evening, George?'

'We aren't supposed to know all the answers, but one thing I do know is that your heart, Aaron, has always been the key to his return. Can't you see? It carries the crystal energy from the cave where Arthur was born, but now you need to believe in what you are here for. I know you do, or you would've run for another same-old life. Remember what you've learnt about your Lakota ancestors from Merlin and Logan. Native Americans were masters of ritual and ceremony, needing several essential ingredients to increase the power of their magic. Purification, prayer offering, prayer repetition, the absence of doubters, secrecy and… I'm sure there's something else, what is it?' George went absent and snapped back to the present. 'It'll come to me. Everything is in its right place today. Even stars are aligning to help your cause. You hold the key to so many hearts. I think Madalane knew from the moment she saw your battered body fall from the vaults, but Beorn and his men needed a little convincing. They now know what's going to happen, it took a little Edinburgh whisky to persuade them. Jesus, those men can drink! I lost count of how many times I fell off Arthur's Seat. They know this isn't about returning an ancient member of royalty.'

I looked at the uneven horizon, unable to look George in his reptilian eye, thinking about how the molten rock I sat on had been pushed from the depths of the Earth to become something new on the surface. My denial weakened. I nodded in recollection of finding myself in Cape Town for the first time, nearly thirty years after my birth, but still half-empty and now I knew why. As George talked, fear diminished and acceptance arrived.

'Are you staying?' I asked.

'I need to rest, if I'm given my free will back. That would be my choice. I've been awake for centuries, and anyway, once you've got stoned with Merlin the bucket list is done, really.' George looked down at his feet where the grass had wrapped itself around his ankles in the brief time we'd spent talking. He lifted his feet one at a time, just managing to break free and bottom-shuffle backwards up the small hill next to the oval for a ringside seat. 'Mother is claiming me, Aaron. Either way, whether you succeed or not, I think this ends for me today, at last. You can never be sure, though.' George smiled.

In all my time in Scotland I had never seen such a clear blue sky. The haze shimmered above the deep red and brown grasses. The giant lava walls basked in the sun, revelling in heat they once radiated themselves as they burst forth from Mother's core millions of years ago. The heat tightened and tuned the earth-drum's skin. I looked down at the grass dug by Stag's manic ploughing months ago and picked up a clump of the turf, revolving it in front of my eyes, expecting to find something special. Aside from its perfect putting-green appearance, I found nothing else unusual so I delved my hand into the soil it came from. My hand clawed through the soil with ease. My forearm was buried in no time and my knuckles found the prize with a crunch. Stag joined me at the edge of the circle, huffing and scraping his feet. I stretched my fingertips out and Braille-read the super-smooth surface as the earth swallowed my arms to the shoulders.

Stag lowered an antler, motioning for me to climb onto his back. As soon as my feet were secured in his ivy stirrups and my hands cuffed to his antlers by their green reins, he hit the grass with missile force and ploughed huge strips onto the marshland. The debris and shaking made it impossible to see, until he stood still and the dust settled. He bayed like a jet-wash into the shallow hole to clear the remaining debris. I peered through his branches at the sight before my disbelieving eyes.

My love of the night, the darkness and Crow, had given birth to an infatuation of all things black, including crystals. It was nature without the light. First and foremost, the colour reminded me where I'd come from. It told me of the insanity and bottomless hole which gave my soul its final dark night before the light came: before the first rays of hope appeared. As I learnt more of its powers, I understood more about black's protective properties and how some of Mother's manifestations of it were talismans which aided on journeys of transformations. Obsidian was such a crystal. It wasn't a rare crystal, but I had never come across one in all my visits to crystal shops and mind-body-spirit fayres. Until now, when the largest crystal I'd laid eyes on gleamed as the sun belted its solar flares onto the black quartz where a multidimensional star screamed its high-frequencies into the crater.

Stag released my feet and hands. I knew where to go. I would've dived into the black abyss if magic allowed. My hands prickled fiercely with Reiki. I knelt down to see my reflection and fizzing silver aura. I hadn't drummed for so long. I raised my hands above my head in a fitting 'Hail Mary' pose and let loose, slamming my palms onto the black earth-drum skin.

Boom! The first beat took me back to Cape Town in an instant. I remembered the first night at rehab as if it was yesterday. A memory which was just one of the built-in defence mechanisms made to prevent me relapsing. But it wasn't the first-day-at-school feeling I remembered as I collapsed onto my bed, it was Table Mountain calling me; it was Mother calling me.

Stag bayed into the shallow; reared up on his hind legs and hammered his front feet onto the black glass. Boom!

The noise defined the word awesome. He grunted in satisfaction and stood back to give me centre stage. I slammed my hands again and let them fly on their own, bringing back the rhythms they'd played so long ago during my solitary nights in the local woods near my house when the goat skin sent soundwaves ricocheting around the forest and my joints weaved streams of smoke through the branches. I fell into a trance with ease, occasionally opening my eyes to look at my silver aura as it swirled around me. I was in my element: alone in nature with my spirit ally, drumming on Mother's volcanic skin, transforming into what or who? At that moment, I didn't care. My hands took on a life of their own, shifting slightly here and there to find slight intonations of tone. The many hours of drum lessons beneath the baobab trees of a Gambian guest house now helped to stir a volcano for the first time in six million years.

I evoked the Reiki symbols in my mind's eye and an image of Tintagel drifted into view. I afforded a smile as I realised what was happening – I was journeying. My body drummed in Scotland while my soul summoned dragon lines and a sleeping king.

Heat and cold swirled around my hands, tickling me like a small captured rodent. I walked up the familiar steps, through the main courtyard to the chapel ruins. There I found the priest, wondering, hoping, crying, praying that today would be the day he held the rope long enough to pull it to gather the largest congregation of spirits the island had ever seen. I knew exactly what to do and where to focus. The sun charged my psychic batteries and a power rose within me.

'Caw… caw… caw,' I sang. We were one now.

I watched and waited for the priest to arrive. Cosmic energy flowed into the top of my head to my heart and down each arm to my hands. Flashing lights and floating colours tinted Tintagel. Oh how I craved the energy now.

The babbling sound of twenty school children rattled my concentration as they filed out of the courtyard and onto the area where the chapel ruins stood. My hands stuttered, missing a beat. I heard Crow laugh inside me. The children stood on the grass and sat on the walls, filling the sacred space. A teacher in a light blue anorak led them into the chapel and began talking about historic dates, Dark Ages, Romans, Mediterranean trade routes and other aspects of the island's long life. I hovered over them, fixated, drone-like from hundreds of miles away, and watched the priest appear from the far side of the island.

The children near the entrance to the chapel were the first to scream. Girls and boys clutched each other, shivering as the ice-cold energy of his presence parted them as he walked down the aisle to where the small spire once stood. The teacher turned white as the priest walked through him. He ushered the crying incontinent children out of the chapel to where the walled garden once stood. He looked back at the chapel, uncertain about what he saw there. The priest walked with his shoulders back and his head held straight. His mission was nigh.

He knelt to pray and sang a quiet Gregorian chant with his hands pressed to the Earth, summoning the rope which dangled next to his head. He stood, gripped it with his right hand and flexed his fingers. His face marvelled at the long-lost sense of touch as he felt the coarse fibres on his palms. The first ring was tentative. Cause and effect in the material world had been absent for hundreds of years. The tones were so clear and sharp. Father Francis wasn't used to the weight of the bronze, or anything for that matter, but the second tug was made with conviction, and passion, reverberating across the island and out to sea, northwards. His left hand gripped the rope above his right and he threw his body into the third, bending at the waist with each pull.

Tourists stopped in their tracks and looked around quizzically, asking each other if they could hear something. Some looked in a confused way over at Tintagel's parish church on the mainland, wondering if the bell's tolls were coming from there. Others turned in circles looking for its source. The priest kept pulling and the bell kept ringing, stirring spirits and a king from his sleep.

Time lost its place; the afternoon vanished. The remaining tourists made their way back to the courtyard and down the steps, away from the island, but the bell kept ringing.

The shepherds arrived first, herding their sheep to the far end of the island to leave room for the families, miners, tradesmen, soldiers and all manner of royal attendants who'd lived there at one point in its history. Some climbed up from the broiling sea, stirred by the increase in spirit and star energy above the land where the Great Bear prepared for dusk and the chance to shine. They hauled themselves over the cliff edges and grew out of the ruins, taking their rightful places on the land just once more. Twelve black horses fit for knights stood on the mainland where the main entrance would've led them and their Grail-seeking riders into the main courtyard, before dismounting for a feast in the great hall. They reared on their hind legs in unison, neighing at the island, and smashing stone with their feet as they leapt into the gap and onto the floor of the Great Hall. One of the horses left the others and walked the pathway to the end of the island to join the thousand spirits summoned by the church bell. The priest let go of the rope as the horse passed the chapel, leaving the bell's tolls to fade, giving rise to the crashing symbols of the sea and the steady clip-clop of its hooves. The crowd parted for the horse as it moved to the farthest tip of the island, looking north, waiting, wanting.

The Michael and Mary ley lines passed thirty miles from Tintagel through Bodmin Moor. Thirty miles from the largest single gathering of spirits North Cornwall had ever known, which magnetically pulled on the lines to open the channel for Arthur's journey through the Bristol Channel and north through Wales to the Ardnamurchan vortex, floating above the farthest tip of mainland Britain where a recovered drug addict drummed with all his crystal heart for a new life, a new beginning – and a chance to make a difference.

The sun began its downward arc. George sat like a crumpled ball of tin foil on the hillock. There wasn't a cloud in the sky to bring the biblical amounts of purifying rain Merlin spoke of. A ball of heat from the cowrie shells in my crane bag warmed my heart. I opened the bag and shuffled the hot shells on my palms. They glowed like embers. Unable to manage their heat, I scattered them over the grass oval and watched as they melted into the ground.

The sun turned lava orange as it met the horizon and the Pole Star took its place on the ever-changing canvas covering a wilderness infused with Celtic magic. Stag bulldozed me, half-tranced, onto his back. He bound us together with ivy and left the obsidian drum reverberating and smeared with my sweat. We ran a thousand yards to the highest crater wall with his nostrils streaming smoke-clouds of sage. He stilled himself and bowed his head to Mother to receive her touch on his cheek and then raised his mouth to the sky and roared with all the might of the Underworld. Again and again he emptied his lungs into the wilderness to mirror Father Francis' intentions, by calling Ardnamurchan's own congregation on the self-made Sabbath.

My ears rang with tinnitus which had always been there since I'd found Led Zeppelin, but his roaring made it ten times louder. Stag returned me to the obsidian at a walking pace. I rested my hands on each crook of his antlers. Ivy wrapped around my wrists as I touched him. Each new connection sent a small burst of energy through me as our hearts merged and then settled together as one. Nothing had sprouted from the ground where the cowrie shells were sown, but I knew we were being watched. I braced myself, scanning the skyline above the crater walls as dusk arrived.

The day disappeared into magical half-light and spirits emerged from behind the veil.

I heard the song before I saw them, mistaking it for a gust of wind careering off the ocean and whistling through gaps in the magma-chamber walls. If angels sang instead of playing harps at Heaven's gates, they would've made the same sound. Madalane appeared from the Sanna Bay side with her sisterhood following in a 'v' shape, like beautiful migrating birds returning home with their song flowing over the ridge. George lifted his heavy head and planted the lance into the hillock, imbued with strength by the divine feminine sounds. Madalane sang, spreading her arms to signal for the other women to fan out, a hundred feet from me at the centre of the obsidian, forming the familiar horseshoe shape the spirits seemed to prefer when addressing me. They lowered their voices, then cupped their hands and knelt to Mother Earth in a sweeping movement rehearsed for hundreds of years with this moment in mind.

Madalane's hands lit up first. She stood leaving a small flame flickering in front of her. The others followed, lighting flames left and right of Madalane with the fire that had once consumed them as they stood tied to stakes, screaming for their loved ones.

The volcano's cauldron took on a holy atmosphere, with flame, song, prayer and a deep moving silence too sacred to be disturbed by drumming. I waited for Beorn's divine masculine reinforcements to arrive. Night fell fast. I placed my hands on the obsidian and looked into the black crystal ball where Avebury's spiralling daytime energy uncoiled from the stone circle centres. George groaned on the hillock. It was turning into his self-made burial mound. In the darkness, I saw so clearly. The Great Bear constellation glowed above us with the Pole Star ripping a hole in the black canvas of the night. I flicked between the vision of Tintagel in my mind's eye and Ardnamurchan's volcanic stage with Mother's serpent energy unravelling before me on the widescreen, just waiting for the call to action.

The stage was set. Thousands of spirits, given their physical forms back for one night, waited on top of Arthur's soul in Cornwall, but half the cast were missing in Scotland and George was disappearing, waist-high, into the Earth. The firelight lit his blood-caked armour, an unfitting epitaph to England's fallen, sinking saint.

A slight twitching of the brown grass which framed the oval signalled a change in the climate. All day, the lack of wind had instilled an otherworldly feel to a coastline frequently battered by all manner of elements driven into the mainland by the Atlantic. It was the calm of all calms before the most supernatural of storms. The wind gathered pace and rushed into the land. The witches and their flames stood fast, protected by the approaching forces. A high screen of white cloud crossed over the volcano, shutting out the stars, providing the perfect backdrop for rolling balls of blackness, crackling with energy from whatever lay inside their elemental masses. They bellowed above us, waking George from his desperate slumber.

'He's brought the rain,' he gasped, and began crying into his folded arms, rocking like a baby cradled by his loving, forgiving Earth Mother.

George wasn't referring to me but to the presence inside the clouds that slowed and hovered above us – Logan had arrived. As the wind lulled, there was a brief silence as the weather positioned itself and then the sound of giant flapping wings began, just as I'd heard it in the desert during Oka's death ceremony. But this time it was in the present, raging above us. Everyone looked up, even Stag, to see the tips of giant stone wings drive through the clouds and slap us with rain catapulted by their movement. George fell onto his back, crying uncontrollably as the guilt and eternal pain of the doldrums in which he'd dwindled for so long lifted.

Energy pressed into my forehead and down through the top of my skull, straight to my crystal heart where I held Tintagel and Ardnamurchan present, waiting for definitive movement in the Michael and Mary dragon lines. The concentration was intense. We had Madalane's divine feminine energies, mirroring the Mary line, but where was the other half?

'Beorn! Bring them forward,' George screamed with all his might before collapsing.

Rhythm ruffled the air as their feet drummed on the caldera. A line of men emerged out of the darkness, hitting shields with their swords and axes, grunting, lifting their feet high, stamping, and spitting earth from their mouths as they came under the golden glow of the witches' firelight and the piercing white starlight. Among the men were boys hiding behind their hips, no higher than their fathers' waists; Beorn stood at their centre, level with Madalane, emotion tearing him apart.

There was a place for their ultimate reunion: not on Earth, but above the volcano in the heavens where their longing could be satisfied, honoured, and where the men's grief and the women's tortured souls could finally be laid to rest as they were once before – together. The route to those heavens was through the positive vortex, a column of energy I felt heating up around me. I sat at its centre, sensing the men's stomping rhythm reverberating far and wide, out to sea, south. Stag walked around the inside of the divine circle: a silent roll-call by the lord of the Earth's beasts, making sure all who needed to return home were present and correct. When he was finished he joined me on the obsidian and bayed at the tumbling storm clouds.

The first drop of rain felt like ice as it touched my sun and wind-burnt skin; the second touched my head and then my hands before the bombardment started. The rain rapped on the few patches of George's armour not yet covered by dragon blood or ancient cement. For all the storms he'd weathered during the centuries spent penancing, none of them had washed the stale stench of death from his holy armour. George turned his head to look at the pellets of water pummelling his shoulder-plate as it drilled through the inch-thick filth, exposing the steel for the first time since he slaughtered Mother's daughter. Chunks of blood and mud fell away as the sound of rain filled the air with its unanimous chorus. George turned his face to the sky to taste the rain with a tongue which turned from that of a reptile to his own. He raised his fingertips to touch his skin for the first time in countless histories as the water washed his face clean. His sobs turned to laughter as the last purifying drops of the new-born Thunderbird's rain wiped his slate clean. The wings gathered pace, driving squalls of water into the volcanic cauldron with every thunderous flap. George stood on his shaky feet to revel in the spectacle of his soul being set free. Sections of his armour fell away one by one as he waved his arms, shouting at the sky in jubilation. As his breastplates fell to the ground and dissolved into Mother's earthy ether, I saw him for the first time. A young soldier, fit for the gallant saint he had set out to be. All that remained of the sainthood was his lance. George kissed its glistening tip, threw it to me, pressed his hands together in a praying clasp over his heart, smiled, and disappeared before my eyes.

The hush that followed brought a lump to my throat. Stag stepped out of the oval, leaving me alone. I felt hollow. The men and women took one step back with their eyes firmly on me as the black clouds dissolved to unveil Logan in all his supernatural glory. A stone eagle the size of a 747 circled the crater, banking majestically over Sanna Bay before heading for its target – me. It screamed to signal its dive to the centre of the circle. I did a double-take at the metal rod I held in my hand and then up at the giant storm-bird. George hadn't thrown me a souvenir; he'd left me with a lightning conductor. I tried to let go of the lance, but it seized my fingers and pulled my arm up to the sky as the eagle moved over me and crashed its wings together.

I had always wondered if lighting would visit me a third time. Each time it had struck me it set me on a new course and the bolt which charged down the lance into me was no exception. The million vaults didn't render me unconscious like my psychedelic encounter.

My life flashed before my eyes as the heavenly fire coursed through my veins and burst out of my chest, arching left and right in heart-shaped loops hundreds of feet high before returning back to my feet.

Ardnamurchan's chamber resonated with my and the thousand heartbeats merged by the Golden Ratio of love. A frequency of the purest healing emotion sparked by the lightning bolt, shining the brightest beacon for Arthur to find his way to us.

'Boom boom!' the earth drum called.

I turned my focus to Cornwall as the stone Thunderbird flew high into the clear starlit sky, squawking with joy. Tintagel's congregation knelt to the island's turf and looked to the Great Bear above them. The tremors threw some to the ground and the more fragile of the ruins collapsed as more landslides sent tons of stone crashing into the sea.

Michael and Mary heard the calling. They felt the love and yearning in the north and uncoiled, darting out of Avebury's stone circle and drilling into the island, shattering more fragile ruins; then they paused to collect their bounty and exploded out of Merlin's cave into the sea. The torpedo of energy dived and then surfaced, leaping out of the water with a primordial roar sending shockwaves north as it swam with untamed fervour towards us.

In the minutes before Arthur arrived I looked, for one last time, at the souls standing around me, holding the space for what I had once thought to be the place where Arthur would take his first steps on Ardnamurchan's earth, but the truth had only come to me in the lightning as it blasted any dregs of denial out of me. The real eventuality was never for the Arthur of old to tackle the imbalances of our world. It was as street-signs and spirits had primed me – for someone new to carry his soul and wield its power.

I looked up at the stars and saw the long serpent-like flame swirling through the air and diving down to engulf me. Heartbeats pounded love into the circle as I said goodbye to my old life, my old skin. Oh how it burned; I screamed as all the pain I had ever put it through left me.

#

The crackling of wood burning brought me back to the night. The noise and scents were fresh and new. I opened my eyes and looked at the fading ghost of my yesteryear doppelganger sitting on the other side of a small fire. He faded and left me with the men and women brought together by the power of quest. Beorn's army no longer held weapons or grimaced with pain and longing. They walked to the women with babies, farming tools and bundles of corn, reuniting as they had been once before and ascended to the heavens in a momentary column of light, quicker than the beat of a heart.

Stag brushed his nose against my back and grunted, assured the demons had finally left me. I climbed onto him and the ivy wrapped around me; a man's voice spoke from the fire.

'You are a guardian now – use my powers wisely,' he said.

The voice startled Stag. I wrestled with the ivy reins to steady him and caught a glimpse of a fiery face looking at me before the flames dwindled and died. I listened to the rhythm of a thousand drums rising up from Mother's core and kicked my heels into Stag, launching into the night with my untamed soul craving adventure, and my heart yearning for someone to love.

Tim Bennett
Awaken

Aaron is supposed to help those less fortunate, but he's been consumed by drug addiction and is praying for his heart to stop beating. Close to death, he's thrown a lifeline - rehab in Cape Town. However, the odds are stacked against him, only one in three people make it to the other side. Aaron needs all his strength to make it through rehab and come to terms with the damage caused by addiction. He isn't alone though, the forces of nature have a special interest in him and send help from a crow. As he embarks on a journey of transformation and self-discovery, he realises that his experience in Cape Town holds the key to his destiny.

Available now in paperback and ebook